the
EXTREMELY
EPIC VIKING TALE
of
YONDERSAAY

AOIFE LENNON-RITCHIE

THE EXTREMELY EPIC VIKING TALE OF YONDERSAAY by Aoife Lennon-Ritchie
All rights reserved. Published in the United States of America by Month9Books, LLC.
No part of this book may be used or reproduced in any manner whatsoever without written permission of the publisher, except in the case of brief quotations embodied in critical articles and reviews.
EPub ISBN: 978-1-942664-67-3 Mobi ISBN: 978-1-942664-68-0
Paperback ISBN: 978-1-942664-52-9

Published by Tantrum Books for Month9Books, Raleigh, NC 27609
Cover illustration by Meaghan McIsaac
Cover design by Najla Qamber Designs

For Jack, Zinzi, and Munro

the
EXTREMELY
EPIC VIKING TALE
of
YONDERSAAY

The Violaceous Amethyst

PRAISE FOR THE EXTREMELY EPIC VIKING TALE OF YONDERSAAY

"This is a great adventure story. Kids will really enjoy the mystery, danger and wit. It's a fun book and would really be a great one for families to read together." - Amber Frazier

"I would definitely recommend this book to my students and others at my school. I would also recommend it to educators to use as a read aloud, to add into their classroom libraries, or recommend to their own students to read. I would also recommend this book to adults who love to read children's books." - Vanessa Ramos

"I liked the relationship between Dani and Ruairi. It felt like a real sibling relationship in that they picked at each other at times, but ultimately they loved each other and worked together." - Holly Bryan

PRONUNCIATION GUIDE

Ruairi	Roo-ri and Rooa-ri are two ways to pronounce this old Irish name.
Yondersaay	Yon-der-say
Róisín	Row (as in row your boat) - sheen. Row-sheen
Róisínín	Row-sheen-een
Fjorgyn Thunderbolt	Fee-yorg-in
Vallhala	Val-hal-ah
Violaceous	Viol (like in violin)-ay-shuss. Viol-ay-shuss
Rarelief	Rare-leaf
Dudo	Dude- oh
Silas Scathe	Sigh-lass Scathe, rhymes with bathe
King of Groenland	Groan-land
Harofith	Har (like in Harry)-oh-fith (rhymes with 'with'). Har-oh-fith.
Odin	Oh-dinn
Hamish Sinclair	Hay-mish Sinkler
Eoin Lerwick	Oh-win Ler-wick
Hjorvarth	Hee-yor-varth (like Garth)
Asgrim Finehair	As-grim Fine-hair
Isdrab Graylock	Iz-drab Gray-lock
Brokk	Rhymes with lock
Tiuz	Tee-ooze
Docteur Tchopemov	Doctor Chop 'em off
Fritjof	Fritt-yoff
Jarl	Yarl

PART I

YONDERSAAY

Please Use Other Door

"Ruairi!" Mum shrieked over her shoulder as she reversed the car out of the driveway. "Is that homework on your lap? It's the last day of school before the holidays. Please tell me I'm not going to get a call today."

"It's not homework, Mum —" Ruairi Miller said, careful not to let his parents see the sign he was writing.

"—It's extra credit," Ruairi's big sister, Dani, put in. "It's part of a very important and good project that Ruairi and I are doing for Mr. De Villiers."

"That's nice, you two … Mr. De Villiers," Mum said, swerving the car in too wide an arc onto the road, "Is he that lovely man who starts wearing Christmas jumpers the day after Halloween?"

"That's him," Dani mumbled.

"Ah yes, and he's forever singing that one Christmas

song. What is it now? *The Holly and the Ivy*," Mum said, and started to hum.

"*Deck the Halls,*" Ruairi and Dani groaned in unison.

"Fa la la la la, la la la la!" Mum sang.

"Mum, no! Please!"

Dad, in the passenger seat, came up from his smartphone and boomed, "'Tis the season to be *jolly*—"

"Fa la la la la, la la la la!" Mum and Dad sang together.

"See what you've started," Dani shot at Ruairi.

Mum and Dad sang on while Ruairi leaned over and whispered to his sister. "Mum's right. He is a lovely man. We don't need to do this, Dani."

"He needs to learn a lesson, Ruairi," Dani said. "It's a hundred degrees out there; I'm sure you've noticed we don't get snow or holly or even decked halls in South Africa at Christmas. Because why?"

"Because it's summer time in South Africa in December," Ruairi said.

"Right! We're in the middle of *summer*! Every year, it's the same. From November first to the end of school, we get a fa-la-la-la-la-ing reminder that we'll never have a white Christmas, chestnuts roasting on an open fire, boughs of holly—"

"–Or bells that jingle," Ruairi said, wistfully.

"Or bells that jingle! It's a slap in the face, Ruairi; it has to stop. Plus, it's a joke. I'm absolutely positive he'll find it funny. And he'll be proud of us, Ruairi, he loves it when students work for a long time to get a project just right."

"First he'll laugh, then he'll be proud?" Ruairi whispered as loud as he could over the atonal crooning of his parents in the front. "I'm not so sure about that."

"Sing we joyous all together, Fa la la la la, la la la la. Heedless of the wind and weather, Fa la la la la, la la la la" wafted from the front seat like a bad smell.

"This is fun," Mum said, screeching the car along the avenue of the wood surrounding their school. "We should do a Mr. De Villiers and start singing Christmas songs on the first of November every year." She did a U-turn by the school gates and sang one final fa-la-la while she stopped the car.

As the children bundled their school bags, school shoes, and their "project" out of the car, Mum said, "Wait, neither of you have Mr. De Villiers for anything—"

Quick as lightning, Dani said, "Mum, why are you dressed in a lab coat and Granny's old reading glasses?"

"Audition."

"Break a leg!" Dani said, slamming the car door shut.

"Bye, Mum! Bye, Dad!" Dani and Ruairi shouted and ran across the empty parking lot toward the school door. Dani waited until she saw the car careen back down the tree-lined avenue before she said, "Today's the day, Ruairi, my friend. Today's the day."

Ruairi had been having a similar conversation with his big sister every morning for about two months. Because every morning for about two months, Dani had been carrying out her plan. Her long-term plan.

Ruairi liked to remind Dani that it involved great sacrifice from him because it meant arriving at school half an hour before everyone else, and that meant getting out of bed a half hour too early every day. And Ruairi did not appreciate that. He could have let Dani carry out her plan herself, but then who would be there to talk her out of the dangerous variations or to cover for her when she nearly got caught?

This morning, like every morning for the past two months or so, Dani took a bright red jumper with a gaudy green Christmas tree on the front out of her bag and put it on. She scooped fistfuls of breadcrumbs from the Ziploc bag she had concealed in her book bag. Then she spread all the crumbs out over one particular parking space. She looked up into the branches of the trees all around the car park, and down the avenue, and smiled.

Dani and Ruairi went inside to wait.

The day before this day and every day of the past two months, just before the teachers arrived, Dani took her phone out of her pocket and pressed Play on a particular recording; it sounded a bit like a tinny *click-clack*. Then she and Ruairi went inside to their classrooms as normal.

Since today was *the* day, Dani didn't play her sound. Instead, just as the first teacher arrived—and the first teacher to arrive was, as always, Mr. De Villiers—Dani and Ruairi slipped inside the school building.

Through the glass front door, Dani and Ruairi watched Mr. De Villiers's large car nose through the gates toward his parking space. Ruairi suddenly remembered something.

"Dani! The sign!" he said, gesturing to the "project" in his hands. "I forgot." He slipped outside and stuck the sign to the front of the door with the tape he had in his pocket.

He dashed back inside just as the teacher climbed out of his car, wearing his bright red-and-green Christmas jumper. Mr. De Villiers was merrily singing the same song he sang every single day from November first to the end of school, and was almost at the end.

"Follow me in merry measure, Fa la la la la, la la la la. While I tell of Yuletide treasure, Fa la la la la, la la la la," he sang as he approached the door to the school. He climbed the first of three steps and reached his hand into his pocket. On the second step, he took his hand out of his pocket and raised his car alarm in the air. On the third step, just before he clicked his alarm, right as he reached out for the door handle, he stopped.

"'Please use other door,' eh?" he said, reading out loud the sign that Ruairi had just that minute stuck onto the entrance to the building. Mr. De Villiers shrugged and turned back. He descended the steps one by one and started to walk around the building to look for another open door. As he passed his car, he remembered his alarm and pressed the button.

The last thing Ruairi heard before the onslaught was the tinny "click-clack" of Mr. De Villiers's car alarm. For as soon as he pressed the button, the hundreds and hundreds and hundreds of pigeons and doves and hadedas that had been perched among the branches of the surrounding elms and oaks flew down and launched themselves at the crumbs Dani had scattered for them. Since the bread crumbs had been strategically placed around, about, and under Mr. De Villiers's car, all the airborne creatures soared onto and around and under Mr. De Villiers's cumbersome 4x4. He clutched at his chest and stumbled backward in a blind panic as the winged multitude descended on him.

It was when the screaming started that Ruairi turned to Dani and said, "I don't think he finds it funny. I don't think he finds it funny at all."

Dani immediately bolted out the door and ran to Mr. De Villiers's aid. Singing serenely to him, she took him by the elbow and led him through the door of the school building. Ruairi dashed out to take Mr. De Villiers's other elbow as they approached. Slowly and calmly, dissipating all pigeon-induced panic, they into the building, quietly singing Fa la la la la, la la la la.

Would the Miller Siblings Kindly
Come to the Principal's Office

"You do realize that man is probably traumatized for life," Ruairi said to Dani as they sat in tiny plastic chairs outside the principal's office.

"Why are these chairs so small?" Dani said, looking around at her chair and all the chairs.

"That's what you're thinking about right now? We're about to be expelled on the last day of school before Christmas, and you're wondering why they have tiny chairs."

"Relax, Ruairi. They can't prove a thing." Dani scrumpled herself further down into the chair. She was almost convincing, looking like she wasn't just as terrified as Ruairi.

"You're still wearing your Christmas jumper," Ruairi said flatly. Dani glanced down, gasped at the lurid colors, and whipped the thing over her head. Ruairi stiffened as the door to the principal's office opened and the principal came out and stood in front of them.

"Daniella and Ruairi, I'm afraid you're going to have to go home early today," Mrs. Nkosi informed them gravely. "Because," she broke into a huge grin, "this delightful woman has come to take you home." Mrs. Nkosi moved out of the way to reveal a beaming Granny Miller in her good maroon coat and her good maroon hat with the puffin feathers.

"My younglings," Granny said, "I have a huge surprise for you! I'll tell you when we get to your house. Oh, who am I joking. I could never keep a surprise for that long. It's dependent on Mum and Dad agreeing, so it's not definite yet, but … I'm taking us all home to Yondersaay for Christmas this year!" She let out a squeal of delight.

Ruairi was stunned. Dani leaped out of her tiny chair and bounded over to her great-great-great-grandmother and enveloped her in a hug. Ruairi could see that mixed up in Dani's happiness at the sight of Granny Miller was enormous relief.

As the three moved toward the door, Dani turned back to the principal and quietly asked, "Mrs. Nkosi, how is Mr. De Villiers doing?"

"He's fine. We were very worried at first. He had completely stopped singing *Deck the Halls*—completely stopped. But he's fa-la-la-ing away again now. We've decided to take that as a good sign.

"Don't worry. And thank you both for taking such good care of him this morning. I wonder if we'll ever find out who was clever enough to spend almost two months coming to school half an hour early to train those blasted rats-with-wings to descend for bread crumbs when they saw a person in a Christmas jumper and heard a car alarm.

I wouldn't be surprised if we never find her. Or her little brother." And Mrs. Nkosi shook Granny's hand and went back into her office.

"What a nice woman," Granny said. "You know, I would have been here to collect you much earlier, but there was a "Please Use Other Door" sign on the door to the building. I went around the building but couldn't find another open door, and when I came back, the sign was still there, so naturally I went around again. And again. Luckily, a frazzled-looking man with a very bright jumper came out to check his car, and I noticed the door actually did open. All righty, then. Let's go convince Mum and Dad that we should all Christmas in Yondersaay."

Going to Yondersaay

"Ready to go, Mum and Dad?" Granny bellowed down the Millers' front hallway. Ruairi and Dani struggled in after her, laden down with her piles and piles of trunks and hatboxes and suitcases.

"Not quite yet," Mum said, and the three heard a door slam at the back of the house.

"Well, get a move on!" Granny shouted. "The taxi is picking us up in an hour to take us to the airport. We can't miss that flight as there's only a thirty-minute layover in Dubai, and there's only one flight this week that will take us from there to Copenhagen and on to Berlin, and from there, it's a wee hop to Dublin airport, a wee-er one to Inverness, and in the middle of all that, there's the ferry, the catamaran, and the helicopter until finally we catch the Yonder Air flight to Yondersaay."

Mum emerged from the living room looking less than

delighted with the sudden change in Christmas plans. "We're nearly ready, Granny." She turned to her children. "Has Granny told you? She's feeling a little bit homesick, so Dad and I have agreed that we'll all go up to Yondersaay for Christmas this year. On three conditions—" Dani and Ruairi started whooping and cheering immediately and took no notice of Mum's three conditions, which were all about safety and good manners and the usual nonsense.

They hugged their mum and shouted, "Yaaaaaay, we're going to Yondersaay!"

"Mum," Granny said, and Ruairi saw Granny finally taking in her great-great-granddaughter-in-law, "why are you dressed as a Victorian governess?"

"Audition," Mum said, struggling out of her corset.

"Oh, for a play, is it?"

"Good lord, no. Commercial."

"Would you not go in for one of those lovely plays in the Theatre on the Bay or the Baxter?"

"No, no, no. Somebody I know might come along and see me and then I'd see them and I'd have to run off the stage."

"My dear, what will you do if you actually get booked on one of these commercials?"

"Honestly, Granny, who can think that far ahead?"

Ruairi and Dani went upstairs at supersonic speeds to pack their suitcases, remembering that unlike in South Africa, it was icy and snowy on Yondersaay at this time of year. Dani upended drawers onto the floor; Ruairi tossed items out of the wardrobe. With everything everywhere, they absolutely couldn't find a single thing they needed.

Mum and Dad were downstairs in the living room. Ruairi could hear little snippets of their conversation.

"It is important to be seen to be committed to the job

in these hard times. We all have to prove our worth," Dad was saying.

Dani put her head over the railing at the top of the stairs and shouted, "Mum, where's my purple jumper? Mum! My purple jumper!"

"But they can't expect you to miss out on Christmas with your family," Mum said as she came to the bottom of the stairs. "It's in the ironing basket, Dani. Get Ruairi's fleece while you're there, and don't forget it's cold on Yondersaay now—not like when we're usually there—bring your snow boots and thermal socks."

"You don't understand—" Dad was saying.

"I understand. You're talking about commitment—"

"I can't find it, Mum! My purple jumper. Where is my purple jumper?"

Mum and Dad's heads popped into view at the bottom of the stairs. "Watch your tone, young lady!" they snapped, together. Then their heads disappeared, and the living room door slammed shut. Ruairi and Dani stopped what they were doing and came to the top of the stairs. They stood looking at the closed door.

"It's all your fault," Ruairi said, close to tears.

Dani put her arm around her little brother's shoulder. "It's not my fault, it's not anybody's fault."

"I know," he said, as they ambled back to their packing.

—— ◦ ——

"Cheer up, guys," Mum said from her position in front of them in the line. "You'll see him in a day or two."

Ruairi glanced back past airport security one last time

to see if he could still see Dad waving, but he couldn't. He collected his shoes and belt and backpack and caught up with Dani, Mum, and Granny at the gate.

"You heard Dad," Mum said as Ruairi reached her. "He's going to call in a favor at the department and get parachute-dropped with his inflatable dinghy backpack from one of their stealth recon drones on their routine sweep of the North Atlantic. Shouldn't take him long to paddle to Yondersaay from the drop point."

"And if they're not going near Yondersaay?" Dani asked.

"Then he'll find another way; you know Dad." Mum led them to their seats. "Granny?"

"Yes, dear?"

"We have such a long journey ahead of us—lots of flying and sailing and waiting in waiting rooms. And then more flying and sailing and waiting and driving."

"Yes, dear, we do."

"Will you tell us one of your stories to keep us going?" Mum said.

"Well, now," Granny said, "I suppose that would be one way to pass the time. But what if nobody wants to hear my stories?"

"We do, Granny," Ruairi said. "Only not the one about the one-eyed tortoise who took a hundred years to lay an egg."

"Or the one about how handbags were invented," Dani said.

"You don't like those stories?" Granny asked, and Dani and Ruairi shook their heads.

The Millers found their row and took their seats.

"Hmm, let me see." Granny closed her eyes and thought for a moment. "It wasn't today or yesterday …" Granny began. This was the way she always began her stories.

"Granny, you're supposed to say 'Once upon a time,'" Dani said.

"No, Dani. 'Once upon a time,' is the ordinary way to begin an ordinary story. There are no ordinary stories about Yondersaay. Besides, when you hear a story that begins 'Once upon a time,' you start out with a set of expectations. You are not surprised when the beans turn out to be magic beans or when the frog turns into a prince. You expect everything to end 'happily ever after' with the baddies getting their comeuppance and the goodies getting married. This is not one of those stories. *This* is a *true* story; it actually happened. There are no poison apples or handsome frogs, and I'm sorry to tell you, Yondersaay stories don't all end up 'happily ever after.'"

"Okay, Granny," Dani said as Granny wedged herself into her seat. "As you were …"

The King of the Danes

"It wasn't today or yesterday," Granny began again. "It was a long, long time ago when the world was warmer, and some believed the sun moved around the earth. There was a Viking of old called King Dudo the Mightily Impressive, lord over all Denmark. King Dudo was a big man, broad and tall, with tanned skin tight across bulging muscles and long reddish-blond hair that fell in thick waves to his elbows—a mighty warrior. All who fought with him worshipped him, and those who fought against him trembled in fear at the very sight of him. An adventurer, he pillaged and plundered as far north as the turn in the world and as far south as the oceans of sand.

"One bright autumn, King Dudo and his warriors set sail from their homeland to the northern-most seas of the world. They wore thick layers of skins and furs against the cold of the northern air.

"Among their number on this westward voyage was a famous monk from the lower lands called Brother Brian the Devout and Handy with Numbers. Brother Brian had the gift of navigation and was an expert star-reader. His job was to guide King Dudo and his Viking warriors to the northern lands.

"After roiling upon the waves for many weeks, their supplies diminishing, and cramp and fatigue setting in, the Vikings were anxious for the sight of land. Surprised they had not found land yet, some began to doubt Brother Brian's ability. A whispering campaign started at the backs of the longships: "Brother Brian has gotten us lost!"

"Now, while it is true that Brother Brian was tasked with getting the Vikings safely to and from the lands of the north, only King Dudo knew that Brian had another task—another *secret* task.

"It had long been suspected that in the middle of the northern-most seas, between the homelands of the Danes and the far-off lands, below the turn in the world but beyond the craggy cliffs of Land of the Scots, lay an island. This island was often the subject of the songs and tales of the kingdom's official storytellers, the court skalders. The stories described it as an enchanted island, cloaked in secrecy. The island was called Yondersaay.

"Viking legend tells that after death, the most worthy Viking warriors would meet in Valhalla, the Hall of the Dead, for a final battle. Anything a Viking had buried in his earthly life would be his once more. His true armor, weaponry, or wealth stayed buried in the earth while its ghostly copy awaited him in the afterlife. So it was, every Viking, before he died, buried his prized weapons and his most coveted jewels in preparation for this final battle.

"Now, the stories go, this lost island in the middle of the

sea happened to be the place where all the Viking warriors of old went to bury their treasures. The riches buried on the island were said to include the most intricate and exquisite objects ever invented, mined, or styled. Some of the weaponry dated back to the first-ever pieces of forged iron, and other pieces displayed the most modern sophistication. Since these riches were sung about the world over by the skalders and other storytellers, the stories eventually made it all the way to the southern lands of Brother Brian's home.

"Yondersaay was widely believed to be the burial place not just of the treasures of generations of Vikings but also of the Gifts of Odin."

"Tell us about the Gifts of Odin again, Granny," Dani said.

"The Gifts of Odin are weapons, jewels, and treasures that were given to the Viking god Odin, the father of all Vikings, throughout his many lifetimes. Some of the gifts were specifically crafted for Odin, and some were imbued with enchantments and powers. Not all the gifts were of this world; some were presents from other gods. Of course, you've heard of a few—the Black Heart of the Dragon's Eye, for instance, and the Violaceous Amethyst. Then there's the Tome of Tiuz and the Fjorgyn Thunderbolt. And there are other, more obscure ones, like the Sword of Lapis Lazuli and its mate, the Asiatic Shield, and the Cup of Memory, to name the most famous of the least famous.

"Rumors of this magnificent cache of treasure traveled far and wide. To ensure the island would not be sacked and plundered, Odin cast an enchantment upon it. The island disappeared from sight and became unreachable. Or, to be more specific, *almost* unreachable," Granny continued as she unfastened her seat belt and pulled down her tray table. The Millers were all together in the middle of the plane in a row of four seats. Granny had taken off her hat and coat upon entering the plane, and Ruairi could see she was wearing her stretchy trousers.

"Granny," Mum said, "you're not supposed to pull down your tray table until they serve the food. It's not *safe* in the event of an emergency landing."

Just at that precise moment, Ruairi saw a very smiley, very tanned flight attendant turn out of the galley pushing a trolley piled high with trays of food.

"You were saying, Mum?" Granny grinned at Mum.

"Never mind," Mum mumbled.

The flight attendant pushed her trolley down the aisle, handing out trays of food. "Chicken or beef?" she said to Granny with a big smile when she got to their row.

"Yes, please." Granny smiled back at her. The flight attendant held the chicken tray in one hand and the beef tray in the other. She seemed confused.

"You can just put them both down here, thank you." The flight attendant looked at Granny. Granny did not break eye contact. The flight attendant hesitated for just a second, then put both trays in front of Granny.

"Oh, and the vegetarian option too, please." Granny manoeuvered the chicken tray halfway on top of the beef tray to make room for the vegetarian. She turned back to Dani and Ruairi and continued with her story before the flight attendant had a chance to object.

"Dudo's favorite skalder's tale tells of a great king who would one day breach the island's enchanted fortifications. A lone warrior with neither weaponry nor army with no council to advise him and no magic to aid him would conquer the jewel-filled island and become its king and master. It is not known how he was to achieve it, what power or ruse he would employ, what deal he would strike, or indeed, whom he would fight. The only thing known for sure was that one lone someone, one great warrior, would do the business, make it to the island, and scoop the loot.

"King Dudo was an intelligent man. He didn't believe there was such a thing as an enchanted island in the middle of the sea stuffed full of gold and jewels. All the same, he did think there was a teeny possibility there was an island off the beaten track that had remained undiscovered for a ton of years, which just might, be a nice place to go and have a look around. Who knew, there might be some pleasant-looking trinkets buried there.

"It was with this in mind that King Dudo the Mightily Impressive enlisted the renowned star-gazing monk, Brother Brian the Devout and Handy with Numbers.

"Brother Brian spent a long time researching the island for King Dudo. He scrupulously documented all known Viking tales and songs about the island. He cross-referenced them with stories from other places, drawing up charts, plotting graphs, and double-checking his maps of the skies with the leading astronomers. When he felt he knew the exact location of the enchanted island, he dispatched a messenger pigeon to King Dudo and went to the upper lands to lead King Dudo the Mightily Impressive to the treasure.

"King Dudo had asked Brother Brian to keep all this hush-hush. He didn't want his men to think he believed in fairy stories. They were just going to go out of their way a little to look for the island, maybe pretend they were lost for a day or two. If they didn't find it, no harm done; they'd be back on course and in the northern lands before they knew it. Although Brother Brian was a monk who wore a habit that looked a lot like a dress, he was no less concerned about his reputation among the Viking men. He was super psyched to be on first-name terms with the most powerful man in the land, so he gave King Dudo a wink and assured him that yes, of course, this would be their little secret."

The Little Secret

Granny had to shout now because of the noise of the wind on the gangplank of the ferry she, Dani, Ruairi, and Mum were boarding. Granny was eating the steaming hot pie Mum had gotten for her in a sailor bar in the port. They huddled close together and shuffled up the gangplank in their winter clothes.

"About three weeks into the voyage," Granny bellowed, "a few days after the warriors started wondering why they hadn't found land yet, dusk fell on a clear, calm ocean. The night was full of light from the crystalline moon, and Brother Brian turned a little in his position in the prow of the lead longship and made a long slow nod of the head toward King Dudo, closing his eyes as his head reached its lowest position. It was a very cool move. Brother Brian had been practicing it in his head for *weeks*. He waited for King Dudo to take his seat beside him.

"'We are close,' Brian said to Dudo and looked to the stars, then back down at the books and scrolls and charts laid all about him and back up to the stars again. 'All my information, all my years of training, and all my expertise tell me we are very close.'

"The boat glided quietly through the water. Most of the Vikings were sleeping. Not so much as a seabird disturbed the stillness of the night. The monk and the king looked hopefully all around; it felt to them that they could see for miles. If the island was there, they would see it.

"They looked and looked. An hour passed, two hours passed, then three. But no land came into view. All of a sudden, King Dudo swung his head around to the left. 'Shh!' he hissed. Brother Brian swivelled his gaze around and looked hard, but he couldn't see anything. 'It sounded like—' King Dudo said, stopping short.

"'Like what, my lord?' Brian asked.

"'Oh, nothing, it's ridiculous … but for a minute there, I thought I heard children laughing.'

Brother Brian gasped, clutched his chest, and went pale.

"'It's nothing,' King Dudo continued. 'The ocean is playing tricks on my mind.' Dudo's shoulders sagged, and he let out a big sigh. 'This is ridiculous! What am I thinking? A magical island in the middle of the ocean … Enough. Time to let it go. Let's get back on track and deliver my men to land.'

"The monk did as King Dudo said and altered the course of the fleet of longships, turning them back a little so they pointed toward a known headland."

"Granny," Ruairi interrupted. "Why did Brother Brian go pale? Did he see something? Did he see Yondersaay?"

"Good guess, Ruairi," Granny said. "But no. King

Dudo didn't notice Brother Brian's near fainting when he told him he'd heard laughing children. Nor did he notice Brother Brian immediately turning and marking the precise location of the laughing children in his charts. Brother Brian the Devout and Handy with Numbers would never, *ever* be coming this way again.

"You see, Brother Brian was a deeply superstitious man. In the lower lands where he grew up, a lot of the horror stories told around the campfire were about voices. If you heard a voice and couldn't see the body it came from, chances were you were being haunted by a ghost. The most terrifying ghost stories Brother Brian had ever heard started with the sinister laughter of a bodyless child.

"When Brother Brian made it back to his monastery in the lower lands, he wrote a travel guide based on his voyages with the Danes. *Brother Brian's Northern-Most Sea Excursions: Hospitable Hostelries and Bloodiest Battlegrounds*, became the best-selling book about the area and was reprinted edition after edition. At the back of the manuscript was an extensive glossary with maps and directions, and all studiously avoided this particular patch of haunted ocean. So every traveler who traveled the northern-most seas and who used Brother Brian's *Excursions* as their guide—and the publishing house will brag that that is absolutely everyone who traveled the northern-most seas—followed Brother Brian's routes. And *all* Brother Brian's routes avoided this spot."

"I think we have that book at home somewhere," Dani said.

"Of course you do," Granny said. "You're Yondersaanians, so you're bound to have one."

"Half-Yondersaanian," Ruairi said, glancing at Mum. With the same blondish-reddish hair as Dani's, Mum was often taken for a Yondersaanian, but in fact she wasn't Yondersaanian, she was Irish.

"Never mind," Granny said, "You can't have everything."

"I can hear you," Mum said, not looking up from the extra-thick, super-comprehensive, safety guide she had requested from the flight attendant.

"Where were we? Oh, yes," Granny went on as the plane landed and bumped along the runway. "Now, Brother Brian, convinced he had made a terrible mistake in his calculations, spent the rest of the voyage going over his charts and calculations. At the end of a month of calculations and recalculations, Brian was utterly confused. Certain he had made a mistake but unable to find it, he vowed to beg King Dudo's forgiveness, if King Dudo were ever to be found alive, of course. 'I'm terribly sorry, my liege,' he had decided he would say, if it turned out King Dudo hadn't died a gruesome and bloody death like everyone believed. 'I beg your mercy and forgiveness. It is to my shame and embarrassment that I admit to a heedlessness and recklessness in my long division and multiplication. I think I must have forgotten to carry the one.'"

"Granny, I'm going to have to stop you there," Dani said matter-of-factly as she handed her passport over to be stamped at customs.

"Oh, yes?" Granny asked, squeezing through the space between the control booths. Ruairi, putting all his strength into it, shoved her heartily until she popped out the other side. She put her newly stamped passport into her handbag and led the way into the arrivals hall.

"Wasn't King Dudo in the boat with Brother Brian just a minute ago?" Dani asked patiently while Ruairi came close to hear. "Why does Brother Brian think King Dudo died a gruesome death?"

"A gruesome and *bloody* death," Ruairi said in hushed tones, putting his passport back in his inside pocket with all his boarding passes.

"I haven't gotten to that part yet," Granny said. "If you'd listened carefully, you'd have heard me say Brother Brian took a month of sweating over his calculations to find out what mistake he'd made with his sums."

"Yes, I remember that bit," Dani was stumped.

"Well, a lot can happen in a month, Dani. May I continue?" Granny looked around at Mum, Ruairi, and Dani who all smiled and nodded.

"Still confused," Dani said, "but do go on."

"Now," Granny said as the Millers made their way from the arrivals hall up two flights on the escalator to the departures hall where they stood in the queue to get on their next flight. "Where was I? Oh, yes, I remember …

"Leading the fleet of longships away from the patch of water that had terrified him witless, Brother Brian gestured in a northwesterly direction toward a jutting headland familiar to all who had traveled this way with King Dudo before. Just in time too. The Vikings were so hungry by now that Brother Brian was starting to look tasty.

"'Too gristly,' Brother Brian overheard one of them say.

"'He'll be all right with a bit of salt,' said another.

"'Look! Look!' Brother Brian screeched hysterically as he was being surrounded. 'Land!'

"They disembarked as the sun rose. The Vikings had camped in this cold and inhospitable land when they had traveled west in the past. They created makeshift shelter, and they were hopeful of finding something to hunt in the nearby wood.

"The forest was one of snow-covered trees that began inland some way from the bay. A team was dispatched to bring firewood to the camp and to begin the hunt for fresh meat.

"A man of action, Dudo was of this hunting party. When they reached the trees, two men set about gathering wood into slings to drag back to camp. The rest fanned out as silently as they could manage, given the crispness of the icy slush underfoot. King Dudo positioned himself on the flank of the group as they all crept softly into the depths of the forest.

"Reaching the edge of the dense plot of trees, Dudo was distracted by a tiny bird with soft purple feathers off to his right. The bird took flight. Following, King Dudo found himself emerging alone from under the dim forest canopy into a field of light between the tree-brown dankness and the sea-blue stillness. Trees to his left; to his right, the sea. Nothing else.

"Enchanted by the spectacular beauty of this place, Dudo walked across a white hollow toward the water. His men continued forward in their hunting circle, not noticing the king had wandered out of position. King Dudo looked out across the vast ocean toward his homeland. He tried to imagine what his Danish subjects were doing at that precise moment—sleeping, eating, or working in the fields. He reflected that he was a lucky man. He had sailed the waves, explored foreign lands, and had seen beauty of a kind most of his subjects could not even imagine.

"King Dudo was startled out of his reverie by a low grumbling noise not twenty feet behind him. He turned, slowly. Before him, a giant white bear padded noiselessly out of the woods. The king looked at the bear, and the bear looked back. The bear slavered. It bared its teeth, and juices slobbered from them.

"King Dudo was trapped. There was no escape. He

could not go backward—there was only icy cold water behind him; he could not go forward—there was only the bear. The hollow was narrow—there was no space to go around. He could not call out to his men for fear of startling or angering the white bear. He stood as still as he could, trying to come up with a plan. "The bear continued toward King Dudo and made its way down into the hollow. As it did so, King Dudo the Mightily Impressive heard the loudest *crack* he had ever heard and felt the earth move beneath his feet."

"I CAN'T HEAR YOU VERY WELL NOW, GRANNY," Dani shouted to her great-great-great-grandmother, who was seated right beside her on top of their luggage and the thousands of boxes in the hold of the cargo plane taking them on the next stage of their journey.

"LET'S WAIT TILL WE LAND," Granny screeched back. "WE'RE NEARLY THERE NOW."

"WHAT DID YOU SAY?" Ruairi shouted at Granny.

"WE'RE NEARLY THERE!" Granny said.

"WHAT?" Mum shouted over the noise of the engines of the cavernous plane. Granny pointed out the window at the airport building that appeared closer every second.

Dudo and the Bear

"With the sudden noise, Dudo felt the white hollow of earth start to shift beneath his feet," Granny said, once they'd landed and had walked across the tarmac into the airport building. "It had broken clean off from the rest of the headland and had started to drift out to sea.

"The loud crack was not heard only by King Dudo. Immediately, the voices of his men broke through the trees, and the sounds of twigs breaking and branches creaking let him know they were coming. He hoped they would not get to him too late.

"The loud crack was not heard only by King Dudo and his men. The white bear was standing just beyond the fissure and seemed terrified by the thunderous split and the movement of the ground. The enormous white bear reared up on its hind legs and bellowed a deafening roar directly into the face of brave King Dudo the Mightily Impressive.

"The roar was loud enough and angry enough and scary enough to spread a ripple of terror through the men now rapidly approaching the edge of the woods and the space where the snowy ledge used to be. The warriors got there just in time to see their lord and king float gently away on a sliver of ice. His only company: an enormous, ravenous, snow-white polar bear.

"Intent on saving his king, one of the warriors jumped straight into the water. He was stunned so badly by the icy cold that not only did he not save Dudo, he could not even swim and in fact required his own rescue party. Two men remained behind to save their overzealous companion while the rest ran at full speed back through the woods to their fellows on the beach. They shouted as loudly as they could to raise the alarm even before they were in sight.

"They jumped into their boats; the rowers sliced the water with all their strength and ploughed through the waves, around the headland, in the direction of King Dudo and the white bear. They put their full might into each stroke of the oars, cutting the blue water like hot swords through melting butter.

"A thick gray fog had been resting atop the trees since they had set foot on land, threatening to descend. And now, at this most crucial of moments, the promise was fulfilled, and the fog tumbled down past them. It stirred up the waves and blocked their view entirely. Men ran along the decks of the boats casting about for signs of their king.

"This Viking squad was a hardy bunch, so desperation did not set in immediately. They kept on their course. They took turns shouting for their king and remaining quiet, listening for a response. But they heard nothing. Not a sound but their own shrieks and eventually their own sighs of despair.

"What was that, dear?" Granny stopped her story abruptly and turned toward Dani and Ruairi.

Dani and Ruairi looked at each other and at Granny Miller.

"What?" Ruairi asked.

"What did you say, my dear? Did you ask me something?"

"No, Granny," Ruairi said, casting about. "Nobody said a thing."

"Oh! I could have sworn … Oh well, if you say you didn't say anything … if you're sure now."

"No, Granny. We didn't so much as open our mouths," Dani said.

"Well, if you're sure. Now. Where was I? Oh, yes." Granny settled back into the comfiness of the armchair in the corner of the departure lounge and sipped the cocoa Mum had bought her at the coffee shop. "And so it was that King Dudo's lifeless body washed up on the unfamiliar shore of an unfamiliar land in the middle of the northernmost seas."

"Nooooo!" Dani and Ruairi shouted out together.

"What, my dears?" Granny calmly looked over her glasses as Dani and Ruairi jumped up from where they had been lying on the floor of the airport concourse.

"No, Granny!" Dani said frantically. "That's not where we were; we were floating away on the ice with the bear and the Vikings and the fog and the Vikings were calling out trying to find King Dudo."

"Is he dead?" Ruairi whispered anxiously to his mother; this wasn't a Dudo story he had heard Granny tell before. Mum shrugged, she didn't know.

"Oh, yes. That's right, that's right. Well. They didn't find him," Granny said and continued. "And so it was that

King Dudo's lifeless body washed up on the unfamiliar shore of an unfamiliar—"

"But the bear, Granny! What about the bear?" Dani asked.

"Yes, Granny, the bear! What happened with the bear?" Ruairi wanted to know.

Granny was looking a little confused now. "What bear now?"

"The bear!"

"The ravenous snow-white bear!"

"The ravenous bear … the ravenous bear. No. Doesn't ring a bell."

"The big white bear that broke off from the land with King Dudo, the one with the fangs and the slavering and the … the … big-ness," Ruairi said, demonstrating how big the bear was with his arms.

"Oh, right, I'm with you now. *That* bear. The *ravenous* bear. Yes, but," Granny paused, "are you sure you want to hear about the bear?" She looked at the two of them. They nodded.

"It's just, well, I thought maybe you'd rather not hear about the bear. Ruairi was looking a bit queasy, and Dani was getting very agitated when I started talking about the bear. Maybe you're not old enough for the bear story yet. It can get quite gruesome. It looked like it was getting to be a bit too much for you."

Dani and Ruairi sat down and tried to look as unagitated and unqueasy as they could.

"Oh no, Granny," Dani said, "not at all. We were just worried that maybe the hot chocolate wasn't chocolaty enough for you, or that you maybe needed another pie. That's what had gotten us worried."

"Yeah," Ruairi went on, "not the bear. No way. I

couldn't care less about the bear. In fact, if you don't tell us about what happened on the floe with the ravenous, slavering, snow-white bear, we won't mind one bit, not one bit. Only—"

"Only?" Granny looked amused.

"Only," Dani went on, "it might get a bit confusing later on, you know, if there are details pertinent to the rest of the story, and we don't know about them. It would probably be good background, for later on, you understand."

"Ah, yes, I see, for later on. Yes, I understand," Granny said and flashed a quick smile at Mum.

"Well, in that case, very well." Granny muttered to herself. "The fog, the Vikings shouting, the ravenous bear … yes, yes, I know where we are, but we'll have to pause a few minutes. They've just announced our flight. This is the last one, my younglings; the next time we set foot on land, we will be on Yondersaay."

The Ravenous Bear

"King Dudo stood perfectly still on the edge of the ice floe," Granny said as soon as they were all settled on the Yonder Air flight to Yondersaay, and she had unbuckled her seat belt and lowered her tray table. "You're both sure you want me to tell this story?"

"YES!" Ruairi and Dani said.

"Well, okay, if you me want to," Dani said more calmly.

Ruairi glanced toward the galley and saw the Yonder Air flight attendant roll the dinner cart out of the galley kitchen and into their aisle. Ruairi could see Mum looking out for it—Granny Miller had lowered her tray table mere seconds before every meal and every snack was served on every flight they'd been on all day.

"Dudo studied the bear, and the bear studied Dudo," Granny went on. "Staying as still as he could, Dudo wondered, could he fight the bear? He looked at the massive creature. Powerfully built, sinewy and strong, it was twice the width of the king, at least. On its hind legs, it was over three times as high. One swipe of a paw would knock the life out of the biggest, strongest Viking in King Dudo's army.

"Dudo had noted the bear's poise and grace when it had padded so elegantly out of the woods to face him. This animal was equally at home on the ice and in the water. There was no way King Dudo could wrong-foot this magnificent creature, which had spent all of its life walking and running on snow and ice, and get it to lose its balance. Even if somehow, against all probability, King Dudo did manage to topple the bear into the water, there would be absolutely nothing to stop the bear from climbing back to where it was right now, growling and snarling mere feet from him. Nothing in the world.

"So, attacking? No. Wrong-footing? Not a chance. Escaping? King Dudo had seen what had happened to the brave but foolish warrior who had tried to save him. The king could not spend more than a few minutes in the water and survive.

"King Dudo thought and thought about what to do. He had once been told that lullabies calmed farm animals ahead of a procedure by an animal doctor. He was reluctant to give singing a go. For one thing, his men might hear him and think he was daft, even though he wasn't sure how close they were; he hadn't heard them calling for him in a while. For another thing, he had about the worst singing voice in the Land of the Danes.

"King Dudo counted his options on his fingers. The bear let out a low, grumbling roar. It came back down onto four legs and snarled, softly inching closer and closer across the ice. Running out of time, King Dudo, threw all his doubts out of his mind. With as much vigor and energy as he could muster, he opened his mouth and started to sing.

"When King Dudo was a little boy and was upset or low with an illness, the song his mother sang to soothe and comfort him was about the tight grip love has on the heart. About how helplessly changed you are when you meet your Heart's True Love.

"The song was more than a simple love song. There persisted a subtle note of sadness. Though it spoke eloquently of the power and fire of love, her song also spoke of the vagaries of it, the shifts in the depths of love over the years.

"The bear was at first perplexed by King Dudo's singing and stopped in its tracks. It cocked its head to the side as though trying to figure out what was happening, as if to say, 'Why is lunch behaving in this strange manner?'

"King Dudo closed his eyes and sang, certain this was his last moment alive. He allowed the song to envelope his heart. He thought about his mother and the love in her life. He felt the loss she must have felt when he grew up and grew away from her. Dudo thought of his parents' love for each other, which was still as strong now as the day they first laid eyes on each other and knew they had found their Heart's True Love. He thought of their love for him, as unblemished and pure as the white of this bear's fur.

"Acutely, he felt the loss of never having experienced true love of his own. King Dudo was not a married man and was not particularly young. Nevertheless, before this day, he held a firm belief that he would meet his Heart's True Love. On this patch of ice in the middle of the northern-most seas, it occurred to him that now he never would.

"King Dudo found himself wishing a last hopeless wish. He sang, and he wished; he wished, and he sang. The wish that emanated from his heart as he sang to the bear was 'let me live to spend a year, a month, a day, with my Heart's True Love. Let me live just that long.'

"King Dudo was approaching the end of his song. There were at least two other verses, but he couldn't remember anything more. He considered starting from the beginning again since it seemed to be working—he was still alive. Instead, he hummed a bit after the song had ended and slowly went quiet. He couldn't hear anything. The snarling was gone. The growling had stopped. There was no soft padding of paws on snow and ice.

"Slowly, King Dudo opened one eye. And then the other. The bear was no longer there.

"On the ice in front of King Dudo was not the enormous, angry, ravenous, snow-white polar bear. Instead, there stood, wet and dripping, a woman!"

"The woman's skin was as white as the bear's fur had been. Her hair was long and wild and a shade of red King Dudo had never seen before. Her eyes, a piercing blue, were trained directly on him. She stood straight and strong, almost close enough to touch. Soaking and shivering, wearing only a simple dress, she was wet from head to toe."

"No WAY!" Ruairi jumped up on his seat. "Did the bear turn into a woman? Did it, Granny? Did it?"

"Was it his wish coming true?" Dani asked. "Did the bear turn into his Heart's True Love?"

Distracted by a passing Yonder Air flight attendant, Granny grabbed his arm and said, as sweetly as she could, "You wouldn't mind grabbing me an extra few packets of peanuts, would you? I'm peckish."

"Certainly, madam," he said and went to get them for her.

"Granny, are you sure about all this? There was a

woman there?" Ruairi cocked his head.

"Yes, I'm sure,"

The flight attendant came back with a tray of peanut packets. Granny took nine.

"Well, let's come back to that in a moment, shall we," Ruairi said, looking puzzled. "Answer me this, Granny—why did King Dudo's lifeless body wash up on the shore of the hidden island?"

"Ah, that's a very good question. And it's very simple to answer." Granny fanned out her packets of peanuts on her tray, opened them all up, and continued with her story.

"King Dudo could not believe his eyes. The bear was somehow gone and in its place stood a woman. The woman stretched out one arm to him and took a step toward King Dudo. King Dudo was startled out of his mind. He instinctively let out a shriek and jumped away. There was nothing behind him to land on, so King Dudo tumbled backward. He somersaulted, head over heels, round and round in the air. Seconds before his body made contact with the iciest waves he ever had the misfortune to plunge head over heels into, he smacked his head on the edge of the floating ice and was knocked out cold. The woman raced to the edge of the little white island. She knelt down and thrust her arm into the water after King Dudo to try to catch him. She almost had him when a wave came under the icy island, rocking it up, and swept King Dudo out of her reach.

"The sea had not exactly been calm, as you know, but now it was positively roiling. King Dudo and the bear had floated a long way, and the floe was now close to shore. A different shore. The tide was going in. King Dudo was unconscious in the water.

"The woman regained her balance as soon as the wave

passed. She stood up and made a most elegant dive into the water. She powered down beneath the waves forming above her head. Darting after Dudo as he drifted deeper and deeper, she grabbed his hand. She surfaced, hauling King Dudo behind her with all her might, and swam toward shore. She got him onto the sandy beach and dragged him as far from the water's edge as she could. She looked quickly around, jumped back into the water, and swam away."

"Wow."

"Wow indeed, Ruairi," Granny said. "King Dudo woke up on a crisp, clear morning in a strange bed. He made to rise but felt a searing pain in his head. A wooziness came over him, and he half lay, half sat, propped up on the softest, plumpest, most luxurious duck down pillows he had ever felt. Though, of course, King Dudo didn't know them as 'pillows.' They were called *downdles* back then. Pillows were not invented yet. As you know, pillows were invented in 1427 in a small hospital town in the south of France by a pioneering Polish surgeon called Docteur Tchopemov.

"Docteur Tchopemov had specialized in amputations, like most respectable physicians in Europe at the time—"

"Um, Granny?" Dani said, twiddling her thumbs.

"Yes, Dani?" Granny smiled benignly at Dani.

"I'm sure the story of Docteur Tchopemov is utterly fascinating, I really am. I'm positive, in fact, but do you think you should tell us now?"

"What do you mean?"

"Maybe," Ruairi said, tentatively, "you could tell us about Dudo first of all and come back to the story about how pillows were invented later?"

"Well," Granny said, pondering this, "it's not a vital part of the story, I will grant you that. But, actually, now that you stop me a moment, I think I would rather like to have a wee rest before we land on Yondersaay, if you don't mind. I'm pooped." And Granny pinned up her tray table and pressed the button on the armrest that made her chair swing back almost flat.

"But, Granny! What about the rest of the story?" Dani said.

"What about King Dudo and the woman who turned into a bear?" Ruairi said.

"Ursula?" Granny asked from a fully reclined position. She let out a big yawn. "But I've already told you about all of that, no?"

Dani and Ruairi shook their heads.

"It's been a very long day," Granny said. "And we'll be there before you know it. A quick rest and Robert's your mother's brother." Ruairi looked puzzled. "Bob's your uncle!" Granny clarified.

"But, Granny," Dani said. "We can't leave it! The suspense will *kill* us."

"And Mum's brother is called Tony," Ruairi muttered as Mum grinned.

"Forget it," Dani said. "We'll have to wait. She's already asleep. Listen."

Granny let out a nasal snore that sounded half like a rocket taking off and half like a kitten purring.

"Try to get some sleep, my darlings," Mum said. "Granny's right. It has been a long day. We'll be on Yondersaay very soon now."

Landing on Yondersaay

Ruairi didn't remember falling asleep.

"It's time to wake up now, folks," Granny said as she roused him. "We're here. We're finally here on Yondersaay."

Ruairi woke up and looked around him. Dani was waking up too.

"You know," Granny said as she wrapped her scarf around and around her neck, "not very many people have ever been to Yondersaay. If they have, they always tell me they fell asleep on the plane and forgot how long they were in the air. They look back out the window to see the cliffs at the top of the country they're flying from, the sea splashes up, and they fall asleep. Strange, no? And," she continued, "no ordinary people ever come to Yondersaay. Only people who are invited."

"Were we invited?" Ruairi asked. "I don't remember being invited. You just told us we were going!"

"Well, you're Yondersaanian, and you've been here about a hundred times."

"Nine," Mum corrected. "Nine or ten. And you were in my tummy the first time, both of you. Though of course not at the same time."

"That would be weird!" Ruairi said.

"Not for twins!" Dani said.

"You're sort of twins, though, aren't you?" Granny said winking at them. "You're *Irish twins*—born less than a year apart."

"But more special even than *Irish twins*," Dani said, grinning at her little brother. "Born less than a year apart—"

"—and within the same year," Ruairi finished, grinning back at his sister.

"And of course, we're not Irish."

"Oi!" Mum said. "You're half Irish."

"Yeah, but we do our best to keep that quiet," Dani said as she dodged the glove Mum threw at her.

"I can't WAIT for my birthday next week!" Ruairi said. "Because then I'll be the same age as you! And you won't be able to boss me around."

"Only for three days. Then it'll be the new year and my birthday!" Dani said. "And then I can boss you all I like. Like now!"

"I'd like to see you try!"

The Millers' plane was the only one at the landing strip. The plug door opened, and a powerful blast of icy wind sent a ripple of shivers, like a Mexican wave, down the plane among the passengers. Ruairi was quickly reminded, as if he could have forgotten, it was cold on Yondersaay at Christmastime. He and his family dressed up warm for the two-minute walk down the steps of the plane at the end of the runway into the tiny terminal building. Ruairi loved the crunch his boots made on the layers of snow on the ground, and he loved the way the soft flakes of snow landed on his face and melted into mush. The first thing Ruairi always noticed was that there were no trees in any direction, unlike at home where there were massive big trees all down the street. But he always forgot when he was back at home again, so noticing the lack of trees every time he came to Yondersaay was always a bit of a surprise for him. As far as he knew, there were only three or four trees on the entire island.

When the Millers got inside the terminal building, their bags were already there waiting for them. The terminal building was just one big room—one departures desk, one baggage carousel, one café, one lost luggage hatch. The baggage carousel didn't move at all. Ruairi could see this disappointed Dani. She was itching to jump on and have a go on it when no one was looking, like last time.

Ruairi looked about the hall for super speedy baggage handlers, but all he could see were a few really, really old people dotted about the place in plastic chairs or on wooden benches looking like they had been dropped off en masse at naptime. They all knew Granny Miller. They waved or smiled or raised their hats, and Granny waved back.

Ruairi noticed the guy manning the cafe wasn't ridiculously old. In fact, he wasn't old at all. Nor was the man in the lost luggage booth. He looked at the dude behind the bar and back to the man in the lost luggage booth, and back again.

They seemed to be the same person. The man handing out "Visit Yondersaay" leaflets—pointless exercise Ruairi thought since they were already there, visiting Yondersaay—was also identical, as was the man filling the vending machines, and the man outside brushing the new snow from the pathway. Granny could see him looking at them.

"They're the five twins."

"What?" Ruairi said.

"The five twins."

"Twins come in twos, Granny," Dani said.

"Nonsense! Well, maybe they do, but not here, not these twins. Five of them came at once." She walked on before Dani had a chance to object.

The Millers collected their bags, showed their passports to the man in the uniform, and walked outside into the snow to find their car.

"Hello, Morag," Granny said to the twin clearing the snow from the path.

"Hello there, Mrs. Miller," Morag said in a very squeaky voice. Dani raised her eyebrows at Ruairi.

By the time the rented mauve car turned into the driveway of Granny's cottage in Yondersaay Village, it was already dark. The Millers were so tired they could hardly remember how long they had been traveling. It seemed like weeks.

Dani went upstairs to unpack everyone's pajamas while Ruairi helped Mum in the kitchen. Prepared, as always, Mum had brought the essentials and made a quick dinner to tide everyone over. Remembering that on Yondersaay dinner is called "tea," she fried omelettes and grilled and buttered toast while Granny chopped wood for the fire.

After tea, Ruairi nudged Dani, and she said as casually as she could, "I think the Roo-ster and I should be allowed to stay up late tonight, Mum. There's absolutely no way we could possibly get to sleep."

"No way at all," Ruairi said, stifling a yawn.

"Darlings, we're all exhausted. It has been a long day. Now go upstairs and get ready for bed."

"But, Mum—"

"That's enough now. You'll thank me tomorrow. You'll have so much energy you'll be able to run all over the island and do everything you want to do. I'll be up in a minute to kiss you good night. And, Ruairi, I will be checking your teeth."

Ruairi and Dani looked to Granny Miller for an intervention, but she was already dozing on the sofa and was no use at all. They trudged upstairs and started to get ready for bed, Mum following close behind.

Ruairi had just rubbed some toothpaste on the front ones so it smelled like he'd brushed his teeth, but when she leaned down to kiss him, Mum did not make him go brush his teeth properly. Instead, she cuddled him and Dani close. Mum didn't go to bed. Ruairi heard her go back downstairs, light the fire, and make herself comfortable on the squeaky sofa with the loose springs. But soon, everything went quiet.

Granny was asleep in her bed. Mum was asleep in front of the fire. But no one was asleep in Dani's bed, nor in Ruairi's bed. In fact, there was no one awake in their beds either. Because while Mum was downstairs drifting off and Granny was in her bedroom tucking her hair into her lacy nightcap and sliding her comfortable slippers under her bed, Dani and Ruairi were putting on clothes and coats and hats and scarves and wellies over their pajamas and climbing out of their window and onto the roof of the garage.

"If Mum thinks we could fall asleep now, she's *mad!*" Dani said to Ruairi as they shimmied down the rose trellis on the side of the garage that faced away from the road.

"I know," said Ruairi as Dani jumped over him and landed on the ground with a soft tumble. "We only just got here, and it's not even that late." They looked up at the sky—it was pitch-black. They looked around—the lights were off in all of the houses on Gargle View Avenue. Everywhere was quiet except for a solitary owl *toowit-toowooing* softly some way off.

"I think it probably is quite late, Ruairi."

"Yeah, but not *that* late." He shrugged. "Okay, what's the plan? Where to?"

"Let's see if any dead bodies have washed up on the shore. Murdered bodies wash up here all the time. They float in from all over," Dani said, frightening Ruairi more than a little. They vaulted over the garden wall, hunched down, and padded as quickly and as quietly as they could in the direction of the harbor.

"Or we could skim stones across the River Gargle," Ruairi said quickly. "There will most likely be people at the harbor, fishermen and suchlike. We might be seen at the shore."

"Good thinking, Ruairi. Mum would have a conniption fit if she found out we'd been walking around on our own after dark."

Ruairi gave a sigh of relief.

"Besides," Dani said, "murdered bodies are just as likely to wash up near the mouth of the River Gargle as they are in the harbor." She turned on down the road. Ruairi could tell she was smiling to herself. He was about to suggest going to the Crimson Forest instead, but he remembered just in time that it was haunted. He caught up with Dani and stayed close. They stole up the High Street to the crest of the hill and broke away from the village, turning right before the path to the Crimson Forest. All the time, Ruairi was sticking as close to Dani as he could manage, while simultaneously trying to dawdle and slow her down, and distract her, and veer her off course. He tried to think of ways to convince Dani that finding a bloody, oozing, murdered body would not be cool, and that finding dead things should not be their aim, but he knew he was fighting a losing battle.

The river swerved at the very bottom of the mountain where it took a jump and crashed straight down, transforming into a waterfall for a moment, splashing into a wide, deep whirlpool, eventually flattening out, becoming a river again, and opening out to meet the sea.

"Dans?" Ruairi said.

"Yip?" Dani soldiered on at speed through the soft snow.

"Are they getting divorced?" He kicked some stones with his shoe.

Dani stopped walking and hung back until she was level with her brother. She flung her arm over his shoulder. "Come on," she said, pulling him on. She waited a moment, "I didn't think so before today."

"And now?" Ruairi looked up at her.

"She really wanted him to come with us." She thought for a minute again. "And he said he wanted to come but couldn't because of work. That's something, right?"

"It is?" Ruairi said as they came up on the whirlpool.

"I think we should be more worried when they don't fight, Ruairi. When they're both okay that he can't come with us."

"I suppo—" Ruairi heard a noise that made him stop in his tracks. He grabbed Dani's arm and pulled her down to a crouch.

"I think there's somebody there," Dani whispered.

Ruairi was petrified. "A murdered body?"

"Don't be silly. Murdered bodies are dead bodies—they

don't make noise. Let's go closer and see who it is."

"Or we could go back? Maybe we should go back; I think we should go back," Ruairi shot out, rapid-fire. Dani was already moving closer. She got down on all fours and crawled to the edge of the river. She could see all around the pool from there.

"Look, can you see that?" she said to Ruairi when he joined her. It was very dark, and they were far away from the few lights that were still on in the village. After a second or two of looking hard, Ruairi could make out two dark shapes on the other side of the water.

One was a massive, hulking man, slowly weaving up and down the pool banks with what looked like an upright vacuum cleaner. Closer to the edge was another man. He was dreadfully thin, and perhaps it was the way he was standing, but he was uncommonly crooked-looking and a bit stooped. He had a very pointy nose and a very pointy chin, and he watched while the massive person heaved himself backward and forward waving his vacuum cleaner from side to side. A voice came from farther back, and Dani and Ruairi saw two more people.

"With all due respect, it's past two a.m., and we've been looking for a solid year now. I think it's time to call it a night," one of the two men said.

"It must be a metal detector. They're looking for something," Dani whispered to Ruairi.

"But why are they looking now? They'll never find anything in the dark."

"I don't know."

The pointy man turned to face the man who spoke; he addressed him sharply. "Enough! I know it is here somewhere. I can feel it. The proximity of it simmers the marrow of my bones. We will continue our search here until daybreak, and tomorrow we will go back through the Crimson Forest one more time and we'll comb through every branch, every leaf, literally every—"

"SHH!"

He was interrupted by the huge man with the metal detector.

"Shh!" the massive man said again and took a step toward the edge of the pool. He looked through the darkness across the river toward the spot on the ground where Dani and Ruairi lay. "What's that?" He pointed in their direction.

Dani and Ruairi looked at each other accusingly.

"I didn't say anything," Ruairi said.

"Well neither did I!"

"There's something glowing," the man said. The other three came close to the edge to have a look.

Dani and Ruairi slowly looked down at themselves, and they saw, all along the bottoms of their jackets and all around the necks and around the cuffs and even in places on their hats and scarves—a glow in the dark.

"Mum!" they whispered together.

Ruairi and Dani scrambled as fast as they could out of sight of the men and ducked behind a boulder.

"I don't see anything," the crooked man said.

"It moved!" the big man called.

Mum, who was terrified of anything bad happening to her children, had sewn yards and yards of fluorescent, glow-in-the-dark tape onto every visible inch of their clothing.

As soon as they were out of sight, Dani and Ruairi took off their jackets and turned them inside out. They turned their hats inside out and tucked their scarves well inside the tops of their coats. They gave each other the once-over, and when they were sure there was no more reflective material visible, they signaled to each other and got ready to make a run for it.

"When did she manage to do all this?" Ruairi said. "Granny only gave us our new winter coats this morning!"

"She must have sewn it on in the plane while we were sleeping," Dani said.

"Sometimes that woman goes too far."

"There's definitely something there," the big man said. "I'm going to take a look." He started toward the bridge.

That was all Dani and Ruairi needed to hear. They bolted out from behind the boulder and ran as fast as they could toward the village and home, never once looking back.

Almost out of breath, they ran down the hill, right in the middle of the High Street, not caring if they made noise now, and onto Gargle View Avenue. The wind was picking up, and the snow was really starting to come down. Taking care not to slip on the fresh snow, they jumped over the garden wall and climbed up the rose trellis on the side of the garage. They tumbled through the open window, undressed, and got into bed as quickly as they possibly could.

"No way did they see who we were," Ruairi said.

"No. Absolutely no way. It was way too dark, and we were quick as lightning. Ruairi, you're becoming super fast. I could hardly keep up with you."

"Thanks, Dans." Ruairi grinned from ear to ear. "I think it's all the broccoli I've been eating."

"You do eat a lot of broccoli."

They both drifted into a fast and sound sleep. Ruairi's last thought just before his dreams began—more an image than a thought; it flashed across his mind and was gone forever—was of two sets of tracks in the snow.

The Butcher, The Baker

Ruairi sprawled out beside Dani on the rug in front of the fire where they were both eating toast and pretending to read their books.

"What do you think they were looking for?" Dani asked Ruairi.

"Maybe it was a dead body." Ruairi went pale.

"Why would they be looking for a dead body with a metal detector? A dead body wouldn't beep. Only something metal would."

"Maybe it had lots of fillings."

"What are you two talking about?" Granny asked from her armchair.

"Nothing, Granny," Dani and Ruairi said quickly.

Dani looked intently at her book and whispered to Ruairi out the side of her mouth. "Let's get dressed and go for a walk by the river, just to have another little look around."

Ruairi was not sure he wanted to do that. "What if they're still there?" he asked.

"No chance, not in broad daylight," Dani said. "Anyway, didn't the one say they were going to go to the Crimson Forest in the morning?"

"Oh yeah."

"I want the pair of you to hurry up with your breakfast. We have a full day ahead of us," Mum said, coming down the stairs with her arms full of coats and gloves and hats. "There's so much to do to get everything ready for Christmas Day. We'll need some milk from the dairy where we'll also get some cheeses and some lovely thick cream for the pudding, which we'll get at the baker's. Ooh, and some crusty brown bread for the smoked salmon from the smokehouse, which we'll eat before the turkey and ham from the butcher's, which wouldn't be Christmassy at all without some Brussels sprouts—" Mum handed out all their coats as she spoke. Granny stuffed two buttered pancakes into her mouth and four slices of toast into her handbag. "—which we'll get at the greengrocer's. We'll find everything else we need there, except the brandy for the brandy butter, which we'll have to take a turn out to the distiller's to get. And if we go the long way through the Crimson Forest, we'll hunt for some holly and mistletoe to decorate the table." Ruairi froze at this. Trying not to look as scared as he felt, he glanced at Dani who was nodding and smiling.

"Let's do all that today," Mum went on, "and tomorrow we can spend the entire day dressing the Christmas tree, building snowmen, eating chocolates, which we'll get at the greengrocer's, and watching Christmas films on telly.

"Wrap up warm, my darlings. There's a nip in the air, and though the snow looks soft as velvet, it comes down quite sharp. It will take an icy bite out of your noses and cheeks if you let it … Why are your coats inside-out?"

"Um …" Ruairi said.

"Ah …" Dani said.

"To keep them clean!" Ruairi said and shot a worried glance at Dani.

"Obviously!" Dani grabbed her hat and pulling it right down so Mum couldn't see her face. Mum shrugged and put on layers and layers of coats and scarves and four pairs of gloves. Ruairi knew Mum loved the snow but didn't think it was safe to get too cold.

The crisp light of the new day ran up the High Street and along the side avenues, across the hill at the top of the village, and fell downward into the Crimson Forest and the River Gargle before bouncing back off the mountain in a cold yellow glow. The Millers headed toward the High Street. It was bright and sunny, clear and dry. And cold. Very cold. There was no sign that it would snow again soon but the ground was thickly covered in a fresh layer of white. The houses all looked as if their roofs were thatched with white straw; there was at least a foot of snow on top of every building. Cars that hadn't been driven for a day or two looked like massive snowballs. All the Millers wore their winter boots and heavy winter coats, not just Mum. They were wrapped up like presents; the only parts that showed were their cheeks. Their bright red cheeks. Which were almost as red as their hair.

They weren't dawdling, but it still took them nearly an

hour to get the two blocks from Gargle View Cottage to the bottom of the High Street. Everyone they met along the way knew Granny Miller and wanted to stop and ask her how she was and say how they hardly recognized Dani and Ruairi anymore, they'd grown so much, and to chat about what a lovely sunny day, if a bit cold, it was turning out to be. The woman from the pharmacist's, the postman, and a short little fat hairy man who was arguing with his very tall, very thin wife stopped them and had a quick chat. A big, balding man, the draper, drove up to them in a tiny blue car the size of a bumper car at the dodgems, and had a conversation out his window. *Everybody* knew them and wanted to say hello.

Granny Miller and Mum didn't seem to mind all of this. Granny Miller grew up here, and Mum grew up in an even smaller place. They were both well used to it. Ruairi was baffled, but it appeared that they actually enjoyed it even. To him, however, and to Dani, it was *torture*.

"Hurry *up,* Mum," Dani whispered.

Ruairi said, "I am getting dangerously cold and *dangerously bored.*"

"Wear the crown of patience, Ruairi," Mum said.

"This is why we never come shopping with you at home!" Dani said. "Remind us never to fall for your trickery again!"

"Isn't it *unsafe* to be this cold? And this bored? You're being irresponsible. You're not thinking of our well-being." Ruairi stood behind the tall, thin woman Mum was talking to and mouthed, "*Please*, let's *go*!" He made a face at her behind the woman's back, so Mum finally said good-bye. From then on, when they met people, they waved to them and said things like, "Hi, how are you? Lovely to see you. Yes, it's a lovely day," but they didn't stop walking.

Their first stop, when they finally got there, on this wintry morning on the day before Christmas Eve, was the butcher's shop.

When Ruairi made it through the door, some incomer was asking the butcher, out of politeness, while she was waiting for her ham to be sliced and wrapped, why he'd decided to become a butcher. He let out a sigh, crossed his arms, and rolled his eyes at her. The colored bits went so far up in his head that Ruairi thought they would get stuck up there and then what would he do.

"I'm Hamish Sinclair, and the Sinclairs are the butchers like the Andersons are the teachers and the MacFadyens are the whiskey-makers," he boomed at her. "Because if I wasn't a butcher, then there would be no such thing as a Sunday roast or a midsummer barbecue or a chicken sandwich. On Sundays, there'd be carrots and potatoes and parsnips and a big gap in the middle of the table. It would be confusing. People would still be hungry after Sunday lunch, and they wouldn't know why.

"And what would be done with all the extra animals, I ask you? The island would be positively chock-a-block with over-woolly sheep and geriatric cows. Not to mention the ferocious smell of poo. People wouldn't be able to walk for poo. There'd be poo everywhere. And you're mad if you think I'm going to spend my days going around cleaning up cow poo and herding pigs and chickens off the High Street so people can walk down it."

When his eyes did flicker over Ruairi and Dani, they gasped. Hamish seemed utterly indifferent to them, and despite themselves, Dani and Ruairi found themselves inching forward so they could look more closely at him.

"That's the man from the River Gargle whirlpool," Dani whispered to Ruairi without moving her lips.

"Definitely. He's even bigger in real life."

"He was in real life last night," Dani said.

"I mean up close. He's even more massive up close. What is he? Half-giant, half-gorilla?"

"Or one quarter mountain, three quarters abominable snowman?"

Eventually they stopped whispering and just stood there, trying very hard not to stare at Hamish Sinclair.

Hamish Sinclair was poured into white wellies and a white butcher's coat that looked like a sausage skin on him. If you pronged him with a fork, he might explode. He wore a white hairnet under a baseball cap. There was a chance he wasn't pleased about the hairnet, it wasn't the most manly-looking accessory; Ruairi imagined a great deal of effort had gone into disguising it and tucking the edges under the cap.

The butcher's shoulders were wider than the entire meat counter. His head skimmed the shop ceiling. And to say he was hairy was an understatement; his forearms needed hairnets.

The thing that made Hamish not just big but scarily big was not his height or his width or his hugely muscular arms and thighs. What made the difference was his voice—so deep, so booming, and so loud that even if he were tiny it would give the impression of a giant speaking. He wasn't smiling, and he wasn't talking cheerfully about the weather, like everyone else they'd met on the island.

Mum and Granny ordered a turkey and a ham for Christmas dinner and sausages and bacon and black and white pudding for tea. They ordered venison for venison stew and sliced meats for sandwiches. They talked about getting a turducken—a chicken inside a duck inside a turkey—for Christmas dinner instead of a turkey and a ham but decided against it in the end.

"Raising chickens inside ducks inside turkeys could be cruel if not carried out in a closely monitored and regulated environment," Mum ventured. "A chicken couldn't possibly have much quality of life if it grew up inside the bum of a duck. And the poor turkey with both a chicken and a duck in its bum. What if the chicken and the duck didn't get on and started pecking? It doesn't bear thinking about."

"Is it organic?" Granny wanted to know.

"Free-range," Hamish grunted.

"All the same, best not," Granny said. "Maybe next year."

"I'll have your order run over to Gargle View Cottage later this afternoon, Granny Miller," Hamish said. He did not ask for Granny's name because he already knew it. He did not ask for Granny's address because he already knew that too. Ruairi was not thrilled that this particular person knew where they lived, but everybody knew everybody on Yondersaay, so of course he knew Granny's address. Mum thanked Hamish Sinclair and wished him a Merry Christmas, and they all left the shop.

"Watch out for the mad one on your way out—she's back from her break, out there yelling 'No meat!'" Hamish Sinclair called out to them as they were leaving. "*Real* men eat nothing BUT meat … and the occasional Cadbury's creme egg."

Ruairi had a quick glance back into the shop on his way out the door. He caught Hamish Sinclair looking straight at him. Ruairi couldn't move—he was held in the stare. He felt Dani tug at his arm and let himself be led out of the shop. The last thing Ruairi saw as they exited was the giant butcher picking up a tiny phone, and dialling a number.

A very angry woman about Mum's age was pacing outside the butcher's shop. She was shouting, "Meat is murder! Meat is an atrocity!" in such a furious way that

Ruairi was more than a little frightened of her. She was wearing old trousers made of patches and a coat that may well have been made out of her own hair and bits of things swept off the floor.

"Meat is murder! You're a *murderer*!" she shouted viciously at Granny as she stepped across the picket line. "You may as well have slit the cow's throat yourself—" She paused, and her face cracked into a big grin. Her shoulders relaxed, and she became positively sweet. "Granny Miller! Is that you? I didn't recognize you for a minute there! You're looking fierce well. How are you? Lovely day, isn't it?"

Granny squinted at the protester. "Little Alice Cogle! I don't believe it. It must be years! Well, how are you? You know you haven't changed a bit."

Alice blushed and said that Granny Miller was very kind to say so. "I'm the best—doing very well."

"And you're doing this now, Alice," Granny said as she looked around uncertainly at the posters and placards on the ground. "How are you finding it?"

"Well, the hours are good, you know, nine to five, which suits me down to the ground. And you? Are you back for the Christmas, is it?" Alice Cogle asked.

Dani and Ruairi wandered on up the street toward the bakery, which was just a few doors down from the butcher's shop. They went quickly and didn't even glance in the window of the new boutique in case Mum noticed it and decided she wanted to go in for a browse.

"Exactly right. I'm here with the family for the few days," Granny was saying to Alice Cogle as Ruairi turned the handle on the bakery door. "I have to say it's lovely to be home at this time of year."

"Of course! It's usually for the summer we have you," Alice said.

"That's right. And have you stopped doing part-time work for Eoin Lerwick at the greengrocer's?" Granny asked.

Granny Miller and Alice Cogle's muffled conversation carried into the bakery a few minutes later when the door opened for Mum, who had stopped to look in the window of the new boutique. "That's odd!" Granny Miller said, as the door swung closed.

Ruairi barely heard it, because as soon as he set foot inside the door his attention was utterly, wholly, and absolutely taken over by the delicious tarts and cakes and buns in front of them. Both he and Dani were suddenly *starving*. The shop was three times the size it was the last time they were here on their summer holidays two and a half years earlier. There were café tables now and an espresso machine on one of the counters. Mum sat down and ordered a coffee, and two hot chocolates for Dani and Ruairi. She said they could have one thing each. Ruairi hadn't the slightest idea how he would ever come to a decision.

═══ ● ═══

You would never know by looking at him that Lewis MacAvinney wasn't just the man who stood behind the counter at the bakery. He also had a medical degree and two PhDs: one in romantic literature, the other in astrophysics.

"It is my understanding," Granny had once told Mum, "that when he goes to Germany, they have to call him Herr Doctor Doctor Doctor MacAvinney."

"That could get exhausting after a while," Mum had said.

"He's rich too but still as sweet and kind now, as a multimillionaire Doctor Doctor Doctor, as he was when he was the best in his troop of Cub Scouts at helping old people cross the street," Granny had explained.

"He would have gotten plenty of practice at that on Yondersaay. Everyone here is *ancient*," Dani had muttered to Ruairi, who burst out laughing.

"Lewis holds patents for a hundred different inventions," Granny went on "mostly in the astrophysics field. All the same, you can't keep a Yondersaay boy away from home for long. You know, he's constantly developing new and interesting cakes and breads for the shop. I'm not sure any of them have worked as planned so far, but I love it when he tries them out on me.

"Last I heard, he was working on a raspberry shortcake that sticks its tongue out at you; a coconut crumble that lifts itself up into the shape of a hula dancer, and sings, "Tallulah does the hula in Hawaii," and crumbles into a pile on the plate. The Current Bun™ with its caffeine-free jolt of energy gives you a little electric shock – I recommend you avoid that one. My favourites are the French sticks that are rude to you, and the "wry" bread that makes droll witticisms about the state of the economy or the shape of your nose."

Lewis came over to the Millers' table with his notebook. "What can I get for you, Granny Miller?" Ruairi liked his voice, it was quiet and kind sounding, and Ruairi saw he made Granny instantly relaxed. Granny tumbled into a heap in a giant armchair and ordered a pot of tea and a raspberry shortcake. When Lewis handed the raspberry shortcake to Granny, he stood and watched it for a minute. It didn't stick its tongue out at her. Lewis MacAvinney gave a little sigh, and made a note in his notebook.

Mum hadn't ordered anything to eat, so Lewis brought her over a plate with samples of about ten different cakes.

"How come she gets all of that?" Ruairi asked, looking from his limp pain au chocolat to Mum's massive plate of cakes and back at his pain au chocolat again.

Lewis gave Mum a big smile and said "Hi," in a very shy way. Mum looked at him, and he blushed behind his little spectacles, turned away, and went back behind the counter.

Dani looked anxiously at her mother. Ruairi whispered to Mum, "You don't think he's nicer than Dad, do you, Mum?"

"Don't be ridiculous, Ruairi. Of course not. Besides, Lewis is demonstrating the Christmas spirit, nothing more." Mum looked directly at both Dani and Ruairi as she spoke.

Dani shrugged and said, "If you say so," and Mum went to the counter to put in her order for cake and plum pudding for Christmas day.

While she was gone, Dani and Ruairi stuffed as many of Mum's cakes into their mouths as they could. Dani poked Ruairi under his arm just as he filled his mouth with a cream bun, which made him snigger and snort cream up his nose. Ruairi's eyes shot open extrawide midsnigger. Dani followed his gaze out the front window. Standing there, in his hairnet and sausage-skin coat, chattering animatedly with two other men who were behind him in the shadows, jabbing his finger in Ruairi's direction, was none other than the butcher, Hamish Sinclair.

Dudo Meets Jarl Olaf

Ruairi looked at the men and spun around to look behind him. There was no one else near him. "They're looking at me! He's pointing at me!" he whispered to Dani while he wiped cream off his face and shrank back into his armchair. "You said they couldn't have seen us last night," he said to Dani.

"Couldn't have!" Dani said. "There must be a simple explanation. Oh no. Mum's ready to go. Let's try to stall her and stay here. Maybe they'll go away and we can sneak out when they're not looking."

"What do you think they want?" Ruairi asked, his lower lip starting to tremble.

"I don't know, Ruairi."

"Maybe they're not looking at me at all. Maybe they want a loaf of bread or something ..."

"Maybe," Dani said. Then, turning to Mum, she said,

"We're a bit pooped now, and it's getting cold. And Granny's all snug in her armchair. I think it would be a good idea to rest a bit before we do the rest of the shopping."

"Not a bad idea, Dani. I'll order us all some more coffees and hot chocolates," Mum said. She glanced at her nearly empty plate. Dani and Ruairi avoided her eye. "And if Granny's up to it, maybe she could tell us a bit more about King Dudo and the mystery woman and the buried treasure."

"Only if you want to, Granny," Dani said, trying not to appear eager.

"Yes, Granny, only if you're not too tired," Ruairi said, scraping his chair around in front of Granny so he could hear better and so he was out of view of the window at the front of the shop.

"It would be my pleasure," Granny said, "but we will need more cakes too, Mum."

"Sure thing, Granny," Mum said, "but keep room for tea. I'm making smoked salmon pâté with crusty bread from here and smoked salmon from the smokehouse followed by a cassoulet of duck leg and—"

"Now. Where were we?" Granny said, cutting Mum off. "Ah, yes. King Dudo was propped up on the most luxurious and softest *downdles* he had ever had the good fortune to be propped up against.

"He had a nosy look at his surroundings. He was in a very nice dwelling place. It was smaller than he was used to, but then again, he was the King of the Danes—he was used to the very best of everything, downdles excepted.

"He felt there were people nearby. He heard muffled voices outside the room. 'No, I will not!' he thought he heard. And 'FORGET IT!'"

"Dudo cleared his throat loudly so whoever was there would know that he was awake. The voices stopped, and several feet shuffled away. An elderly man popped his head around the entranceway.

"'Ah,' he said, 'you have awoken. Welcome to my humble home. You are most welcome. I am Jarl Olaf Barelegs the Balding on Top. Welcome.'

"'A jarl?' King Dudo bowed to the elderly man. On his way back up from the bow, he noticed that the man was not wearing trousers or leg coverings of any kind. Instead, he wore a very short kilt. 'I thank you for your warm welcome. You are lord of this country?'

"'Indeed, I am lord of this place; however, you are not in any country. You have landed on the island of Yondersaay.'"

Dani and Ruairi beamed. "Yondersaay!" they said.

Granny looked at them over her glasses and continued. "King Dudo gasped, 'Yondersaay!'

"Jarl Olaf Barelegs the Balding on Top nodded gravely. 'Yes, King Dudo,' for he knew that King Dudo was King Dudo.

"'You know that I am King Dudo!'

"'But of course, King Dudo. You have the bearing of a king, mighty and brave, and exceptionally clever. Plus, your name was stitched onto your underwear.'

"'Ah,' said King Dudo.

"'You have breached the boundary of the enchanted island in the middle of the northern-most seas,' the jarl continued. 'You have arrived at a place you've most probably been told doesn't exist. But exist it does and on it you are.'

"King Dudo was speechless. The one place he'd always dreamed of finding, and now, here he was.

"'Rest, King Dudo. I will send my daughter to tend to you. She will find fresh clothes for you and will fetch you some mead and bread …'"

"The woman from the ice!" Ruairi said. "I bet his

daughter is the woman who turned into the bear—no, wait; the bear who turned into the woman—on the ice, when King Dudo sang and cracked his head and fell in! I bet it's her!"

"Ursula?" Granny said. "Well, let's see. Jarl Olaf left the dwelling place, and King Dudo waited for the jarl's daughter to arrive. He hoped against all hope that the woman he was waiting for was the woman who had appeared before him on the ice. He wished it in his heart and in his bones. He heard a rustling and looked to the entranceway.

"Before him stood the jarl's daughter. She had pale skin and blue eyes. She was a true beauty. She smiled at him and walked toward him with his new set of clothes. There was grace and elegance in every movement. She came to him, put a hand on his shoulder and gently asked him what the matter was. 'Are you ill, my liege? You look so desolate.' She asked him this because King Dudo had a look of such sadness on his face. His whole body gave off an air of melancholy and disappointment.

"The beautiful girl smiling sweetly at him and tenderly touching his shoulder, was *not* the girl from the ice. 'I am very well. Nothing is the matter,' he said to her. He forced a smile and accepted the clothes."

"It's not her? Where is she?" Dani asked. "What happened to her?"

"Did she turn back into a bear again?" Ruairi asked.

"Maybe we never see her again," Granny said.

"I think that's improbable," Dani said with finality.

"Oh, you do, do you? And why do you think that?"

"Because in stories people always end up with their Heart's True Love. And they get married and live Happily Ever After." Dani folded her arms.

"But this isn't some *story*, Dani. This is real life. It

wasn't today or yesterday, but it did really happen. It's a sad fact that in real life people don't always end up with their Heart's True Love. And in real life, sometimes—and I'm warning you now before we go any further—sometimes the baddy doesn't get his comeuppance. And sometimes ... sometimes the good person dies."

Dani leaned over to Ruairi, who was a little distressed at this news, and whispered, "I still think he'll see her again."

"Well, as it happens," said Granny, sighing, "the next day King Dudo was feeling much stronger and decided to go for a walk outside. He wanted to have a look around the island. He came out of the dwelling place into the light of the morning, and who should he see but a red-haired, blue-eyed, pale-skinned woman!"

"I KNEW IT!" Dani shouted, and both Dani and Ruairi leaped up onto their bakery chairs, which were surprisingly bouncy, and started jumping up and down shouting and screaming,

"Yay! He's found his Heart's True Love!" Ruairi shouted.

" He's found his Heart's True Love! We knew he would. We knew he would," Dani echoed.

Mum shushed them.

Granny ignored them and continued with her story. "Dudo was frozen to the spot. He stared at the woman. She was carrying an empty pail toward the dwelling place. She glanced at him as she approached and turned away again as though she hadn't even noticed him. She walked straight past, an inch from him, and into the dwelling place and out of his sight."

"Oh," said Dani, and stopped jumping.

"It's her twin sister!" Ruairi said and sat down on the chair. "Her *evil* twin sister." He narrowed his eyes.

Granny went on. "She came back out of the dwelling.

This time her pail was filled with garments. She walked by King Dudo without even looking in his direction, around the back, and out of sight again.

"King Dudo was startled and a little embarrassed. Even if she didn't have feelings for him, she should at least remember him, no? King Dudo walked in the direction the woman had gone and saw she had walked to a gargling brook at the back of the property. She was up to her knees in the brook, her skirts hitched high and fastened by a ribbon at her waist. She was singing a little tune and washing the garments she had carried there. King Dudo approached the bank of the brook and called out, 'Well, hello there!'

"The woman looked up at King Dudo, politely smiled, said, 'hello,' and went back to her washing.

"The king was bewildered. He really had expected more of a reaction than that. He was King Dudo the Mightily Impressive after all! Lord over all Denmark, the glorious King of all Danes! He was a handsome man and brave and known throughout the world as being Mightily Impressive. Mightily Impressive, I tell you! And brave! He was not used to this sort of reaction from a woman, especially a peasant woman who washes her own clothes. He was used to women blushing coyly when he approached them. They were, as a rule, only too delighted to have the king say such pithy things to them as 'well, hello there.' The king was confused and a little bit angry. He turned around and stomped off to find the jarl.

"King Dudo found the jarl at the harbor shooting the breeze with some of the local men. Jarl Olaf greeted him warmly and introduced him to the men. 'This is Soxolf the Unshod,' the jarl began.

"'Very pleased to meet you, Soxolf,' King Dudo said, holding out his hand to shake. Soxolf folded his arms, stuck out his chin, and turned his head away. The jarl continued introducing the men in quick-fire succession. 'Bling of Brand Island, Magnan the Generous, Avorage the Ordinary, Thorar the Smoldering, and Pal the Friendly.'

"The men were a surly bunch, except for Pal the Friendly who smiled and waved until Soxolf kicked him in the shin and Avorage poked him in the ribs with his elbow. Dudo noticed Pal was a little unsure of himself. He adopted the posture of the other men—he folded his arms and stuck his nose in the air. All the same, he did glance back at Dudo every now and then and smile at him. Magnan grunted, and Bling spat on the ground near Dudo's feet.

"The king noticed all this of course and was more than a little put out by it. He was sorely tempted to say 'Don't you know who I am?' and he almost did. The jarl, however, noticing that King Dudo was getting angry, got up and told the king he would take him on a walk and show him the island.

"'You must understand,' said the jarl as they walked away. 'Everyone is frightened that you will try to sack and pillage the island. They think you may be their enemy, and they do not think I should have welcomed you to my home.'

"'Ah!' said King Dudo. 'Now I understand. Thank you, Jarl Olaf.' They walked on, and Jarl Olaf took King Dudo through the shaded valley of the Crimson Forest, which was filled with bushes and shrubberies and the prettiest little flowers, just like it is now. Back then, of course, there were also thousands and thousands of trees of all kinds.

"As they walked, King Dudo had turned to the jarl a number of times as though he was about to say something.

"'Do you have a question to ask me, my lord?' the jarl asked King Dudo. Dudo was at this moment kicking an imaginary stone in front of him and whistling in a most tuneless manner.

"'No, not a thing, not a thing. Whatever could have given you that impression?' King Dudo said. 'But if you insist,' he continued, 'I suppose I could come up with some random thing to ask you—nothing important, you understand. Nothing I've been thinking about all morning or anything like that.'

"'I understand, my lord, but yes, please, if you could grasp some random query out of thin air, I would be very happy to try to answer it. I love answering random unimportant questions,' the jarl said.

"'Oh, good,' said the king. 'Well, in that case, just to please you, you understand, could you tell me …'

"'Yes?'

"'Do you know …?'

"'Yes?' The jarl waited patiently.

"'There's a girl,' the king said.

"'A girl?' the jarl asked, nodding sagely and stifling a grin.

"'Yes, I was just wondering who she was and if she also might think that I'm a grotesque enemy just out to plunder and pillage.'

"'We have many beautiful girls here on Yondersaay. I, of course, know every single one of them, as I know all people on my island. We are all one big loving community,' the jarl said and swirled his arms around in the air to demonstrate this closeness. 'Describe her for me.'

"'She has skin the color of polished ivory.'

"'Pale skin. Yes.'

"'And eyes reminiscent of bluebells.'

"'Blue eyes. Yes.'

"'And hair the strangest color of red I have ever seen. It is the color of a sunset over the oceans of sand, the color the sea goes before a rain, the color—'

"'Red hai—No!'

"'No?'

"'No. I know no one like that.'

"'But—'

"'Nope. I'm afraid not. Nuh-uh.'

"'But you just said you knew everyone on the island, that you were just one big loving community.' The king swirled his arms in the air the way the jarl had done. 'Besides, you must know her; she was in your house just now.'

"'Oh, *that* red-haired girl. Oh, yes,' said Jarl Olaf, looking a little defeated.

"'Yes?'

"'Yes. But she's no one.'

"'*Really?*' King Dudo said, narrowing his eyes.

"'Just a servant girl, a mere peasant,' the jarl continued. He leaned toward the king and said to him in a low voice, 'It is widely believed that she has, um, very hairy toes. And she's not a good sort. And she has smelly knees by all accounts. You are not interested in her. No, no, no. We'll forget you even saw her. Very hairy toes.' And Jarl Olaf Barelegs the Balding on Top led King Dudo the Mightily Impressive through the forest to a spot under a taut young oak where a luscious picnic had been laid out in preparation for them.

"'I wish to introduce you to someone,' the jarl said to the king as they sat by the picnic. All of a sudden, he heard a voice from above him.

"'Hello,' said the voice. King Dudo was startled. He looked up but could see no one. He looked all around—no one. He got up and walked around the tree—no sign of a living person who could have spoken.

"'I have decided,' the jarl said, 'to be utterly forthcoming with you about the island, King Dudo. I think it is right that you should have answers to your questions about Yondersaay's secrets. It is for this reason that I am introducing you to Rarelief the Splendiferous.'

"At that, the jarl looked straight up. King Dudo also looked straight up. Just then, the tree moved forward and down as though taking a bow.

"'I am very pleased to make your acquaintance, Your Kingship.'

"Now," Granny said, "let's do the rest of the shopping!" She made to heave herself out of her comfy chair.

"But, Granny, that's not the end of the story, is it?" Dani said.

"It can't be," said Ruairi.

"In truth, it is not the end of the story. But it is getting very late," Granny struggled onto her feet. "And we still have oodles of shopping to do. I'll tell you what. If it's all right with Mum, you can stay up late tonight, and I'll tell you what happens next."

Dani sneaked a glance out through the shop's front window. The coast was clear, so she gave a quick nod to Ruairi. They both turned to their mother.

"We'll be very good all day," Ruairi promised.

"Yes, and we'll help with the dishes," Dani said.

"And we'll brush our teeth," Ruairi added.

"Well it *is* the night before Christmas Eve," Mum said, and Ruairi could almost see the cogs going around in Mum's head as she weighed up the dangers of lack of sleep and overexcitement. "Oh, all right then," she finally said, and Dani and Ruairi gave a cheer.

The three redheads and the one ex-redhead all said good-bye to Lewis MacAvinney, who raised a hand in a shy wave to Mum. Granny shot Mum a sly look, and Dani shot her a worried one, and out they spilled into Yondersaay Village.

At the Greengrocer's

Dani came out of the shop first, puffing herself up and doing her best to make sure Ruairi couldn't be seen behind her. She glanced left, then right, and walked out, falling into step on the outside of Ruairi and just ahead of Granny and Mum.

"I see what you're doing," Ruairi said.

"What do you mean?" Dani avoided Ruairi's eye.

"You were trying to block me out, like a big bodyguard. You do know we're pretty much exactly the same size." Ruairi rolled his eyes.

"I'm *much* taller than you," Dani said.

"I bet if we measured again tonight, I'd be slightly taller than you now." Ruairi smiled as he spoke.

"Complete rubbish! I am at least one sixteenth of an inch taller than you."

"You won't mind if we measure then?" Ruairi raised

one eyebrow.

"Fine. But just remember, even if you do end up taller than me one day," Dani switched into a sing-song voice, "you'll always be my wickle brother!"

"But only for three hundred and sixty-two days of the year! For the other three, I'll be the same age as you *and* taller than you!"

"Dream on, little man!" Dani chanted. "Dream on!"

"Anyway …" Ruairi said, coming closer to Dani so Mum and Granny couldn't hear. "That butcher guy was looking at me funny back there, wasn't he?"

"Maybe he just needed a loaf of bread, but I highly doubt it. There was nothing stopping him from coming in to get it, and why was he pointing you out to those two others? Besides, he was looking at you in an extremely odd way when we were in his shop too."

"That's what I thought. Are you sure? I mean, definitely, totally sure?" Ruairi started to fidget. "They couldn't possibly have gotten a good look at us last night," he assured himself.

Dani thought a moment. "Maybe that's not why he was looking at you like that."

"Then why?" Ruairi asked.

Granny swung open the door to the greengrocer's at the bottom of the village. If Dani and Ruairi had been thrilled and delighted with the changes they found in the bakery since they had last been on the island, their reaction was equal and opposite when they walked into the greengrocer's.

This was the place Dani and Ruairi liked most on the island because of the "Thing" Eoin Lerwick had. They were not quite sure what the "Thing" was, and they knew not to ask for details. Dad had winked at them and put a finger to his lips when he had told them about it years ago, so they knew it was all hush-hush. He had whispered to them that Eoin Lerwick had a "Thing" for Granny Miller.

Every time they went into the shop, Eoin Lerwick would get them whatever sweets they wanted from the rows of jars on the shelves behind the counter and let them play with all the toys. Ruairi's favorite sweets were the grape gobstoppers that took a week of sucking to get to the purple liquorice in the center. Dani could not be doing with something that took a week to get to the good bit. Her favorites were the lemon sherbets—the sticky ones with the powdery sour center—that you could suck for a bit, or crack in one go if you wanted.

Eoin Lerwick would sit the two of them down and tell them the most amazing stories. They were always terrifying or hilarious, sometimes both. He would often act them out as well. It was lovely to see Granny laughing so hard. They had been best friends growing up and knew each other inside out. Eoin had two pet ravens called Thought and Memory, and he could make them do tricks. He could speak to them, and they understood him. At least that's what it looked like. They would rest on his shoulders and swoop around the shop like synchronized swimmers in the air, and they would fetch anything Eoin asked them to fetch. Once, in the middle of summer, he asked Thought to fly out, find a snowflake, and bring it back for Granny Miller. Thought was gone a very long time, and they'd all but forgotten about her and were about to leave when in she flew, the tips of her wings covered in snowflakes. She had hovered just above Granny's head and beat them softly, a tiny blizzard of snowflakes fluttering down onto her upturned face.

On this particular day before Christmas Eve, Eoin Lerwick was nowhere in sight. His birds were distinctly absent, and the shop was, quite frankly, a dump. It was dark and dirty. As they walked in and looked around, they noticed all the lights were off, and there was no produce in the front window or in crates on the street like usual. There was hardly any stock on the shelves, and what was there was covered in dust. It was like the shop had closed down years ago.

Dani and Ruairi wandered about, trying not to touch anything; it was all so rank. Ruairi flipped over the part of the counter that swung on its hinges and went to have a look at the jars of sweets. Dani vaulted over, getting a layer of filth on her hands. The jars were either empty or full of a putrid, oozing mess. Dani made retching noises, which made Ruairi smile. Ruairi pulled down the jar of grape gobstoppers and opened it. There was one sweet in there. It looked bigger than he remembered them being. Rougher but shinier. And more purplish, somehow. He reached in and pulled it out. Ruairi was turning the gobstopper over in his hand when there was a surge in the putrid smell of rancid flesh and rotting vegetation. A slow movement at the corner of his eye made him turn around.

Silently, as if he'd slithered out of nowhere, a lanky sliver of a man with greasy hair, a pointy nose, and a pointy chin appeared in the center aisle before Granny. Ruairi tapped Dani on the shin with his foot, and she looked too.

"With your permission," the man said as he bent down to move a crate out of Granny's way.

"Hello, Mr. Scathe. Is Eoin here, please?" Granny asked stiffly.

"You have *literally* just missed him," Mr. Scathe said to Granny in a voice that was at once high-pitched and quiet.

As soon as he spoke, Ruairi and Dani gasped. Ruairi instinctively stepped out from behind the counter, and putting the gobstopper in his pocket so he could close the counter flap, came and stood shoulder to shoulder with Dani. As quickly as they could, they moved backward toward the door and away from the man. Dani and Ruairi stood safely behind their mum and granny and stuck their elbows into each other's ribs, but they didn't make eye contact. They didn't need to.

"I will leave a message for him. See I'm writing it down now, and I'll give it to him just as soon as he comes back," Mr. Scathe continued, his gaze briefly landing on Ruairi. Granny started to speak again, but he cut her off. "No, I'm afraid I don't know how long he'll be. He didn't say. I'll *literally* get him to call you as soon as he gets back." His mouth turned into a greasy smile. His eyes didn't change at all.

Ruairi wanted to leave. The shop smelled like everything had gone off. He had no doubt that this was the stooped man from the River Gargle the night before.

On their way back from the distillery, Mum suggested they finish up now and go home—it was very dark by this time of course, and it was icy cold. It was starting to snow. Nighttime snowfall on Yondersaay is a very beautiful thing. Ruairi looked into the sky and saw emptiness all the way up into the black. The snow fell from just there, it seemed, tumbling softly down as though someone were standing on a ladder and sprinkling it from that height and no higher.

Mum herded everyone back toward the High Street and shouted over the sound of the wind that it was the perfect night for hot chocolate with roasted marshmallows and Granny's story in front of the fire. "And if you're up to it, if you're not too tired—"

"We're not tired, Mum," Ruairi said as brightly as he could.

"Well if you want to, we can decorate the Christmas tree tonight while we listen to the story instead of waiting until tomorrow."

Dani and Ruairi said they would like to stay up to decorate the Christmas tree and hear the rest of the story and roast marshmallows. So they all hurried toward home.

"My dear," Granny said to Mum, "do you remember the last time we saw Eoin Lerwick? It's so very odd. I can pick out the time when he and I were no more than Ruairi's age, and we had gotten lost exploring the caves on Mount Violaceous. One of Eoin's birds, tiny then, found us and led us out. And I can remember this trip to the beach and that trip out on the boat to the mainland and picnics in the Crimson Forest when we were Dani's age and even your age, Mum, but not for the life of me can I remember anything more recent than that. It is very puzzling."

"Very puzzling, Granny!" Mum said. "Let's give him a ring when we get home."

"That's an extremely smart idea, Mum!"

The wind picked up and blew hard against them and the family of Millers thrust forward into the wind and made for home.

The Night before Christmas Eve

Back at Gargle View Cottage, Mum put some logs on the fire while Granny, after a quick snack of a roast leg of lamb, a barmbrack, and a cantaloupe melon, unearthed the box of Christmas tree decorations in the attic. Dani and Ruairi put on their pajamas and helped Granny down the stairs with the box.

"I don't want you to get upset now, you two, but, I have something to tell you," Mum said as they prepared to start. "Dad may not be coming."

"What do you mean he may not be coming?" Ruairi said. "Why not? He said he'd be right behind us. He said he just had to go to a meeting."

"Yes," Dani asserted. "He said, 'It's unavoidable, kids. The blah blah blah has to be signed off before Christmas. But,' he said, 'BUT—I'll get parachute-dropped between Greenland and Norway and paddle from there.' He promised!"

"Darling, you *made* him promise. You wouldn't leave until he promised. It's out of my hands, guys. You've got to be grown-up about it. There's nothing we can do," Mum said.

"But there's plenty of time," Dani said. "It's the day before Christmas Eve ... plenty of time."

"He promised," said Ruairi, determined to refuse the marshmallows once they were toasted.

"Come on now, you two. If he doesn't make it here for Christmas, it isn't because he willingly broke his promise to you. It's because ... It's because ..."

"Yes?" Dani and Ruairi said. Granny gave Mum a look now; her eyebrows went up, and her mouth puffed a little.

"It's because of ... the tarantulafish! The waters to the south of the island are tarantulafish-infested waters, you know."

"Rubbish!" snorted Dani as Ruairi turned pale.

"Nonsense!" said Ruairi, getting paler.

"It's true. Granny, isn't it true?"

"What, dear? Tarantulafish. Oh, yes. Once, when I was a little girl, it was rumoured that Dougal MacLaggan went for a swim on the wrong side of the island and got caught in their web. He never came back. Of course, some people say he was actually sent to boarding school on the mainland, but that doesn't make sense to me. Because if he really just went to boarding school on the mainland, why did he never come back? Answer me that! Everyone always comes back to Yondersaay." Then Granny wandered into the kitchen to see if she could fashion a sandwich out of some leftovers.

"Anyway," Ruairi said, "say we did believe in tarantulafish—"

"Which we don't," said Dani.

"Right, which we don't, but say we did … What do they have to do with Dad coming for Christmas?"

"Good question," Mum said. "As you know, there's only one harbor on the island, and it's right here at the bottom of the hill. Usually, lots of boats come to and fro, in and out of the harbor, but today all you could see were the little sailboats and fishing boats bobbing in the water, anchored to the spot. Nothing's come in. And nothing's gone out."

"Let me guess—the tarantulafish are eating all the boats that try to go in or out." Dani was not convinced.

"Close. They're not eating the boats—they only eat meat—they're blocking them. The tarantulafish have a gigantic web under the waves inside a massive burrow that stretches for miles, and they live there for most of the year. Some people think the burrow starts at the mouth of the River Gargle, where the river runs into the sea. Others think it's just off the Beach of Bewilderment.

"The strands of the web seem to be dangerously high in the water at the moment. A few were spotted by the lobster fishermen early this morning when they were coming home after a night in the boats. They narrowly missed being trapped. I spoke to them personally early this morning when I went to the bakery for the croissants. They radioed out a warning and all ferries to and from the island have been suspended until further notice. Dad's rubber dinghy would never make it through," Mum said, folding her arms.

"That won't stop Dad," Ruairi said to Dani. "He'll find a way."

"Dad'll be here. I know he will, there's always the airport or the helipad. He can get the department to loan him a helicopter."

"'Lend,' Dani!" Mum said. "If only there wasn't a storm

on its way in from Shetland … Unfortunately, all flights, in all aircrafts, have also been suspended until further notice."

"Hmm … Funny how we've never heard about these tarantulafish before now. You make us watch the news headlines every night, and never once has the newscaster said anything about tarantulafish," Dani said.

"Yeah!" said Ruairi. "Not once."

"That's not the least bit odd," said Granny, affronted. She was back now with seven sandwiches on a plate. "They are *Yondersaanian* tarantulafish. They belong on the *Yondersaanian* evening news. What would we be doing telling the international news community about our tarantulafish? The idea of it!"

"Turn on the local news then, Granny," Dani said slyly. "Let's see what they have to say about them."

"Well, wouldn't you know? We've just missed the evening news," said Granny.

"Pity," said Mum.

"Convenient," said Dani.

"We'll catch the morning news tomorrow," Granny said. "In the meantime, the mayor has tried to call the fire brigade onto the case because they're trained for such eventualities, being firemen and all."

"Trained to fight imaginary sea creatures?" Dani asked.

"Exactly! Um, no, not quite. They're trained in underwater firefighting," Mum explained.

"Oh! Now I *know* you're talking pants," Dani said "There's no such thing as an underwater fire. That's just impossible."

"Improbable, certainly. Impossible, not at all," Mum said.

"Look out the window," said Granny. "Do you see that mountain?"

"Yes," Dani and Ruairi groaned together.

"You would have to be positively blind not to notice the mountain," Dani said.

"It's Fenrir's Seat," said Ruairi.

"Well, it wasn't always Fenrir's Seat," Granny said. "Good gracious. Do they teach you history at all in that school of yours? A fair while back, when I was a tiny little girl, so not a year or two ago—"

"I'll say," Ruairi whispered to Dani.

Granny shot them a side-eye glance and continued, "Fenrir's Seat was not Fenrir's Seat, but a furiously angry volcano called Volcano Mount Violaceous. Very temperamental, it was. It would erupt at a moment's notice and spew filthy ash all over the island.

"Then, all of a sudden, things changed. One Christmas morning, the island woke up, and there were no rumblings or spewing noises coming down the peaks into the village. All the ash that was already in the air was settling finally, and it wasn't being replaced with new ash. It was like someone had taken a duster to the sky and cleaned away a layer of dirt." Granny walked around the room swiping her napkin backward and forward through the air. "The days were brighter. The sun glistened overhead; some people took to wearing sunglasses. Or *reflectacles* as they were known then. Sunglasses hadn't been invented yet. The sounds of rumbling had stopped too, like someone had turned off a radio in a far away room.

"The mayor put together an expedition squad to scale the peaks of Volcano Mount Violaceous and have a look inside to see what was up. The squad set out shortly after breakfast. I won't bore you with the details of that particular breakfast, but oh, I can still smell the bacon sizzling on the pan, sausages, eggs, mushrooms, grilled tomatoes, and black pudding rounds as thick as your wrist … ah." Granny sighed and looked wistfully into the middle distance.

Ruairi and Dani waited patiently. Ruairi cleared his throat quietly.

Granny glared at them over her spectacles. "My dears, you're possibly a little young, but when you get to my age, you will understand that the details of a good breakfast will be of the utmost importance in any tale. Where was I? Oh, yes. The expedition squad set out toward the Beach of Bewilderment and crossed the River Gargle at Tidal-Pool Bridge." Granny hoisted Ruairi's backpack onto her back and waded across the living room carpet as though she was hiking across sand on a windy day.

"They scaled the peaks of Mount Violaceous on the west side"—Granny climbed up onto a chair, tottered for a minute, and launched herself into the air and landed heavily on another chair—"pausing only for Old Mrs. MacAvinney's delicious packed lunch—crusty bread, thick slices of cheese oozing out—" Granny climbed up on the table by the window, clinging to the curtains like they were a rope. She leaned backward, picked up a sandwich, and took a bite.

"Granny! Be careful! Please!" Ruairi said, running to stand under her with his arms out wide so he could catch her if she fell.

"What happened next, Granny?" Dani was still sitting cross-legged on the carpet.

"They scaled the peaks of Volcano Mount Violaceous." Granny jumped off the table, did a tumble and roll, bounced up, and started to climb the brick fireplace. Ruairi ran and put cushions on the floor underneath her.

"All the while suppressing little butterflies of fear that perhaps old Violaceous was just taking a break and that lava and ash would suddenly spew from the top of the mountain and engulf them in terrifying flames, leaving them either dead or worse. But the little butterflies of fear were all for nothing. It never happened. In fact, nothing happened at all. When they got to the top of the mountain and peered over and looked in, they got the surprise of their lives." Granny jumped back down to the floor.

"The islanders couldn't think of a single historical event that matched this strange occurrence." Granny went to the bookcase and pulled down a dozen books. She put on her reading glasses and leafed through all the books around about her. "The pig farmer, who was also the local geologist, had to call to mind everything he'd ever learned about rocks and volcanoes, but even he couldn't come up with an answer. In the end, they decided it was a mystery. Though they had a theory." Granny came over and sat down on the sofa.

"It looked as though, during the night of Christmas Eve, while everyone was sleeping, dreaming of the presents they would get when they woke up and the wonderful things they would eat on Christmas Day, a sliver of a glacier had been swept south from the North Pole. It slid over the earth as they all slept, swooshed up the side of Mount Violaceous, and fell into the hole at the top of the mountain. It careened into the throat of the volcano and came to rest on top, blocking it up, cooling it off, and sealing in all the fire and ash." Granny paused, ate, and looked at Dani and Ruairi.

"Wow," said Ruairi.

"No one knows how or why the glacier decided to glide into our volcano or even how it got there so quickly. Of course, you know that on Yondersaay, to say 'to move at a glacial pace' means to go as fast as humanly possible."

"So, there was no more volcano?" Ruairi asked.

"Well, that's what it looked like. And slowly, what we

see out the window, the thing that dominates every view on the island, came to be known as Fenrir's Seat. But that's another story for another day." Granny Miller took a bite of her last sandwich.

"I'm still not quite getting the connection, Granny. What exactly does this have to do with the fire brigade?" Dani asked.

"Volcanoes don't just go away," Mum said.

"Exactly right, Mum," Granny said when she'd finished eating. "And the island council were worried that all the ash spewing and lava rumblings were still going on, building up just under the surface of the glacier. The islanders met, debated, took a vote, and decided that the fire brigade should get ready and train just in case one day the volcano blew up underneath the glacier.

"The island geologist reckoned that if the volcano came to life again and erupted, the cap of ice would start melting slowly from the underside, but there would still be a plug of ice sealing the mountain and slowing down the fire. Fire needs oxygen, and none could get in through the thick layers of the tightly packed ice and water. The glacier would stop Mount Violaceous and keep Fenrir in his seat. Everyone at the meeting breathed a sigh of relief.

"They were just about to move to 'other business,' when little Albert MacAvinney, Lewis MacAvinney's granddad, tentatively raised his hand. The mayor called for silence, and everyone turned and looked at the little boy sitting between his grandparents at the back of the hall. 'Yes, little Albert MacAvinney. What is it?'

"'The caves,' little Albert MacAvinney said. 'Air will get in through the caves.'

"And he was dead right. There's a veritable labyrinth of caves in and around and under Fenrir's Seat, with hundreds of openings all over the mountain. Some begin under the sea; some open at the top of the cliffs and work their way down. They meet and mingle out of sight, deep underground. Some lead directly to the belly of the mountain, some to dead ends, and some tunnels lead you to a maze."

"Is that what that big cave at the Beach of Bewilderment is?" Dani said. "The one just over the sand dunes as you come from the beach toward the mountain? Is there a tunnel leading into the volcano there too?"

"Yes, Dani," Granny said. "If you crawl right to the back, there's a hole, a tunnel."

"Can we go and have a look at it? Can we?"

"We're probably not allowed to. That would be dangerous," Ruairi said.

"Yes, indeed, Ruairi," Granny said. "No one's allowed to go wandering around in those tunnels. Besides, I have a feeling it's all blocked up."

"Oh well," Ruairi said.

"I'm sure we can unblock it," Dani mumbled to herself.

"Listen to Granny, Dani," Mum said. "You must never wander around in any of these caves—either of you. It's too dangerous. You may find yourself hopelessly lost, unable to find your way out." Mum looked back to Granny, who continued.

"All eyes turned to little Albert MacAvinney. 'Although it would be very difficult,' he said, 'maybe even impossible to block off all the cave openings from the *out*side, it may be possible to block them off from the *in*side. If the belly of the mountain is filling with water,' little Albert continued, 'someone in the water would be able to see where the tunnels ended. They would be able to see bubbles coming into the melting water and feeding the fire and block off the tunnels. "Everyone in the town hall agreed that little Albert

MacAvinney was exceptionally clever. Old Mrs. MacAvinney, little Albert's grandmother, beamed with pride.

"Hence the fire brigade scuba squad!"

"Sometimes," Mum said, "you can see the firemen in the lake or the swimming pool in their fireman's helmets and fireman's boots and scuba gear doing drills with their hoses, practicing putting out underwater fires. Or carrying massive boulders from one side of the swimming pool to the other—that's when they're practicing blocking up the tunnels and keeping out the bubbles. And, at other times, you see some of them with giant bubble blowers under the water testing other firemen to see if they can spot the bubbles. They often do it all blindfolded, getting ready for the day when Fenrir's Seat becomes Volcano Mount Violaceous once more.

"So they were the obvious choice," Mum continued, "when it emerged that the tarantulafish were mucking about on the ferry route again, to scuba on down there, dismantle the web, and create a clear passage."

"But you can't force them to go," Granny said.

"Why not?" Dani asked.

"It's their job. You just said so." Ruairi was getting suspicious again.

"Ah, you see, actually, it's not their job really," said Mum. "It's just an extra thing they do. The few house fires, chimney fires, oil spills, and road traffic accidents on the island don't warrant a full-time fire service. The firemen and firewomen are also the local farmers and the butcher, the baker, the cobblers, and a couple of university students. And now the draper is saying he's not terrified of the tarantulafish, not absolutely terrified out of his skin of them at all—it's just that the run up to Christmas is his busiest time of year, and he can't leave the shop. And Mr. Lachlann who owns The Bewildered Inn overheard him say that and spread the word so nearly everyone else is saying the same—they're not scared of the tarantulafish, not a bit scared. It's just that Christmas is such a busy time of the year. They can't close their shops. The customers would be up in arms!

"It's not a very busy time of year for the cobbler. But he has a migraine. So he's out too. There's nothing to be done about it," Granny said with finality.

"I'm not buying a word of this," Dani said.

"You're not?" Ruairi whispered to her. And then he said, louder, "No, me neither. We're not buying a word of this!"

"Look, darlings. Let's not let it ruin our holiday," Mum said. "Dad'll get here if and when he can. I just want to prepare you in case he can't make it. You need to be grown-up about it."

"Okay," Ruairi mumbled.

"If you want us to be so grown-up about it," Dani shot back at her mother, "why tell us all that nonsense about tarantulafish and underwater volcanoes? That's not very grown-up!"

"Grown-up it may not be, Dani," Granny said over her glasses, "but it's the truth, the absolute truth, and nothing short of it."

"Whatever," Dani said.

"Come on now, kids," Mum said, "Let's just concentrate on having the best holiday ever," she said as cheerfully as possible. She went into the kitchen and made hot chocolate with roasted marshmallows while Granny, Ruairi, and Dani quietly unpacked the decorations.

Ruairi decided that Mum and Granny were probably as disappointed as he and Dani were about Dad and that there was no point in being huffy with them. There was nothing anyone could do. He would just have to hope the weather changed and Dad got to Yondersaay in time for Christmas.

The Violaceous Amethyst

When the decorations were unpacked, and they were set to trim the tree, Granny continued with her story of King Dudo the Mightily Impressive.

"Where were we? Ah, yes, the jarl had brought King Dudo to the foot of an oak tree in the Crimson Forest. The tree moved forward and down as though taking a bow, and said, 'I am very pleased to make your acquaintance, your kingship.'

"King Dudo stared at the tree, his jaw hanging down. Recovering himself, he said 'The pleasure is mine.' Rarelief the Splendiferous grinned from ear-branch to ear-branch. King Dudo even thought he saw Rarelief blush, but it was very hard to tell—his face was made of bark. The tall, skinny oak tree bent a branch down. King Dudo took hold of a twig, and they shook hands.

"King Dudo settled himself on a knobbly root at the

base of Rarelief the Splendiferous's trunk.

"'I'll leave the two of you to it,'" Jarl Olaf said, swinging his arms and retreating slowly. 'My liege, Rarelief here will tell you all you need to know about this island, its history, and its many secrets. He was here before any of us were born, and he will be here long after we have all returned to the earth and will give you an objective answer to any question you may ask.' And with that, Jarl Olaf Barelegs the Balding on Top shuffled off, and King Dudo and Rarelief the Splendiferous were alone.

"Rarelief recounted the history of the island to King Dudo. Within that history was Rarelief himself. He was a tiny sapling when Odin, the majestic father of all Vikings, decided that of all the Viking lands, Yondersaay was the most perfect place to prepare for Valhalla. Odin made the island his home for a short while to explore the landscape and to get to know the people. He bestowed upon the island many of his own powers. He made it his treasure trove—the place where he and his hundreds of thousands of followers, over many generations, could amass their personal fortunes and weaponries ahead of their final battle.

"He enshrouded the island in a mysterious invisibility and bestowed upon it many secret gifts, all of which Rarelief the Splendiferous relayed in detail to King Dudo."

"What were they, Granny? Will you tell us?" Ruairi asked.

"Ruairi, darling, I'm afraid some are so secret that even I don't know about them. I can tell you about some of the enchantments that Odin bestowed upon the island, and I can also tell you a little bit about each of the Gifts of Odin, but not more than that, I'm afraid. Like I said, the island is shrouded in mystery." With that, Granny, at the top of a twenty-foot stepladder balanced precariously against the tree, let a flutter of silky silver tinsel icicles float down to land evenly on the branches.

"Odin was a great and powerful god who had battled many great and powerful gods during his hundreds of years in existence. A Nordic god of old, he wasn't perhaps quite as all-powerful or all-knowing as you might think. Like people, all gods were not created equal. Some were braver than others, some were stronger, and some were craftier. Odin had accumulated the most amazing objects you'll hear of—some through force of war and combat, and some came to him as gifts and offerings. I will briefly tell you about one treasure." Granny slowly climbed down the twenty-foot stepladder. She approached the little table by the fireplace where Mum had piled mounds of mince pies and slices of Christmas cake and stacks of fluffy white marshmallows for the hungry tree trimmers.

"Let's pick one, Ruairi. Can you remember them all?" Dani said. "There's the Cup of Memory, and the something something Thunderbolt, and the Sword of Lapis Lazuli."

"And the shield that goes with that," Ruairi said.

"The Asiatic Shield."

"Right. And what else?"

"Ooh, ooh!" Dani said. "Tell us about the Black Heart of the Dragon's Eye. That sounds evil."

"I want to hear about The Tome of Tiuz," Ruairi said. "What is a tome and what is a Tiuz?"

Granny, preoccupied, ignored them. She had a sparkly yellow bauble in one hand and a garland of tinsel in the other. She wrapped the garland loosely around her neck like a very shiny scarf and tucked the sparkly yellow bauble under her chin. Then she filled both hands with mince pies and slices of Christmas cake and fluffy marshmallows and slowly and very carefully climbed back up the twenty-foot stepladder beside the Christmas tree. Granny stuffed a few marshmallows into her mouth and the rest into the pocket at the front of her frock.

"I will tell you of one treasure," she said while chewing marshmallows, "one of Odin's most prized possessions. And I will tell you about that particular one because it was created right here on Yondersaay. It's something you haven't listed yet. Its name has something in common with something else on Yondersaay, something big and rocky and lava spewing."

"Volcano Mount Violaceous is big and rocky and lava-spewing," Ruairi said.

"It must be the Violaceous Amethyst!" Dani said.

"Well deduced, the pair of you," Granny said.

Granny took the sparkly yellow bauble in her one free hand and leaned into the tree to hang it. "Odin first came to Yondersaay because he had heard tell that the Yondersaanian Vikings had no equals in their craftiness in war, their surety upon the waves, and their courage in battle. A great battle was underway between the Yondersaanians and some Vikings from Groenland. Odin observed unseen.

"He chose a position high above the waves of the northern-most seas with a clear view of the ocean and island where the two Viking armies battled tirelessly. He also saw a dozen or so Valkyries riding their airborne horses very close to the action.

"The Valkyries were women, equally admired and feared, who carried out the will of Odin, the father of all Vikings - for he could, if he wanted to, decide the outcome of any given Viking battle. The choosers of the slain, the demigoddesses of death, the Valkyries would select the bravest of those who had been killed in battle, gather their souls, and bring them in triumph to the afterlife in Valhalla.

"Odin loved to watch the Valkyries work. Tough and fierce, they were swift, graceful, and deadly. It was not widely known at this time, but if you were to capture and hold a Valkyrie, you could make her grant you a wish. They were also, as a rule, uncommonly beautiful.

"Odin was a known admirer of beautiful women. On this particular day, Odin caught a glimpse of a beautiful Valkyrie, tall and strong and with eyes a deeper blue than the darkest ocean. She had blond hair to her thighs and skin of the palest ivory. She expertly directed her steed among the warriors in battle. Like the other Valkyries, she wore a scarlet corset and held a shield and a spear. Odin was smitten.

"After the battle, Odin called her to him. He learned her name was Svava, and she was more beautiful up close than Odin had imagined. He told her how her strength and grace had captured his heart and invited her to visit the island of the victorious Vikings with him.

"Svava and Odin retreated to Yondersaay, and there they had, em, they had lots of cups of tea."

"Yuck! You're not going to tell us about the 'cups of tea,' Granny? Please tell us there's no 'tea!'" Ruairi said, doing air quotes with his fingers.

"No, Ruairi, I will not tell you about the 'tea' on this occasion. But there may be 'tea' later on in the story. I'm not promising anything!" Granny chuckled as Ruairi pretended to be sick into a bucket.

"I don't mind the kissing so much," Dani said. "I mean 'tea.'"

"You're weird," Ruairi said.

"Much as Svava loved being on Yondersaay with Odin," Granny went on, "she longed to return to battle with her sisters. Odin could not convince her to stay with him.

"Determined to bestow a most special gift upon Odin, Svava thought for days about what to give him. What do you get the god with miraculous powers who has everything? He already had a magical horse and enchanted armor. He already had the ability to change his appearance, to disappear from view, to blend, and to escape. It was a tough one.

"Svava knew that as much as Odin was a revered and worshipped god among his friends and subjects, he was hated by his enemies and not always immune to their powers. One night, she asked him who or what could do him most harm, if they really wanted to.

"He said, 'Few beings exist who are powerful enough to reduce me to dust, and I know of only three who dislike me enough to want me dead.'

"'Who?' Svava asked him.

"'Mr. Jarrig, the Luchrupan, is one. He lives for trickery and mischief. He would have a lot of fun setting a trap for me. Mr. Jarrig is not wholly evil, but he is not wholly good either.

"'The beautiful goddess Queen Olwen and I have a long and tortured history. She has reason to want me out of the way.

"'And lastly, there is Mimir the giant, my old mentor. As you know, Svava, the giants and the gods have been enemies for many a century. We just can't seem to get along for very long. I was very close with Mimir once. A difference of opinion angered him beyond tolerance, however, and we broke from each other after a furious argument.'

"They talked at length about the particular strengths and weaknesses of Jarrig, Olwen, and Mimir. Keeping it secret from Odin and armed with all this new knowledge, Svava went about creating something so transformative, so protecting, and so beautiful, that it would become a legend in its own right.

"Svava cast deep beneath the compressed rock of the Volcano Mount Violaceous to search for the ideal amethyst. Usually, it would take years of excavation, but Svava, with an intuition to match her beauty, uncovered the perfect one in a fraction of that time. She found a faultless stone— small but exquisitely formed and stunning in its opalescence. With the help of her sister Valkyries, she imbued this gem with the powers that would make it a most special parting gift.

"It was particularly powerful because to the uninitiated it just looked like a pretty trinket, something attractive to hang around one's neck. In reality, it possessed the power to protect its bearer from intoxication, from poisoning, from transformation, from manipulation even. The stone also possessed the power, like Odin himself, of changing its appearance. Under ordinary circumstances, all things being equal, its color was a tender purple. But when manipulated by its owner, it could become clear or white, even yellow.

"Svava gave her lover this unique gift, the Violaceous Amethyst, and she was gone. Now, back to Rarelief the Splendiferous."

"That's it?" Dani interrupted, turning to face Granny.

"But what happened to Svava?" Ruairi asked softly.

"I will tell you all about it, but on another occasion. Unless you'd like me to switch to this story?" Granny asked.

"No, Granny, you're probably right," Dani said after a moment.

"We can come back to it another time," Ruairi agreed.

"Well, all righty then. Now, where was I? Oh, yes. " Granny took a few marshmallows from the front pocket of her frock.

"Odin settled on the island and decided it was his ideal hiding place. He protected it and enchanted it and bestowed many secret gifts upon it. Next, he set about finding the best place on the island to hide his treasures.

"To help him make up his mind, he made it possible for everything on the island, every leaf and flower and boulder and brook, to speak with him and to answer his questions. For example, he asked the gargling brook and the River Gargle about seasonal swelling and flooding and found out that the banks are routinely burst in winter and the land all about gets soggy and wet—not a good place to hide valuable treasures. They might get washed away one year, or at the very least be exposed if the soil on top was washed away.

"He asked the boulders on the borders of Mount Violaceous which of their caves would be a good hiding place and was informed that when the volcano blows, everything within the caves gets scorched—not an ideal place to hide garments of war made from leather and hide or tools made of wood. He enquired of the sands on the Beach of Bewilderment about the possibility of digging down and burying the treasure beneath them. He was reminded by a flock of passing puffins that the tarantulafish love shiny things and have a habit of scavenging along the beach. They were likely to dig up the treasures and use them out at sea to line their nests—no longer buried, the treasures could never find their way down to their masters when they reached Valhalla.

"Eventually, one day, at about dusk, Odin took a stroll through the Crimson Forest. He despaired of ever finding the perfect hiding place. He sat down at the base of a very young sapling to have a think about where oh where he could hide the treasures of Valhalla.

"Odin was sitting and thinking when the sun started its descent. Under the canopy of the Crimson Forest trees Odin was barely aware of the time of day. It was only when he felt the warmth of the final rays of the sun on his shoulders that he had a look around him and took in the setting sun's play of light on the kaleidoscopic trees. The autumn leaves were multicolored and magnificent. There was already a colorful blanket of fallen leaves across the forest floor. Odin looked about him and took in the spectacle. 'Beautiful,' he thought to himself.

"As he sat there looking about him, the setting sun broke through the branches high above the young sapling where he sat. A gentle beam fell upon its leaves, and to the Viking god's astonishment, the leaves sparkled purple. Odin had never seen such a thing. Yellowing leaves turning bright purple in the fading evening light. Odin addressed the tree. 'How has this come to be, young sapling? Tell me the secret of your leaves.'

"The sapling turned its branches to Odin and said, 'I'm afraid I cannot tell you, your godship, even if I wanted to. My poor mother here'—he twisted one branch in the direction of a solid, regal-looking oak standing protectively behind him—'is forever fretting that I have some atrocious canker. All my friends keeps predicting it will spread to my branches and my trunk and finally my roots and that I'll be rotted away to pieces in front of them.' The young sapling started to sob.

"'Nonsense,' said Odin. 'Your leaves are glorious and beautiful beyond belief. There is no sign of any illness or disease whatsoever. And I should know—I am a god! And we gods know everything. What is your name?'

"The tree stopped sobbing and looked at Odin. 'Freakylief the Diseased, your godship,' he said, and Odin patted the tree encouragingly.

"'I shall rename you.' Here Odin took a minute to think. 'Henceforth, you shall be known as Rarelief the Splendiferous!'

"For the first time, Rarelief the Splendiferous felt real pleasure. His mother immediately turned to all the other trees to brag about her splendiferous son.

"'And in recognition of your exquisite splendour,' Odin went on, 'I shall bestow upon you a great honor.'"

"Wow, a great honor," Ruairi said, in hushed tones, then after a second, "What great honor?"

"What do you think, dummy?" Dani said. "He buried the treasure underneath him. Jeez, keep up."

"*Cool*! Can we go looking for him tomorrow? Can we go treasure hunting, can we, can we?" he asked Mum and Granny.

"That might be a bit difficult," Granny said.

"Why?" Dani and Ruairi asked together. Granny waited a minute.

Ruairi cottoned on first. "Because there are no trees on the island. Well, hardly any trees on the island."

"Spot-on, Ruairi," Granny said.

Ruairi looked to Dani and said, "Keep up!" Dani elbowed him in the ribs. "Stop it!" Ruairi said and shoved Dani.

"No, *you* stop it," Dani said, flopping on top of Ruairi and wrestling him to the floor.

"Hey!" Mum said sharply. "That's enough, you two!"

Dani and Ruairi ignored her and rolled around the floor flailing at each other and shouting.

"Stop it!"

"No, *you* stop it!"

"*Leave me alone*!"

"All right, that's it. It's time for bed!" Mum shouted.

Dani and Ruairi stopped midflail and looked up. "*What?*" Ruairi said.

"But you said we could stay up and hear the rest of the story!" Dani said.

"That was before you started behaving like hoodlums. Off you go. Go on. Up the stairs." Mum settled onto the sofa and started reading her book.

"But"—Ruairi said, coming up onto his knees beside a similarly kneeling Dani—"you said!"

"Well, I've changed my mind," Mum snapped, without looking at her children. "Good night."

Ruairi and Dani glanced at each other and then back at their mother. "Sorry," they both muttered together and stared at the floor.

"You started it," Ruairi said under his breath to Dani.

Dani glared at him.

"What was that, Ruairi?" Mum said, raising her eyebrows.

"Nothing," he mumbled. "We're sorry; we won't fight anymore. Please can we stay up?"

Mum's gaze flicked to Granny, who was using the break in her storytelling to stuff her gob with whatever food she could reach from her chair. Given that she'd positioned her chair right next to the table, her mouth was positively laden.

"It's up to Granny," Mum said finally. "If she can bear the sight of the two of you a little longer, well, then, you can stay up."

Dani and Ruairi sat side by side. They didn't flop all over each other like usual—they sat stiffly, without touching, and shot reproachful glances back and forth.

Granny nodded, swallowed hard, and started again.

How to Conquer Yondersaay and Become its Lord and Master

"The Crimson Forest is only called the Crimson Forest," Granny began, "because the islanders could never agree on a new name for the area. There are lots of shrubberies and bushlike plants and millions of tiny colorful flowers at certain points in the year in the forest but hardly any trees at all. Not nearly enough to warrant the title 'forest.' All the trees disappeared ages ago. No one remembers when. There are perhaps three or four trees on the whole island, and they're all out of sight in the hollow of the Crimson Forest. And if the treasure was buried under any of them, it would surely have been discovered decades ago.

"Perhaps the naming of the area known as the Crimson Forest was just ironic. The island council voted to change the name a few years ago to Crimson Valley or Crimson Meadow or some such. There was a majority in favor, but it was quite rightly pointed out to the assembled crowd, probably by one of the MacAvinneys, that if the word 'forest' was to be rejected because of the area's lack of forestial qualities, then the word 'crimson' should also be replaced because there was nothing remotely crimsonian about the place either. That's where the islanders came unstuck. They couldn't agree on a new word to replace 'crimson,' and so Crimson Forest remained the name of the area.

"On a sunny day in autumn, a long, long time ago, King Dudo the Mightily Impressive sat and chatted for hours with the only oak tree in the Crimson Forest—Rarelief the Splendiferous.

"Dusk was approaching, a time of day Dudo was eagerly awaiting. He was dying to see the tree's leaves glisten purple in the last beams of sunset. Rarelief sensed this. Rarelief caught Dudo glancing toward the horizon, watching the sun getting lower in the sky. 'It's not going happen,' Rarelief said.

"'What won't happen?'

"'My leaves will not turn a sparkly purple for you, my liege—not for you.'

"'Not for me? Why not?'

"'You're not from here, are you? My king, you were not born here, you do not rule it, you are not part of one of the island's families. King of all the Danes you may be; a Yondersaanian, I can tell you, you are most definitively not. A tree whose leaves turn purple at sunset? Pretty easy to spot, wouldn't you say? Odin would have said. Because Odin did say.

"'In mortal fear that a plunderer, having heard tell a story of a purple-leafed tree, would crack through the island's enchanted border, seek out your man with the purple leaves—that's me, by the way—and shovel out my treasures, he shrouded my transformation from all but those who are born of this island and those who are part of the island's clan. And for extra double sureness, he made the forest a haunted forest. He instructed all the trees and flowers and shrubberies in the art of effective haunting. That was a grand school, that was. So that if someone not of the island, some incomer, wandered in here, they'd be in no hurry to hang around.'

"'What a pity,' King Dudo said. 'I was rather looking forward to seeing your leaves turn purple. Thank you for not haunting me, by the way.'

"'Welcome,' Rarelief said.

"'Rarelief, I must tell you that all my life I have dreamed of adding this island to my kingdom. I had sort of flattered myself that the legend of the one king who will win the island and become its master was about me. I did get here, after all, and well, they don't call me King Dudo the Mightily Impressive for nothing. I'd rather not go to war with the Yondersaanians, but conquering and pillaging and plundering *is* what I do for a living."

"'It wouldn't do you a bit of good.' Rarelief smiled benevolently. 'You cannot take this island by warring alone.'

"'You can't?'

"'No.'

"'Well, how can you then?'

"'There are two ways and two ways alone that this island could be yours. The first way you'd probably love, as it'd make powerful use of your plundering and pillaging abilities, but there's no chance in a gazillion it would work for you. You cannot just make war with the island and the islanders, you know. Oh no. You must extinguish all in the ruling clan's line. For starters, you'd have to ixnay old Baldy there, and for good measure, you'd have to do away with his daughter.'

"'That would be exceptionally rude. They've both been so kind and hospitable,' Dudo said.

"'But even that wouldn't do the deed for you. The jarl has a brother in Land of the Scots. You would have to go there, find him, kill him, and get yourself back here and claim Yondersaay as your own.

"'Now, I'm not saying I know how you got onto Yondersaay yesterday. Because I don't know. Nobody knows. But it's beyond even an idiot's reason that you could ever find your way back again. And then all the killing and the offing and the murdering will have been in vain. Sure, you might have enjoyed it, but if you can't get yourself back to the island, then, you can't become its lord and master.

"'The other night, the jarl told me every single one of the islanders gathered on the shore to have a gander at you and all your mighty ships sailing by. Everyone could see you looking and looking and looking but not seeing. The children were having such a gas looking at you not seeing anything, they made the most odious faces and hand gestures at the lot of you. A couple of the young ones, I'm not naming names, broke into fits of the giggles.

"'My goodness, didn't a panic break out! The islanders thought they were done for then. They saw you look right at them, right into their eyes, as you floated mere yards away. You looked all around, and that spotty fella in the dress looked all around. Then you suddenly turned north and sped away. Everybody breathed a sigh of relief just then, I can tell you.

"'So it's a mystery, an entire, absolute mystery, how you managed to wash up on the beach like you did mere hours later.' Rarelief looked at King Dudo, clearly expecting him to tell him the secret of his arrival on the island.

"King Dudo was silent. Rarelief continued.

"'So you got here once, so you did, and no one has the foggiest how you managed it. It might be the case that someone helped you.' Here, Rarelief paused again, hoping that King Dudo would explain. He raised an eyebrow branch. King Dudo sat and waited for Rarelief to continue, saying nothing. 'Or,' Rarelief continued, 'it might be the case you found the island because you were not looking for the island. You were unconscious and half-drowned—you couldn't have been seeking it out. At the very moment you reached the perimeters of the island, because you did not actively desire it, being unconscious and half-drowned, you were somehow able to wiggle yourself in through the enchanted boundaries and wash ashore.' Rarelief paused. 'Or it might be the case that somebody helped you,' here he narrowed his bark eyes.

"King Dudo still said nothing.

"'Someone would've had to have helped you. Because you washed up on the beach, and you're not bewildered. Well, as far as I can tell.'

"'Bewildered?' Dudo said, bewildered.

"'You'll have heard about the Beach of Bewilderment, of course?'

"'Nuh-uh,' Dudo said, shaking his head.

"'Well, if you happen to find yourself wandering alone on the Beach of Bewilderment, caught unawares, it has the powers to discombobulate you. There are instances of people who have gone stark raving bonkers because they happened to wander onto the beach when they had something on their mind. Take Bera Droplaug, the tanner's daughter. She was puzzling out what meal she should serve when her prospective new husband Sverting's hoity-toity parents came to meet with her. She got bewitched by the beach and forever afterward talked only about tapioca pudding and wore a rack of lamb on her head.'

"'Bewildering indeed!'

"'*But*, and I'll say it again, you'll not get yourself here twice. Someone would have to invite you, and as you may or may not have noticed, Your Kingship, the jarl is a kind and trusted leader, and he and his daughter are terribly loved. You'd find it hard to find a single islander on your side if they came to harm by your hand. In fact, everyone on this island would, in all likelihood, become your sworn mortal enemy. For life. To the death.'

"'And the other way?'

"'Pardon?'

"'The other way you can win the island.'

"'Oh, yes, the other way. That way is altogether nicer for everyone involved. I take it you are unwed?' Rarelief asked the king.

"'I have not found my Heart's True Love yet,' Dudo mumbled. 'No. I'm not married.' King Dudo could not disguise his sadness.

"'You're getting on a bit, aren't you?'

"'Hey!'

"'Tad late to be worrying about your Heart's True Love, if you ask me. Probably about time you face facts, settle, take what you can get. A king should marry and bear heirs.'

"'I'm really not that old! Besides, what does it matter to you?'

"'Because,' Rarelief continued, 'the only other way to become master of the island is to marry the jarl's daughter. Then the island will legitimately be yours when the old man kicks the bucket, and much as I love old Baldy there, he does have a terrible wheeze on him, so I daresay he's not long for this world. His daughter is a stunner, isn't she?' Rarelief asked.

"'Hmm.'

"'She is not to your satisfaction?'

"'She's very nice.'

"'I see.'

"'No, I mean, she's lovely. She is beautiful and kind. I am certain she would make a loving and supportive wife. It's just …' King Dudo let out a big sigh. 'She's not my Heart's True Love.'

"'Well, you only just met,' Rarelief said. 'Give her a chance. Take her on a date; get to know each other. But don't wait too long. I gather she is leaving the island soon.'

"'How soon?'

"'At the end of the week.'

"'At the end of the *week?*'

"'Yes, she accompanies her father to their country pile in the southern lands every year when the harshest of the winter months set in. They take all their staff with them. Like I said, he has a bit of a wheeze on him. It gets very cold here in winter. Of course, you could wait until she gets back next summer,' Rarelief continued, 'but do you really want to spend months here on your own waiting for her to get back? Aren't your men out there looking for you? Besides, if you wait, you might miss your chance. The jarl's daughter is no spring chicken herself. She'll be wanting to settle down soon too, I'm sure, and she gets a lot of attention when she goes south—her coloring being unusual in southern lands, her uncommon beauty goes down a bomb there. She's always hotly pursued, and this year she might just say yes. She always says no, you see.'

"'Why? As you say, she's no spring chicken.'

"'Some rubbish about waiting to find her Heart's True Love.'

"'Ah.'

"'So, you'll have to really make her fall for you if you

want her to marry you. And you'd better get moving. You have three days and counting.'

"'By the winged moustaches of Thor, that is not a lot of time!'

"'It should be ample.'

"'*Ample*? Are you kidding me?'

"'Should be no trouble for a charming, impressive hero like yourself.'

"'I suppose there is some truth in that, Rarelief. I *am* incredibly charming and incredibly impressive. I really cannot deny that. I have often been told as much. Often. There's just one problem.'

"'And what would that be now?'

"'I was going to ask you, since you know so much about the island. There's this woman—'

"'Let me stop you there.'

"'Huh?'

"'Forget her.'

"'Why?'

"'If you have any interest in possessing this island and all its treasures and mysteries, and they are plentiful—'

"'Yes, I know, you've told me all about them. In great detail.'

"'If you truly desire this island, you must forget about this other woman and concentrate on the jarl's daughter. She's the only one for you.'

"'Well, she did totally blank me.'

"'Who? This other woman? There you go.'

"'I mean, she didn't even *acknowledge* me. It was embarrassing! I was all, *Well, hello there,* and she was all, *Nothing,* and I was all, *Hi,* and she was all, *Hmph,*' King Dudo said as he folded his arms and turned his back on Rarelief.

"'Like I said, forget her. What's the point? She clearly doesn't get you. You need someone who gets you. Take Olaf's daughter on a date. See if she gets you.'

"'Yeah, but three days …'

"'You're the King of all the Danes, and look at you! How could anyone resist?'

"King Dudo looked at his muscles and his flowing hair and stood tall with his chin in the air and his hands on his hips. "'You are right,' he said proudly. 'I am fantastic. How hard can it be?'"

The Wooing of the Jarl's Daughter

"Dudo went straight back to the village in the harbor, sought out the jarl, and asked his permission to take his daughter on a date.

"'May I have the honor of asking your daughter to come for a walk with me, Your Majesty?' he asked.

"'Why of course you may, my majes, um—liege. Of course you may.'

"'A question,' Dudo said.

"'Ask anything,' said the jarl.

"'What is her name?'

"'Her name?'

"'Yes. What is your daughter called?'

"'Her name is, uh, she's called, um …'

"'Yes?' asked Dudo.

"'Brunhilda.'

"'You seem uncertain.'

"'No, no, her name is Brunhilda. Hilly to me, her father, her daddio, her pops …'

"'Allrighty then,' Dudo said. 'I shall herewith ask the beautiful, what was it again?'

"'Brunhilda. Brunhilda Thunder Thighs.'

"'The beautiful Brunhilda Thunder Thighs on a date. Righto then. Off I go. I'm going. I'm heading in the direction of your house right now to ask, um, Brunhilda on a date. Here I go.' And the king walked off in the direction of the jarl's dwelling place, found the beautiful Brunhilda, and asked her if she fancied going for a stroll. Brunhilda smiled coyly and said she would. She went inside to get her handbag—

"Oh no, wait! Handbags weren't invented yet. Do you want to know when handbags were invented?" Granny asked.

"Noooo!" both Ruairi and Dani said at once.

The Wooing of Brunhilda Thunder Thighs

"He's not really going on a date with the other one, is he?" Ruairi asked.

"Well, let's see," Granny said. "The king asked Brunhilda Thunder Thighs out for a stroll—there was a promenade along the harbor wall, just like there is now, only there weren't so many people inline skating and cycling along it then as there are now, obviously, it being winter."

"And inline skates not having been invented yet. Yes, we get it, Granny." Dani rolled her eyes.

"Oh, now, my dear, young great-great-great-granddaughter, you are quite wrong there. Inline skates were invented by the Yondersaay Vikings not too long before this outing of Dudo and Brunhilda's. They were all the rage. They were invented one foggy spring morning—"

"Granny!" Dani shouted.

Granny stopped and raised her eyebrows at her. "You

wouldn't like me to tell you how they were invented?"

"Not really," Dani said.

"Your loss," Granny said.

"But you're sure, Granny?"

"About what, Ruairi?"

"About inline skates. Are you sure they weren't invented a lot more recently that that?"

"Absolutely. We'll go down to the Yondersaay museum tomorrow, and I'll show you the fossilized remnants of inline skates made from bone, stone, and iron. It is commonly known that those guys who 'invented' inline skates in the eighties had been on holiday on Yondersaay the week before," Granny said, outraged now.

"Suspicious," Ruairi said, narrowing his eyes.

"Very suspicious," Granny said, narrowing her eyes right back. "Anyhoo, back to Dudo and his date. The beautiful, ebony-haired, thunder-thighed Brunhilda ran inside. She said she was going to retrieve her *handle-bagorium*, as handbags were called then, but really she had Ursula help her brush out her long hair and dab some of the red dye powder they used in fabric dyeing onto her high cheeks and her full lips. Ursula squeezed her arm and wished her good luck."

"No, I don't believe it Granny!" Ruairi said. "Ursula can't have wished Brunhilda good luck! She's got to be her mortal enemy! Dudo is her Heart's True Love! He has to be! So how can she be wishing Brunhilda luck? Did she poison the dye? Or put a snake in the handle-bagorium?"

"You'll have to wait and see, Ruairi, but don't bet on it," Granny said. Ruairi was confused. "It's real life. I keep telling you. You can't expect them to break into a catfight just because a handsome man turns up at their village. That's not realistic. Besides, Ursula has paid no attention to Dudo this whole time. And you must remember, King Dudo wants to possess the island of Yondersaay above all else. He's been dreaming about this his entire life, and now here it is, his for the taking. Who says Dudo is Ursula's Heart's True Love, and who says Dudo is even fussed about finding his anymore?" Granny asked.

"I'm not convinced," Dani said. "I want to hear more, Granny. I'm with Ruairi on the poison and the snake. Ursula won't take this lying down!"

"We'll see," Granny said, "but I don't know. I hope you won't be disappointed. Now, where were we? Oh, yes. Unbeknownst to both women, while Ursula was helping Brunhilda get ready for her stroll, the king was spying on them.

"He was peering into the dwelling place through a slat in the window covering. He scrutinized Ursula's face. He had hoped when he saw her there, helping her mistress get ready for a date, that she would be at least a little bit jealous. She didn't look jealous, and he could detect no ill feeling between the two women whatsoever.

"'Huh!' King Dudo thought. 'Just as well. She was not pretending; she has no interest in me after all. It really will be easy to give the beautiful heiress all my wooing attention. I shall woo her good,' he decided.

"Brunhilda emerged a moment later, radiant. She truly was a magnificent-looking woman. She smiled sweetly at the king as she held up her hand for him to kiss.

"'Sheesh,' King Dudo thought. 'She may have been brought up in a tiny habitation on an island in the middle of nowhere with a bunch of farmers, peasants, and fishermen, but she sure does know how this wooing business works.'

"The king and Brunhilda walked slowly along the promenade chatting amiably. It started out a bit awkwardly, as these things often do, but once they'd established that Brunhilda's favorite color was blue and Dudo's was yellow, and that they were both evening people as opposed to morning people, their conversation ambled along quite affably.

"They found that they had rather a lot in common, all things considered. Very soon they were perfectly comfortable in each other's company. Any silences were easily filled with talk about the weather or the choppiness of the waves coming in to shore. Their conversation didn't get very deep, mind you, but it was pleasant enough, and importantly, it was not strained.

"'I suppose you miss your homeland?' Brunhilda ventured as they reached the pier.

"'Not really,' King Dudo said. 'I like seeing new lands and meeting new people.'

"'What a coincidence!' Brunhilda responded. 'Me too!'

"'How wonderful!' King Dudo replied.

"As King Dudo and Brunhilda strolled contentedly along the promenade, they heard ecstatic screeches of laughter coming close up behind them.

"'Watch out!' cried a voice but too late. A startled Brunhilda jumped off the path just as two people, hysterically laughing, hurtled up to them on inline skates. One of them was a big, strong, handsome man, and he was holding the hand of a woman.

"A red-haired woman. Ursula.

"King Dudo wasn't fast enough. The woman crashed straight into him. He tumbled head over toes down the steep incline at the side of the promenade. He found himself lying flat on his back at the bottom of the little hill. He was just about to right himself when Ursula flopped on top of him. The strong, handsome young man, meanwhile, came to a toppling halt a little way up the path, and Brunhilda ran to see if he was hurt.

Face to face at last, albeit lying down and in a very odd position, King Dudo seized the opportunity and addressed the woman from the ice. "'Hi. I'm Dudo,' he said as Ursula jumped up.

"'Yes, I know.' She smiled and leaned a hand down to help him up.

"'We've met before.'

"'Yes, you're the man who said, *Well, hello there*, when I was doing laundry in the brook.'

"'That was not our first meeting.'

Ursula, looking away, absently twiddled her necklace.

"'I believe you saved my life.'

"'It was nothing.'

"'HA! So you admit it! It *was* you! You were on the ice. There was a bear and then there was you—'

"'Hurry up, Ursula!' the strong, handsome man, who happened to have the nicest set of pristine white teeth Dudo had ever seen, called from the promenade.

"'I'm afraid I have to go,' she said and made her way up the verge with great difficulty; she was wearing inline skates after all. Once she hit the path, she bladed off, and she and the strong, handsome man with perfect white teeth glided away hand in hand toward the harbor.

"King Dudo straightened himself and strode to where Brunhilda waited patiently on the promenade. 'Who was that?' King Dudo asked Brunhilda.

"'You know who that is—that's my mis—I mean, my servant girl, Ursula, the one who toils for us. In the fields and in the home. She's a servant. She toils.'

"'No, I mean the man. Who is the man?'

"'Oh, him. That's Thorar the Smoldering. He is the

jar—I mean, my father's right-hand man.'

"'I see. And are they betrothed?'

"'I don't know. I don't think so. He is probably just wooing her. She gets wooed a lot.'

"'She does, eh? I shall take you home now, Brunhilda,' said Dudo and strode purposefully back the way they had just come.

"'What? Oh, if you say so.' Brunhilda ran after King Dudo. 'That was a quick date. You only picked me up ten minutes ago.'

"'Yes, well, I realize now that I have not been doing this right. We need to have more *fun*!'

"'That's great … I think …'

"'I will pick you up here tomorrow. At daybreak!' King Dudo announced with much gravitas and vehemence. 'And we shall have *fun*!'"

Granny stretched herself out on the sofa where she had been since the tree was trimmed to everyone's satisfaction. She sipped the cocoa Mum brought her and snuggled her feet deeper into her cozy slippers.

"It's going less than nicely for Dudo and Brunhilda, is it, Granny?" Ruairi said, slyly.

"Not what you'd call a great first date," Dani said, grinning.

"Maybe he'll ditch Brunhilda and try Ursula instead," Ruairi said.

"It's not like Dudo to give up, now, is it? He is tenacious, and he has set his mind on wooing Brunhilda," Granny said with finality.

"We'll see," Dani said.

"Yeah, Granny," Ruairi said. "We'll see."

The Wooing of Brunhilda Continued: The More Fun Version

"The next morning, a beautiful Brunhilda Thunder Thighs emerged from her dwelling place to find a beaming King Dudo waiting for her. He had two pairs of inline skates.

"'Are you ready for the best date of your life?' he asked an uncertain-looking Brunhilda.

"'Sure, but have you ever skated before, my liege? It's not as easy as it looks. Perhaps we should get you some padding—'

"'Nonsense! I have faced the toughest enemies and tamed the most vicious beasts. I have braved the stormiest seas and climbed the most forbidding peaks. I shall take to skating like a baby dragon takes to barbecuing.'

"'If you say so.'

"Five minutes later, Brunhilda was doing loop de loops and pirouettes around Dudo on the path while Dudo moved along inch by inch, his arms outstretched, his feet barely moving. He had his winged golden helmet on and had *downdles* strapped to his elbows and knees.

"'Yes, I'm getting the hang of it now. See?' He gave Brunhilda a huge smile. 'I haven't fallen once in at least two minutes,' he said as his left leg shot out in front of him and his right leg shot out behind. He did windmills with his arms and managed to balance precariously inches from the ground. Brunhilda rolled her eyes and went to his rescue.

"'Perhaps you were right, Brunhilda. Perhaps a picnic in the forest is the way to go. We've hardly chatted at *all*. I want to get to *know* you,' Dudo said.

"A short while later Brunhilda and Dudo wandered within the shelter of the thousands of trees in the Crimson Forest, and Brunhilda set out a blanket for them in a clearing. They sat and chatted. 'Yes,' thought Dudo, 'this woman is very sweet and very calming. I can be at ease with her. Perhaps she is right for me after all.' He decided that now, a mere two days before Brunhilda was to sail out of his life possibly forever, now was the time to propose. He moved in front of Brunhilda and was just about to arrange himself so that he was on one knee when, from high above, came sounds of screeching laughter very similar to what he and Brunhilda had heard on the path the day before. Turning and looking up what should they see but Ursula and Thorar the Smoldering floating through the air with giant eagle wings strapped to their arms. They had jumped off the top of Volcano Mount Violaceous, which was rumbling and spewing softly in the background.

"Dudo and Brunhilda rose from the blanket. They shaded their eyes from the sun to get a better view. 'I think they're headed this way,' Dudo said as the two gliders swung around in their direction.

"'This is a habitual landing place for eagle gliders. There is moss underfoot—it is soft.' As Brunhilda predicted, Ursula and Thorar made synchronized swoops slowly downward. 'Don't they look grand together? They make a striking couple, no?' Brunhilda asked.

"'Hmm,' said Dudo.

"Ursula and Thorar were perhaps ten feet from the ground when a circling gust blew through the trees and slammed into their wings. They both lost control of their equipment and came tumbling down at a great speed. Ursula's wings came right off her arms, and she splattered straight into King Dudo, who went down with a crash.

"'Mother of—' King Dudo said as he tried to right himself. 'We meet again. You do know how to make an entrance, servant girl.'

"Thorar landed with a bump and rolled and rolled and rolled along the moss-covered forest floor. Brunhilda ran to see if he was hurt. Ursula stood and helped Dudo to his feet.

"'You were telling me yesterday,' King Dudo said, 'of the bear and the ice and our first meeting.'

"'I was?' Ursula responded, shyly glancing at Dudo as she made to follow Brunhilda.

"'Yes. Yes, you were,' Dudo said as he motioned to Ursula to sit down on the picnic blanket. 'The first time you crashed into me and caused me to scramble in the dirt. Sit, please. They will be some time, I think. I saw poor What's-his-name hit his head on a rock but don't fret—my darling Brunhilda will revive him in a tick.' Ursula moved to go and help them. 'You doubt Brunhilda's nursing abilities?' King Dudo asked, pouring beverages for the two of them and motioning once more for Ursula to sit down.

"'No, of course not,' Ursula began. 'It's just—'

"'I think it best to leave the boy's revival to her kind hands,' Dudo said and handed Ursula a drink and a sausage roll. Revive yourself, peasant. Eat and drink,' Dudo said. 'So! You were telling me'—he sat back and crossed his arms—'the bear, the ice; then you showed up. Don't deny it, you admitted it yesterday. Unless you have a twin sister— perhaps an *evil* twin sister—and I find that highly unlikely.'

"'I do not deny it,' Ursula said. 'It was I. I was having a stroll along the beach, and I heard an unearthly wailing sound, and I figured someone or something was in trouble.'

"'I take it you are referring to my singing,' Dudo said, a little deflated.

"'So I took to the water and followed the wailing—I mean singing—and found you and the bear on the ice. I climbed onto the little island, wrestled the bear—'

"'You did what now?'

"'I wrestled the bear and forced it back into the sea—'

"'No, no—hold on a minute. You're telling me you fought with the bear, all on your own—alone, with no help, just you—and you won?'

"'Sure. It was no big thing. We are an island of warriors, you know. To be honest, I did want to ask you why you hadn't fought the bear yourself; it would have seemed a lot simpler a solution than trying to deafen it with your wailing.'

"'I, eh, um, I didn't want to hurt such a magnificent creature,' Dudo said quickly. 'I didn't, you know, think it would be fair.'

"'I see,' Ursula said, unconvinced. 'Then, it was my intention to dive back into the ocean and swim away, but you opened your eyes. I couldn't just swim away.'

"'You couldn't?' Dudo asked, softening for the first time. He sat up straight and looked at her closely. He took her hand in his. 'Because you felt something? You felt something deep inside you, like your heart turning into a million butterflies floating and dancing within your rib cage, and you knew, you just knew that after all the wishing and hoping, after all the years of longing and dreaming, of never meeting your Heart's True Love, you realized that in front of you was—'

"'No,' Ursula said with finality. 'Because you fell off the ice and cracked your head.'

"'Oh. So, it didn't mean anything to you?'

"'Not at all,' she said, and Dudo thought, hoped, she looked a little uncertain.

"'So why bother?' King Dudo asked in a huff.

"'I could hardly let you drown, now, could I? You looked so pathetic.'

"'Pathe*tic*?'

"'Like a wet rat.' Ursula stifled a grin.

"'I have had enough of this insolence, peasant! Servant girl! Away with you!' Dudo snapped around and turned his back on Ursula.

"'You did ask!' Ursula said as she got up from the blanket and walked into the woods, humming, in the direction of Brunhilda and Thorar. From the woods, Dudo could hear Brunhilda and Thorar burst into laughter, clearly at something Ursula had just told them.

"Dudo strode across the clearing and stood at the edge of the trees. 'Brunhilda, Brunhilda, come away. Our picnic has been ruined by these interlopers. I am taking you eagle gliding.'

"'Oh, no no no no,' Brunhilda said, emerging panicked from the trees. 'I don't think that's a good idea, my liege. I'd much rather go back to strolling. Strolling was good. I liked strolling. Let's do some more strolling.'

——— • ———

"The following morning, the day after the eagle gliding date, on Brunhilda's last day before heading south, she and Dudo went for brunch in the harbor. Dudo was not comfortable. He still hadn't gotten used to the brace on his neck. The cast on his leg was itching like madness, and the bruises all over the rest of his body still hurt like all hell.

"'This is just lovely,' Brunhilda said, 'even nicer than strolling, which, of course, you'll be able to do again in six to eight weeks depending on how that break heals. Just lovely. I never much cared for eagle gliding anyway. It's overrated. Of course it was not your fault at all that you careened headfirst off the mountain as soon as you took flight. It was a bad day for wind.'

"'Brunhilda, beautiful Brunhilda, I've been thinking,' Dudo said through his wired jaw.

"'Yes?' Brunhilda replied, sipping elegantly on a beverage.

"'I have something to ask you.' "Dudo heaved himself off his seat and painfully got himself into a position which from certain angles could look like he was on one knee. 'Ow, ow, ow, ow ow,' he said. 'You are a very nice person, and we get on quite nicely, don't we?'

"'I think we do, yes, and thank you. You are a very nice person too. Not very sporty but very nice, yes,' Brunhilda said.

"'One comes to a point in one's life,' King Dudo continued, 'when one thinks one might be better off being with someone else, someone nice, to do things with and share things with and bear heirs with. Do you agree?'

"'Yes, I think I do agree, King Dudo. I think I do. Someone nice is far preferable to someone who is not nice. And one really should get around to bearing heirs before it is too late for one.'

"'In that case, Brunhilda, and I know we don't know each other very well as yet, but I was wondering …'

"'Yes?'

"'I was wondering'—Dudo took Brunhilda's hand and looked earnestly into her eyes and screeched—'YOU HAVE GOT TO BE KIDDING ME!' For just then, Ursula and Thorar, laughing hysterically as usual, came speeding into the harbor riding on the backs of two dolphins. 'No, seriously, come ON! Does that servant girl ever do any work? *Ser*iously!'

"Ursula and Thorar came to a sharp halt at the water's edge next to where Dudo was kneeling before Brunhilda. They sent a wave of saltwater into the air as they halted. Brunhilda nimbly dove out of the way, but Dudo, slow to react, was sent sprawling by masses of icy-cold saltwater.

"Dudo glared at Ursula. Ursula looked back coyly. 'Oops,' she said as she leaped off the dolphin's back onto the promenade beside King Dudo.

"A dripping Dudo, shivering from the icy water, turned to Brunhilda. 'Beautiful Brunhilda,' he said, and as he waited for Brunhilda to come back to him from the dry part of the verge, Dudo thought he saw Ursula's smile fade as she moved away to allow Brunhilda space. But he couldn't be sure. It was this uncertainty that cut Dudo to his core. When the others had laughed at him under the canopy of trees, he knew Ursula had laughed with them, but the timbre of her laugh had lacked the vigour of theirs. When they emerged, he thought he caught a look of sadness on her face. An admission that what she'd said and done did not reflect how she felt about him. It was an impression only, a feeling, and a fleeting one at that. Nothing he could count on; nothing he could grasp firmly and say 'Here, look. This is what you did or this is what you said, and this is how I know my love reflects yours. This is how I'm sure your heart beats in time with mine. And why I can never love another, even the fabulous Brunhilda with her hair of sleek ebony and her thighs of thunder.' But he didn't have that certainty, and with noon blazing its silken presence on Brunhilda's last day on Yondersaay, Dudo's mind was set.

"'Brunhilda,' he mumbled through his wired jaw as he heaved himself back onto his one good knee, 'Darling delightful Brunhilda, will you marry me, today, at sunset?'

"Brunhilda, undoubtedly startled by the sudden mumbling, gasped before eloquently answering, 'Um, all right.'

"Dudo rose and wetly limped as quickly as he could, so not very quickly at all, with as much dignity as he could muster, which wasn't very much at all, away from the harbor toward the dwelling place. 'Wonderful,' he threw back over his shoulder, 'until sunset!'

"His last glance backward took in a startled Brunhilda, a gorgeous Thorar the Smouldering, and although Dudo could not be certain of this, a pale and stricken Ursula, who with an almost imperceptible step back clutched the dirty rock that hung on her neck. As Dudo left, he heard the faintest whisper of Ursula's voice as she hummed sadly and strolled away.

The Wedding of Dudo and Brunhilda

"The wedding of Dudo and Brunhilda," Granny began.

"That can't be right, Granny. Are you sure you're remembering the story correctly?" Dani asked.

"Yes, Granny, how can Dudo marry Brunhilda when Ursula is his Heart's True Love? You sure you're not mixing it up?"

"Do you want to hear the story or not?" Granny said sternly.

"Yes," Dani and Ruairi replied.

"Do you want me to tell it to you the way it really happened, or do you want me to make something up so it all ends Happily Ever After?"

"The real way, Granny," Ruairi said.

"Well, all righty then." Granny looked at Dani and Ruairi and sighed. "We'd better take it upstairs. It is ludicrously late. Go brush your teeth and get into bed, and I'll come up and finish the story up there. I'll just make myself a quick snack while you're getting into your jammies. I've barely eaten a thing all day."

"WE'RE READY!" Dani and Ruairi shouted from their bedroom a few minutes later.

Granny vigorously bounded up the stairs and threw herself into the giant beanbag on the floor of the bedroom with her feet sticking up and out. "Where were we?" Granny settled down deep and began again. "Word of the proposal spread quickly, and as everyone on the island always wanted in on a good party, they all came together in the village and got stuck into preparations for the wedding feast.

"The island's men—fishermen and farmers naturally but also warriors to the core—were a little saddened that the chances of bloody battle between them and the Danes were seriously diminished. They had hoped Dudo would take Rarelief's first option and go off, find his men, ixnay the jarl's line, and scootch back to the island for battle. However, they bore the disappointment stoically and got into the party spirit instead. There was much goat sacrificing and mead drinking in honor of the happy couple.

"As the day wore on, smells of cooking mingled with the smell of the sea and wafted all over the island. Villagers hung banners and lights for the sundown ceremony. As the hour approached, men and women, dressed in their finest gear, which happened to be their battle gear, paraded down the main thoroughfare of the island. They held aloft huge flaming torches, which lit hundreds of giant candles placed all over the settlement.

"They also carried a longship on their shoulders. Usually in Viking times, and you may not know this, Dani and Ruairi, a longship was burned only at funerals. But not on

Yondersaay. There have always been lots of very old people on Yondersaay, and not that many funerals. Yondersaanians rarely got a chance to burn a longship because of the lack of people dying. So it was long the tradition on Yondersaay that longship torching was no longer confined just to funerals, and the locals could and did perform the ritual at any big occasion, happy or sad.

"The villagers began gathering at the point chosen by the bride as the wedding venue. Brunhilda had decided against having the wedding at the harbor, an obvious choice since the sunset over the waves is exquisitely beautiful. It was too close to the promenade, the site of her groom's embarrassment on not one but two occasions. She had decided against the clearing in the Crimson Forest for similar reasons, despite that spot coming alive in a chorus of animal music upon the setting of the sun. She didn't choose anywhere on Mount Violaceous because her groom had fallen off the mountain so disastrously the day before. Instead, running out of options, Brunhilda chose as her wedding site the banks of the gargling brook by the clearing just beyond the dwelling place with the woods behind them and the shimmering sea in front.

"A stunning location without doubt, but Brunhilda was not to know that this was where Dudo had seen Ursula for the first time after his escape from the ice. Brunhilda was not to know that this was where, believing Ursula to be his Heart's True Love, Dudo spoke to her for the very first time. Brunhilda was not to know that this was the spot upon which her groom was hurt more deeply than he had ever been hurt by any savage beast or by an adversary in battle.

"It was here on the banks of the gargling brook by the clearing just beyond the dwelling place with the woods behind them and the shimmering sea in front, that Dudo the Mightily Impressive, arriving for his marriage to the beautiful Brunhilda Thunder Thighs, realized that forevermore he would go through life an incomplete man. For it was on this spot that King Dudo the Mightily Impressive, crushed and broken, was coming to understand that he would never spend a year, a month, or even a day with his Heart's True Love.

"Brunhilda was not to know this.

"He stood, balancing on his crutches, taking care not to move his wired jaw too much, thinking and waiting, as the islanders settled onto chairs and benches and stools behind him. Ursula approached him.

"'Wintersuckle flowers,' she said as she pinned some tiny flowers to his sleeve. 'The bride's handmaiden traditionally bestows these as a gift to the groom on the day of his wedding. They grow wild on the island and survive even the harshest of conditions. They represent continuity, stability, and fertility. May you and your bride have a long and loving life together, and may the gods reward your devotion to each other with many healthy children.'

"Dudo was taken aback by the sweetness and sincerity with which Ursula spoke to him. He saw a gentleness in her face that he had never seen before as she fastened the flowering buds to his clothing. 'I am grateful for this gift,' Dudo said to Ursula, and he looked into her eyes, deep into her eyes for the first time since he saw her on the ice. 'Thank you. You make things seem very clear to me.'

"'I do?'

"'Yes, yes, you do.'

"Ursula blushed and started walking away. 'I will bring your bride to you. As you are alone here on the island, Thorar will stand with you.'

"Dudo turned and welcomed the resplendent Thorar the Smoldering. Thorar smiled and slapped Dudo on the back. 'My congratulations to you both,' he said. 'It is my pleasure to stand with you today.'

"Dudo instinctively turned to watch Ursula leave. He didn't even realize he was doing it. Just as he was about to turn back and chat with Thorar, Ursula glanced back at him.

"Ursula saw Dudo looking at her, and Dudo saw Ursula looking at him. His heart soared. She reddened and looked away. Dudo turned back to Thorar, but he could not concentrate on what the warrior was saying. All he could think about was Ursula and the way she had looked at him just now.

"While he was deep in thought, soft music started up. The village musicians had fanned out along the bridge across the brook and were now playing sultry music that echoed and enhanced the atmosphere of the latening day. They played in the glow of the setting sun and the thousand candles laid out across the bridge.

"The birds were singing their evening tunes, and the night insects had started their mating songs when Brunhilda emerged.

"She truly was a striking bride—beautiful and radiant. White and flowing, her dress set off her raven hair, her blue eyes, her red lips, and ably presented the perfection of her form. It was clear to Dudo, as it was to everyone present, that this woman, his bride, was a natural beauty. From his conversations with her, Dudo knew her heart was just as pure and beautiful.

"Nevertheless, Dudo could not help his heart from yearning for the woman simply attired in an everyday dress with neither makeup nor jeweled adornment, who was walking quietly, her eyes on the ground, behind his bride.

"When the heiress reached the king, their hands were joined by an ancient man in flowing green robes. He was the resident ceremony-official-maker. Dudo had noticed him earlier, snoozing on the ground, propped up against a rock. He had been hoisted into position by the jarl and Thorar while everyone else's attention was diverted by Brunhilda's arrival. Dudo had never seen anyone so old.

"The ceremony-official-maker raised his arms, and the crowd quieted. He began, 'It is with very heavy hearts that we gather here to mourn the loss—' The jarl leaped with great speed to the ceremony-official-maker and whispered something in his ear.

"'WHAT?' the old man shouted. The jarl whispered a bit louder. 'OH, I SEE! A MARRIAGE, NOT A FUNERAL.' The old man turned to the bride and groom and smiled. He slowly raised his arms, closed his eyes, and lowered his head. The assembled wedding guests, everybody on the island, awaited the old man's pronouncement.

"The old man did not move. The jarl cleared his throat. The ceremony-official-maker was standing upright, his head bowed down as though in preparation, and his arms were raised in the air. After a minute, a soft snoring sound came from the old man and carried all the way to the back of the crowd. The jarl gave the old man a swift kick to the ankle. He roused himself with a snort and started speaking again as though he'd never stopped.

"'We are here on this beautiful evening to celebrate the coming together in marriage of'—and here the old man paused, and his eyes flickered toward the jarl who coughed.

"'Cough—Hilda!'

"'Brunhilda! And ...' Again, the old man glanced toward the jarl.

"'Cough—Udo.'

"'And King Dudo of the Danes! Let us hear from the groom,' the old man said and bowed his head again.

"Dudo turned to the assembled crowd. He looked into the faces of his would-be subjects. He thought briefly of the treasures buried deep beneath Rarelief's roots.

"'My liege,' King Dudo said. He spoke loud enough for the entire congregation to hear, but he was addressing the jarl— a man who had been hospitable and generous when he had not needed to be. 'This island represents the culmination of a lifetime's dreaming. Yondersaay would be the jewel in the crown of Denmark. The young men of the island would be a huge asset to my Viking fleet. I would be honored and proud to go into battle with any one of you. My fellow countrymen would hail me as their greatest king for centuries if I were to sail home and proclaim Yondersaay mine.

"'As you know, there have been songs sung and legends told of the mighty king who will single-handedly engineer the island's surrender, who will possess the island despite its being hidden from view in the northern-most seas and inaccessible to the merest mortal. I have come to love this island over the past few days; it has come to feel like home to me. I have seen myself so many nights in my dreams as this one heroic king.'

"Here, King Dudo paused for a moment. He drew a deep breath and continued, 'Your daughter is a genuine beauty. Brunhilda possesses a perfection of heart, mind, and body so pure as to bring light and hope to the most dejected. So it is, indeed, with the heaviest of hearts that I say to you'—and Dudo looked at the jarl and then turned to his bride—'that I lay bare my soul and confess: I am not the king of the legends.' Here King Dudo looked back at the jarl. 'It sorrows me deeply to say I cannot marry your daughter.'

"The crowd drew a collective intake of breath. They gasped in shock. Soxolf the Unshod, silent when Dudo first met him, could plainly be heard, by everyone, to say, 'He's ditching her at the altar? What cretin would do such a thing?'

"'I'm sure he has his reasons,' Pal the Friendly whispered back.

"'My lord,' Dudo continued, despite the crowd's rumblings getting louder and louder, 'I must relinquish my life's dream and leave your island disconsolate, empty-handed, and alone. I hope, nevertheless, my lord, that I will always be welcome at your table. You and yours will always be welcome at mine.'

"King Dudo turned to face Brunhilda. 'It is with the utmost sadness and regret, Brunhilda, that I renege on my promise to marry you. That I should do it today of all days, on your wedding day, while you stand before me at the altar, is unforgivable. I have been a coward and a fool, and I should never have allowed myself to take our courtship this far. You have done nothing wrong, and I will be eternally ashamed at the way I have treated you, at the humiliation I have brought upon you, and the disappointment you must feel.'

"'Actually, to be truthful, I really don't mind,' Brunhilda said, smiling and hugging Dudo. 'Not at all. If we're being a hundred percent honest, I could happily have gone either way.'

"Thorar beamed a glistening, white-toothed smile at Brunhilda. Brunhilda caught the smile and smiled widely back at Thorar.

"'No, I know you're just covering up your humiliation

and disappointment,' Dudo said, slightly affronted. 'My poor, brave Brunhilda.'

"'No. No, I'm really not, my king,' Brunhilda said. 'You are a very nice man, courteous and kind, but frankly, you're not really my type. I'm more into men of action.'

"'Men of action! I am King Dudo the Mightily Impressive!'

"'If you say so.'

"'Poor, sweet, broken-hearted Brunhilda,' Dudo said, patting her on the head.

"Brunhilda shrugged at Dudo and turned toward Thorar the Smoldering, who came to her side and stood close to her. So close that no one in front of them could see that secretly, behind their backs, they were holding hands.

"Dudo turned to address the jarl once more. 'I feel I owe you an explanation, my liege. I have met my Heart's True Love. I simply cannot take another as my wife. It is therefore with ease that I give up this island and the glory it would bring. I would happily give up my throne and my entire fortune for just one day with her. For she is my Heart's True Love.'

"'I see,' the jarl said.

"'It just so happens that this woman, a woman who has spurned me, I might add, is not"—Dudo indicated Brunhilda—"the heiress of Yondersaay. In fact, she is a simple peasant.'

"Throughout all of this, as he spoke, as Brunhilda and Thorar were secretly united, Dudo was aware of Ursula, standing still a few feet away, looking straight ahead. He did not turn toward Ursula as he spoke of his Heart's True Love, nor did he indicate her in any way, nor so much as glance at her. He was simply aware of her.

"The gathered crowd took in the news that there would

be no party. This was disappointing. They were all dressed up now. Soxolf had washed his feet and everything. The people whispered among themselves, trying for the life of them to come up with some reason, any reason, to keep the party on as scheduled. Dudo, in this moment, as the crowd got louder and louder chatting among themselves, allowed his mind to wander.

"His mind paced its way back to all of his encounters with Ursula, from seeing her on the ice to now, this moment. He remembered something, or he figured out something. At least, something occurred to him that hadn't occurred to him before.

"When Dudo had tried to talk to Ursula at the brook and she blanked him, it hurt. It hurt even more when, seemingly unmoved by the encounter in any way, she had hummed a song to herself. Ursula, Dudo now realized, hummed the same song when he saw her in the woods, and the same song was on her lips while she conducted her menial tasks around the dwelling place. In fact, every time King Dudo had seen Ursula, every single time, either as he encountered her or as she wandered away from him, she was humming the same song.

"His mother's song.

"The song Dudo sang to the bear on the ice." Granny said and paused to look at Dani and Ruairi who were bouncing up and down with excitement.

Dani leaned into Ruairi and whispered, "I knew it!"

Granny went on. "The assembled islanders were still chattering away to one another about how and where to best continue the festivities. Their attention was no longer on the wedding party in the clearing; they were neither watching nor listening to what was going on.

"Dudo turned to look at Ursula with his realization

fresh in his mind. Ursula had not moved an inch; she was still standing off a little to the side, looking straight ahead.

"'Look at me,' he said.

"Ursula did not move.

"Dudo limped over to her and softly repeated through his wired jaw, 'Look at me.'

"Ursula looked at the king, and for the first time, Dudo saw what she had not allowed him to see all this time. Dudo saw his heart in her eyes. He saw his love for her reflected there. He saw what he had been looking for his entire life.

"'I will go away now, and you will never see me again,' Dudo said to her almost in a whisper. 'Just tell me one thing before I do.'

"'If I can, my lord,' Ursula said.

"'Tell me you do not love me,' Dudo said.

"Ursula did not speak. She looked away from Dudo; she looked to the jarl and to Brunhilda, trying to get them to tell her what to do. They looked back at her, but their faces held no answers. Ursula turned back to the king and said in a low voice, 'I cannot tell you that.'

"Encouraged, Dudo said, 'I think your heart lies with mine. Tell me it doesn't, and I will leave and I will never come back.'

"'I cannot tell you that, My Liege,' she said.

"'Ursula,' Dudo said, taking her hand in his, 'Ursula Swan White, of the sundown tresses and the sea-ice eyes, tell me I am not your Heart's True Love.'

"Ursula shook her head. 'My liege, I cannot tell you you're not my Heart's True Love.' she said.

"Dudo persisted. 'I defy you. Tell me to go away. Tell me to leave this island and never come back.'

"Ursula looked straight into his face, resolute at last, and said, 'My king, that I can do.' Strong and firm, with tears nevertheless springing into her eyes, she proclaimed, 'I can and I will tell you. Go away and never come back,' Ursula turned from King Dudo, her Heart's True Love.

"Dudo was stunned. 'But why?' He waited for a response, for an explanation, but none came. 'You cannot wound me like this and not tell me why. You cannot shatter my heart into a million pieces and not explain your reasoning.'

"The ceremony-official-maker, who had been right there all the time looking from one to the other and back again as they spoke, looking more and more confused, finally caught up to what was going on. In a very loud voice he said, 'What is this? Is the marriage off? What did he say just now, what did he say? Brunhilda, the heiress of Yondersaay? How preposterous! Brunhilda is not the heiress of Yondersaay.'

"Dudo turned to the ceremony-official-maker. The jarl, Ursula, Thorar, and Brunhilda tried desperately to silence the minister, but he was having none of it and swatted them away like flies as they leaped to shush him.

"'Brunhilda is not the heiress of Yondersaay?' Dudo asked the ceremony-official-maker.

"'What on earth gave you that idea?' the old man said. '*Ursula* is the heiress of Yondersaay.'

"Dudo was astounded. He didn't know what to think. Ursula, the heiress of Yondersaay? He looked to Ursula for an explanation, but it was the jarl who spoke.

"'Let me explain, my lord,' he said. 'It is true what the old man says.' He looked around to him accusingly, but the old man had fallen back to sleep. 'Brunhilda is not my daughter. She is my servant girl. Ursula is my daughter. Do not blame them. I insisted on the deception. I could not risk you marrying my darling daughter just to gain control of the island. This incredible woman deserves to spend her life with someone who loves her for herself, not for her inheritance.

"'I forbade Ursula from having anything to do with you, though I knew how she felt. I made her swear on my life and on the lives of all who live on Yondersaay that she would reject you and turn you away. She thought, we both thought, we were doing what was right for Yondersaay and for our people.

"'Ursula is no longer bound by her oath.' He turned to his daughter. 'I release you from your promise; you must act in the best interests of your heart, not of mine.'

"'It didn't work,' Ursula said, indicating her necklace. For the first time Dudo really noticed her piece of jewelry. It looked like a smooth, clear piece of glass, like something roughly hewn or that had washed up on the beach. It was fastened around her neck on a simple string.

"'It is the Violaceous Amethyst,' the jarl said to Dudo. 'It protects its bearer from intoxication. I was afraid you would ruthlessly and carelessly seduce my daughter if you knew who she was. She wore it and still she loves you. If you had tried to deceive her and manipulate her, it would have kept her safe. You got through to her simply by loving her. And she got through to you simply by being herself.'

"'I thought it was supposed to be purple,' Dudo said.

"'When it is close to the source of its power'—the jarl indicated the Volcano Mount Violaceous from which it was mined—'its hue can be manipulated by its wearer to channel the effects of the lava beneath the earth. Besides, a purple rock hanging around her neck would have been a bit of a giveaway; Rarelief the Splendiferous was certain to have told you about the Violaceous Amethyst.'

"'Fair point,' King Dudo said.

"'I beg your forgiveness, my liege, and your understanding' the jarl continued. 'If you can forgive Ursula for deceiving you under order from me, if in your heart you harbor no ill feelings, you are truly at liberty to woo my daughter, my real daughter, Ursula.' With that, the jarl left the hollow by the gargling river.

"The villagers, having decided that *not* having a new king was a thing they could celebrate, moved the festivities to the harbor. Brunhilda and Thorar, holding hands openly now and hardly able to keep their eyes off each other, followed the islanders to the party on the shore. Dudo and Ursula were soon alone.

"The sounds of revelry carried all the way to the brook where Ursula stood in the fading daylight, barefoot and in her simple dress. The king had never set eyes on anyone so beautiful.

"'I love you,' he said when he was sure they were alone. 'And I always will.'

"'I love you too,' Ursula said.

"'Will you have me as yours?'

"'I will.'

"'Shall we wake him?' Dudo gestured to the minister who was once again snoring under a rock.

"Ursula smiled. 'Yes, but I want to do this properly. I am an heiress, after all.'

"Less than an hour later, as the last of the sun's embers glinted off the water by the pier, Ursula walked toward her Heart's True Love. In the company of her lifelong friends, dressed beautifully, with rubies and emeralds, her hair adorned smelling of the sweetest flowers from the beds of the Crimson Forest, Ursula said, "I do," to King Dudo the Mightily Impressive, brave and noble lord of all Denmark. She took him to be her husband, for better, for worse, for richer, for poorer, for as long as they both drew breath.

"Cheers went up, fireworks sprayed across the sky, and all the inhabitants of Yondersaay made merry until the wee hours of the morning.

"So it was that King Dudo, a lone warrior with neither weaponry nor army, with no council to advise him and no magic to aid him, became next in line to be the lord and master of Yondersaay, the enchanted island in the middle of the northern-most seas.

"The following morning, the jarl headed south with Brunhilda and Thorar. Before he left his dwelling place, he spoke in his private quarters with King Dudo. 'When I die, the island will pass to you and your family. My daughter will bear you heirs, and in your family, the island will stay forever. It may not be traded or forcibly taken. Whosoever takes it forcibly, and believes it his, will be visited by lifelong disappointment. The island will stay in our line, directly or through marriage, forevermore. Should the line end, only then shall he who claims it be the true owner.

"'There is one last thing I must do for you before I leave. I wish to introduce you to someone,' the jarl said. With that, the door to the dwelling place opened and in walked the ancient, stooped, hard-of-hearing, bumbling old ceremony-official-maker who had tried to marry Brunhilda and Dudo and who had succeeded in marrying Ursula and Dudo. Only he didn't look quite so ancient or stooped, and when Dudo spoke to him, he didn't seem quite so hard of hearing nor as bumbling.

"'This is Odin, the father of all Vikings,' the jarl said to Dudo, who couldn't disguise his shock. Dudo dropped to his knees before the mighty Odin, father of all Vikings, keeper of the treasures of Valhalla, and bowed his head.

"'My lord, I am overwhelmed by this great honor. I am

at your service. How may I please you?' Dudo said.

"'Your offer is a kind one,' Odin said, in a voice at once gravelly and pure, 'but it is I who am at your service. Should you or anyone on Yondersaay need aid or protection, you can be certain that I or my friends'—he motioned to two ravens of the darkest black that were resting nearby—'will be close at hand and will battle to protect you. You will one day be lord and master of all Yondersaay, and with that honor comes a heavy duty. The priceless treasures of all the Vikings of old will be under your protection and will remain under your family's protection until the final battle in Valhalla. We shall help you keep it safe.'"

Granny looked up from her puffy bean bag. Both Dani and Ruairi were fighting off sleep as bravely as any Viking warrior fights off the fiercest enemy. "Time to call it a day, my younglings," Granny said, trying to get out of the beanbag as Dani and Ruairi helplessly drifted into a deep sleep. Granny squirmed and wriggled in the puff. She tried to heave herself this way and that, but it was no use, she could not get out. "Mum!" she called. "HELLLP!" There was no response from downstairs. "Maybe I'll sleep here," Granny mumbled as she struggled one more time. "MummEEEEE!"

PART II

CHRISTMAS EVE

Dawn on Christmas Eve Morning

What first made Ruairi suspicious when he woke up on Christmas Eve and looked out his window was not the hundred men running down the island High Street with lit torches in their hands and glistening battle-axes over their shoulders. It was not the fact that these men looked remarkably like the Vikings of old and were dressed— whiskers to big toe—in leather, chain mail, and sheepskin, with horny helmets on their heads. It was not the fact that some of the men in the middle of the crowd were hoiking a massive Viking longship on their shoulders in the direction of the harbor. It was not even the fact that these normally quiet, mild-mannered men—the village shopkeepers and local farmers, the teacher, the distiller, and the publican— were singing with throats upturned to high heaven, "Up HellyAa! Up HellyAa! I'm a Viking. The sea is the place for me. Up HellyAa!" It was the fact that right in among all the other Vikings, a fair bit off to the right at the back a little, Ruairi could see someone who looked a lot like Hamish Sinclair, albeit in a leather skirt, a sheepskin waistcoat, lace-up leather sandals, and a winged helmet. Hamish Sinclair, who maintains that vegetables are for wimps, that real men only eat meat and the occasional Cadbury's creme egg, Hamish Sinclair, Ruairi now saw was, with not a shred of embarrassment, openly and brazenly eating an apple.

Granny and Dani joined Ruairi at the window.

"There's something not quite right here," Ruairi said.

"No flies on you," said Dani.

"I'm flabbergasted!" Granny said as she took it all in. "I can't believe my eyes." She rubbed her eyes hard and looked again. "Are you seeing what I'm seeing?"

"Yuh-huh," Dani and Ruairi said, leaning right out the window now.

"And just to be extra, absolutely, completely sure," Granny said, going pale and clutching her chest. "Is what you're seeing by any chance all my lifelong friends and acquaintances, all the people we know from this island, is it all of them"—Granny took a deep breath—"looking like Vikings and acting like Vikings and doing things the way you'd expect Vikings to be doing?"

"Yuh-huh," Dani and Ruairi said again.

"Is there any chance I haven't woken up yet?" Granny pinched herself all over and collapsed into a heap onto her beanbag.

"We're awake, Granny. It's really happening," Dani said.

"Really," Ruairi said.

"Well, I suppose, it is Christmas Eve." She moved and put her hand under her bum. She lifted her hand out and found that she had collapsed on a mince pie. She looked at it, shrugged, and started to eat it. Dani and Ruairi waited for her to say something. "In all honesty, this does ring a bell."

"What on earth do you mean 'this does ring a bell'?"

"Granny," Dani said, "everyone on Yondersaay is here on the High Street. Look. There's the butcher eating an apple, the draper drinking mead from a helmet, the cobbler setting things alight with a flaming torch. Even the carpenters who live on the far side of the island in Halfdan Hollow are here. They're carrying a longship down the High Street on their shoulders with the lobster fishers. Everyone is a Viking!"

"You're not, strictly speaking, a hundred percent correct in that statement, my dear," Granny Miller said as she held out her arms so Dani and Ruairi could heave her up out of the beanbag. She eyed them both and looked back out the window again. "Everyone on the island is a Viking—except us."

Dani and Ruairi looked down at themselves to make sure they weren't wearing sheepskin and leather, and sure enough, they were both still in their pajamas. "Yes," Ruairi said, looking out the window again, "that's right. Everyone on the island is a Viking except us."

"For as long as I can remember," Granny said, "things frequently seem a little odd or a little not quite right all of a sudden come Christmas morning. People have woken up in places they don't remember going to or have discovered tattoos they didn't have before. It's usually put down to having one too many hot toddies or glasses of mulled wine at Christmas Eve parties. But the draper, well, he's a teetotaler."

"A what?" Dani asked.

"A teetotaler is someone who never drinks. It brings

them out in hives, I believe. The draper woke up one Christmas morning in the crow's nest of a sailboat halfway to Australia. It took him a week to get home. So that was the end of the rum punch theory. There was a whispering suggestion that the draper lost the run of himself on this particular Christmas Eve and had a go at the gin and tonic when no one was looking. They say he only said it took him a week to get home because it took a week for the hives to die down, that he was in his attic the whole time. Now he gets at least one bottle of calamine lotion to put on the hives for Christmas every year as a joke.

"Well," said Granny, "I think it's about time we found out exactly what is going on around here. Let's wake Mum and go out and see what we can see. Look. Everyone's in very good humor, at least; they're all singing and chatting. Maybe we can join in without attracting attention."

"Some of them are doing a weird dance," Dani said.

"Some of them are wearing inline skates!" Ruairi said.

"Told you!" Granny said gleefully as she perched on the windowsill and pressed her forehead to the glass. "It's all very troubling," she murmured. "All the same, it's cheering to see all my old friends having so much fun."

Dani and Ruairi reluctantly turned away from the window. They went down the hall to wake Mum.

"GRANNY!" Dani shrieked from down the hall.

"MUM'S NOT HERE!" Ruairi shouted. Granny leaped off the windowsill and sprinted down the hall.

Ruairi ran downstairs to see if she was asleep on the sofa or in the kitchen. There was no one on the sofa and no one in the kitchen. Granny and Dani followed close behind. "Look," Ruairi said, "there's a bowl and spoon, a cup, and a plate and knife in the sink. Mum must have had her breakfast already."

"Look at this," Dani said. There was a note stuck to the fridge.

Dani read what it said. "'Morning, my darlings. Up early so thought I'd go to the Crimson Forest for holly and ivy. Back soon. Love you, Mum.'"

"We'd better go get her and make sure she's all right," Dani said.

"Or maybe we should wait here until things are back to normal," Ruairi said, fidgeting and trembling a little. "What if she comes back and we're not here? She might go back out again, and then we might come back, and she wouldn't be here so we'd go back out again, and then she'd come back again and see we're not here and go out again, and then we'd come back and go out again, and we'd end up missing each other over and over and over again," he said, hyperventilating as he spoke.

"We'll leave a note, Ruairi. Look," Dani said, calming him, and she turned the paper over and wrote, *Gone out to look for you. We'll be back here every hour on the hour. (Hope you're not a Viking.) Love, Dani and Ruairi.*

"And Granny," said Granny.

Dani wrote, *And Granny.*

"Okay, so let's go," Dani said.

"WAIT!" Granny shouted as Dani and Ruairi scrambled into their wellies and coats. "Not in your pajamas. It's freezing out there! Get upstairs and get into your proper clothes."

"Granny!" Dani and Ruairi pleaded. "It's not that cold, and look, most of the people out there are wearing no more than a few strips of leather!"

"Go! And there'll be some breakfast here waiting for you when you get downstairs." Granny dodged further objections by quickly adding, "Which you can bring with you and eat as you walk."

"I'll bring my backpack too," Dani said, "just in case. It has all sorts of handy things in it like a rope and a torch and a Swiss Army knife and an umbrella and a flare and an alarm and—"

"You watch too much television," Ruairi mumbled as he ran ahead up the stairs.

In precisely four minutes and thirteen seconds—Ruairi was timing it on his watch—Dani, Ruairi, and Granny Miller, in proper winter clothing, were walking among the Vikings on the High Street eating buttered toast. Dani, fearless, was a little ahead of the others.

"Hello!" Dani said loudly to a hugely tall woman and a tiny man who passed close by. The man stopped and looked at her. The woman stopped too. They came up to her and asked her where she got her clothes.

"I have not seen such an assortment of colors before, nor such an abundance on one personage. It is quite a strange arrangement," the woman said.

"Oh, you know, I do what I'm told," Dani said and rolled her eyes toward Granny.

"Well, hello there, Jimmy and Janice! Grand day, isn't it?" Granny said to them.

The McKellans looked befuddled. Janice, in her leather bodice and skirt, turned to her sheepskin-clad husband and whispered very loudly, loudly enough for Granny and everyone else close by to hear, "Is this ancient lady addressing us? She's looking at us. She's smiling at us. She seems to be talking to us."

Her husband whispered back, equally loudly, "Just nod your head, my dear, and smile. Let's take our leave." With that, Janice and Jimmy McKellan, in Viking form, backed slowly away from Granny, Ruairi, and Dani, nodding and smiling all the while. They motioned to a very tall boy, a very small boy, and a middling-sized girl to follow them.

"They have a point, my dears. Look around you. We're the weird ones. Everyone else, as far as they're concerned, is perfectly normal."

Dani, Ruairi, and Granny continued up the High Street. They soon noticed that everyone else was headed down toward the harbor. When they got to the brow of the hill by the bakery, they were able to look out and get a good view of the pier. Hundreds of Vikings, all of whom Granny knew or knew to see, were milling around.

"They're getting ready for a party! Look!" Ruairi said.

On the sandy bit of the shore by the harbor, they could see men stacking a pile of wood and other combustibles. A little farther up, more men were piling earth and sand in a big mound.

"Make way! Make way!" they heard from behind and looked around just in time to see the majority of the fire brigade and the amateur rugby team jog past with a huge longship on their shoulders. They were singing the song that had woken Ruairi that morning.

"Up HellyAa! Up HellyAa! I'm a Viking, fierce to see. The sea's the place for me. Up HellyAa!" They were surrounded by other men with thick legs and wide shoulders carrying lit torches.

Dani and Ruairi stood beside Granny and watched the longship go by.

"Wow, it's massive," Ruairi said, awed.

"Yes, indeed," said Granny.

"Are they going to put it on the water, Granny?" Ruairi asked. "Can we have a go on it? Once we find Mum, of course."

"My guess is that it's destined for that big pile of wood down there on the shore."

"What a shame to torch it. It's fantastic. they sail it first maybe?"

"Do you know Ruairi, I have no idea. Believe it or not, I am very old, granted, and you might find this hard to believe, but I am not old enough to have been around in Viking times. The stories are all I have to go on."

"That might not be true, Granny," Dani said. "Maybe you were a Viking before, one other Christmas Eve, and you just don't remember it. You said strange things happen every Christmas morning and no one can figure out why. Maybe everyone changes into a Viking every single Christmas Eve and they forget all about it when they wake up. Maybe you have been a Viking one day of the year for all of your life."

"And you forgot," Ruairi said.

"Yeah, Granny, and you forgot," Dani said.

Granny's eyes opened wide. "I need a minute to think about this," she said. "I'm flabbergasted." Granny stumbled backward to the bench on the footpath. "Flabbergasted!" She plopped down onto it. "Impossible!"

"I don't think it is impossible, Granny," Dani said.

"Improbable, then." Granny took a deep breath.

"I don't know," Dani and Ruairi said together.

"No no no no no no, I can't take all of this in!"

"Look!" Dani shouted. "It's Mum!"

"Where? Where?" Ruairi asked. He couldn't get a good look because of the crowds of people, so he jumped up on the bench beside Granny and looked down the hill over their heads toward the harbor. "I don't see her! I don't see her!" he said.

"There! There!" Dani said and took off down the hill.

"Wait, Dani! Wait!" Ruairi said, instantly worried, but she was off.

"Come, Ruairi," Granny said, and she held on to his arm and chased after Dani.

"Slow down!" called Ruairi as Granny nimbly threaded through the crowd in pursuit of her great-great-great-granddaughter, dragging a flustered Ruairi behind her. If Granny lost her grip, Ruairi reflected, he would spot her easily in the crowd; her head popped up as she ran, and she had puffin feathers in her maroon hat that spiked high into the sky.

Ruairi ducked out of the way as a herd of Viking men went charging by swinging battle-axes and swords in the air. One of them bumped the big draper's tiny blue car. The alarm screeched and startled them out of their wits. They attacked the tiny blue car with their battle-axes and swords. They jumped on the hood, stamped on the roof, and kicked in a door.

The kicking Viking stood aside as another man charged across the street with his shield up and his sword outstretched. He emitted a piercing war cry and slashed his sword into the rear tire—which burst with a *pop* and deflated with a long, low *hiss*. The car alarm shrieked and shrieked and shrieked.

Granny and Ruairi caught up with Dani about halfway down the hill. Dani was standing in front of a Viking woman.

"You look so different, Mum," Dani said to the woman. The Viking woman turned to Dani and smiled a smile Granny and Ruairi had seen a million times. They were both so relieved when she smiled that smile. It really was Mum.

"Thank you. I think."

"Oh, yes. It's a compliment, you look, you look ..." Dani gave her mother a once-over. Mum was wearing a tight leather bodice with a fringed leather skirt that was shorter than either Dani or Ruairi had ever seen their mother wear. Her hair was down and wavy but not at all styled. It was what Mum would have called straggly, and it looked really nice. Mum was standing with another Viking woman Ruairi recognized as Alice Cogle, but it was clear from the way Alice stood back a bit from them that the recognition was not mutual. Alice was wrapping a twirling piece of golden jewelry around the upper part of Mum's arm.

"I like the bracelet," Dani said.

"It's beautiful, isn't it?" Mum said. "It's from him." At that, Mum turned and looked to a tall, handsome man who was standing just beside her.

Alice leaned in to Granny confidentially. "He is wooing her!" she said.

Ruairi, Dani, and Granny turned and saw the village baker. "Lewis MacAvinney!" they said together.

"Yay for Mum." Granny gave Mum a wry smile.

"Granny!" Dani said, appalled. "It's Mum! Mums don't get wooed! Anyway, she's already been wooed— she's married to Dad, remember?" Ruairi retreated behind Granny.

"No, no, I'm not married. You are mistaken," Mum said. "I have not yet decided if I want to be wooed by this man." Here she tilted her head toward Lewis MacAvinney, barely looking at him. "But I am free to be wooed. I have not yet found my Heart's True Love."

"You *are* married, and you have two children!" Dani said.

"I have not borne any offspring, my dear, but I can tell you," she said, turning and looking properly at Dani, "I do have dreams of one day having children, and in those dreams, my daughter is brave and strong of character, just like you seem to be." Mum and Dani looked at each other closely. "Now, if you'll excuse me ..." Mum smiled at Dani and leaned down to catch a name.

"Dani," Dani whispered, incredulous. "Daniela. YOU DON'T RECOGNIZE ME?"

"Oh, but of course I do, Dani-Daniela. Sure, I do. Actually, no, no, I don't recognize you, but you do look very familiar."

"Familiar? I look like you! I'm your *daughter*," Dani said, gulping.

But Mum didn't hear the last bit because at just that moment, the burly Viking Lewis MacAvinney had grabbed Mum by the hand and was leading her down the street toward the festivities. Mum turned back and quickly grabbed Alice's hand. "Aldis the Irregular, where I go, you go," she said. And they were gone.

Ruairi was just about to follow Dani and Granny, who took off after Mum, when he felt a presence beside him. He turned around and found himself nose to buckle with a very ornate belt. He heard a low grumble and slowly turned his gaze upwards. Standing right in front of him, fixing him directly, was hairy-looking, scary-looking Hamish Sinclair.

The Red King of Denmark

"It's well you might appear to be just a schoolboy, but I remember what you were to look like when I was to see you," Hamish Sinclair said as he put one arm around Ruairi's middle, lifted him clean off the ground, and carried him away, in the opposite direction of Granny and Dani, up the High Street.

"'Look out for him,' the skalder did be telling us all last thing at night when we'd had our tea and our bath and the spuds dug out from behind our ears and we were drifting off to sleep in our beds. 'He'll be pale and slight, light-colored eyes like the fins of gray or blue or greeny-blue dolphins, and hair the color of copper.'

"And here you are, pale and coppery as they come. He warned us you'd be slippery and make up a story, for why would the true Red King of Denmark come to the island he wants to claim from its people and not pretend he was just an ordinary ginger?

"You can deny it, if you like, but everyone knows, and so do I, that there's a secret sign, a way to tell for sure that your blood is blue and from what line you come. I just … right at this minute in time, can't for the life of me quite remember what it is," said Hamish. "You're coming with me till we can find out the true meaning of this and till I can remember what it is I am to do with you."

"There's no need for that," Ruairi said, indicating a bench they were passing. "We can sit there while you remember. Really, this bench is a good place for remembering. Maybe I'll remember something before you remember something, and then we'll have all our remembering done right here on this bench." Ruairi was trying to sound as reasonable as possible. Hamish paused and considered Ruairi's suggestion. Ruairi gave a big grin. His arms were pinned at his sides, and Hamish's massive arm was wrapped around him as though the boy were a big loaf of bread.

"Let's sit," Ruairi said, still grinning.

"No, no. Come with me. The jarl will know. We will ask the jarl."

"Can't we just phone him?" Ruairi asked as he maneuvered himself in Hamish's arm and had a quick look down the High Street. He could see Granny stopping and looking around for him. "I have a cell phone. We could just sit here nicely on the bench, side by side, remembering, and we could give him a quick ring and see what he thinks. What do you say?"

Granny had spotted Ruairi; they locked eyes. Ruairi could see that Granny was calling after Dani. Would Dani hear her over the noise of the crowd?

Hamish was moving away from the bench as Ruairi spoke. As he reached the tip of the High Street, Ruairi managed to catch a glimpse of Granny and Dani, Granny's head popping up and Dani's fluorescent winter gear sparkling through the crowds, both of them sprinting in his direction. Hamish's strides were longer and faster than Ruairi thought possible, even for such a big man. He was striding in the direction of the Crimson Forest.

Rarelief the Splendiferous

Dani and Granny reached the edge of the Crimson Forest just in time to see Hamish Sinclair, with Ruairi tucked under his arm, wading through a shallow part of the River Gargle, just before the whirlpool. He climbed easily onto the bank at the far side and took off at a trot toward the foot of Mount Violaceous.

"Why didn't he use whirlpool bridge, I wonder?" Dani asked Granny.

"He's not the brightest, Dani. Maybe he doesn't know what it is, maybe bridges hadn't been invented yet in Viking times."

"You think?" Dani said. "Let's get after him; we could make up a good bit of time by not having to wade across like he did." They took off again through the Crimson Forest, a sheltered valley cocooned in the shade of towering Mount Violaceous, a forest in name only, toward the River Gargle.

It was still very early in the morning on this particular Christmas Eve, but as Granny and Dani made their way across, the thick snow of the High Street gave way to a carpet of colorful winter flowers poking through the white. Meandering in and out of tufts of shrubberies, clouds were obscuring the sun, and away from the openness of the village and the harbor, they found the area dark.

"It's quite gloomy in here, isn't it, Granny?"

"Ah!" Granny shrieked and spun around.

"What is it?" Dani asked.

Granny looked all around and could see no one. "Nothing," she said. "I thought I felt something, but it must be my imagination." She turned around and headed toward the river again.

"Ah! Ah!" Dani shouted and grabbed the back of her head. "Somebody threw something at me!"

"Ow!" Granny said, grabbing her shin. "And at me! Quick! Behind here." Granny and Dani hid themselves behind the only oak tree in the whole forest, perhaps the only oak tree on the entire island. They made it just in time—they narrowly missed being pelted with hundreds of little missiles that went hurtling by them and into the oak.

Dani bent down to pick one up. "It looks like an acorn," she said.

Granny risked a look around the broad tree. "There's no one, no one at all. But, look! Look at those two skinny elm trees over there."

"They're moving. They're shaking," Dani said.

"They're laughing at you," said a booming voice from above.

Granny and Dani both screamed. They hugged each other and looked up. The oak tree was talking to them.

The oak tree chuckled a bit, and as he did so, a smattering

of colorful leaves sprinkled down onto the forest bed. "Allow me to introduce myself." The oak made a theatrical bow, moving one enormous branch down and bending it in front of him, and bending another down behind him like actors do at the end of a play. "My name is Rarelief the Splendiferous."

Granny and Dani didn't know what to say. Dani walked all the way around Rarelief and looked him up and down. She picked one of his fallen leaves off the ground and examined it. "So you really exist!" she said.

"You're the guardian of Odin's treasure!" Granny said.

"I do. I am."

"But how is that possible?" Granny said. "People must have looked here for the treasure millions of times over the years. How could they not have found it?"

"I know how to keep it safe," Rarelief said and tapped his nose with a branch. "Those two fellas over there, by the bye, are Dizzie and Dozie, the incorrigible elm twins, who even though they're many hundreds of years old, simply refuse to stop acting the cod. They do, however, do their haunting job fierce well, don't you think? You have to hand it to them. You did feel haunted, didn't you? Didn't you?"

"Is that what they were doing? Haunting us?" Dani asked. "It's sort of hard to feel haunted in a forest with no trees."

"Whisht, would you! You don't want to hurt their feelings!"

"No, of course not, no. They did an excellent job," Dani said and shouted to the two elms, "EXCELLENT JOB, YOU TWO, OF HAUNTING! EXCELLENT JOB!" She gave them two thumbs up. Granny smiled awkwardly and did the two-thumbs-up sign too.

"But I sort of do see what you mean," Rarelief said. "It's

not easy to do our job, you know, with entirely three trees in the whole forest. We only get to do this whole haunting lark one day of the year now as well. The island being all normal the rest of the year nowadays."

Rarelief looked disconsolately at the few acorns the elms managed to pitch at Granny and Dani. "But we do our best. The shrubberies are fantastic haunters, but I reckon they're a little on the short side. You may not have noticed them scratching at you as you wandered past them. They also do a good *oohing* noise when the wind is up. But it's not very windy today, sorry to say. As for the hundreds of thousands of tiny flowers, well, the less said about them, the better. Their idea of haunting is to look slightly less pretty than usual. Not very effective. But sterling efforts," Rarelief said, stressing the last bit and saying "sterling efforts" very loudly. The flowers looked pleased and flickered for a minute so that all their colorful petals caught what little sun there was and transformed themselves, for that instant, from very pretty flowers to stunningly beautiful ones. Then they turned back into their haunting poses.

"If you had a few more trees," Granny was saying.

"We do. There are thousands of trees," Rarelief explained. "They're just not here."

"Where are they?" Dani asked.

"I've spent most of my life on this island, Mr. Rarelief, sir," Granny said. "And I confess to never having seen more than you, Dizzie, and Dozie here, anywhere on the island, ever."

"But you say there used to be trees, Mr. Rarelief?" Dani asked.

"Yes, thousands of us. Right here in the Crimson Forest. All the way from the dip in the valley beyond the village." He pointed back the way Granny and Dani had come and turned a branch toward the mountain. "All the way to where the incline starts to become steep and where the lush earth becomes solid rock, this entire valley, was home to my family, our families," he said, indicating the two elms. "Mostly elms and oaks and some other kinds too. But they're all gone now."

"Where have they gone to?" Dani asked again.

"They were stolen!" said Rarelief.

"Stolen?" Dani repeated.

"How could anyone steal thousands and thousands of trees?" Granny asked.

"It's a long story," Rarelief said.

Granny made to settle herself on the ground. "I love a good story," she said.

"But Granny, we have to find Ruairi!" Dani said.

"The little red-haired boy who came hurtling through here under the arm of the massive, huge Viking?" Rarelief asked.

"Yes," Dani said.

"Ah, I could tell you a thing or two about that as well. You have time—they won't sacrifice him till the Great Yuletide Sacrificial Festival at sundown, and we're hours away from that yet. You're better off being armed with the knowledge of old Rarelief here before you go any farther. Many surprises lie up yonder that way."

"*Sacrifice* him?" Dani and Granny said together.

"Yes, yes. Apparently he's the Red King of Denmark," Rarelief said by way of explanation.

"He's not the Red King of anything! He's my little brother!" Dani said.

"It will do no use to insist on it. They'll have made up their minds," Rarelief said.

"We'd better get after him then, Granny," Dani said.

"You have time, and I have things to tell you that will save you more time in the long run. Things you cannot know about the island and her secrets."

"All the same, Mr. Rarelief," Granny said. "We'd really much rather get on. Good-bye now."

"Good-bye," Dani said. They ran off in the direction of the River Gargle.

Rarelief hummed a little hum to himself. He swept the snow off one of the knobbly roots that stuck out of the ground and piled dry leaves on top of it.

"What are you doing?" Dizzie called over to him.

"I'm making a comfy bench for the girl and the old lady."

"But they've gone, Rarelief. They couldn't get out of here fast enough. You'll not see them again," Dozie said.

"Wanna bet?" Rarelief asked.

The elms bent toward each other and whispered. They looked up and said, "Yes, we do!"

"Oh, goodie," Rarelief said. "If they're back within five minutes, you take that family of squirrels that are forever tickling me every time they go up and down my trunk and give them a comfy new home in your branches."

"Deal," Dozie said, "and if they're not back within five minutes, you take all the new birds that are hatched from nests in our branches until they're potty-trained." With this, Dizzie and Dozie turned their lower branches so that Rarelief could see white splashes of bird poo all along the length of the wood.

"You're on!" Rarelief said.

A puffy green shrubbery a little way off in a clearing said he had a very good view of the sun and would be official timekeeper. All three trees, so all the trees in the entirety of the Crimson Forest and all the shrubberies and all the pretty flowers turned and looked toward the river. And waited.

A couple of minutes passed. Everyone was tense; no one made a sound. Even the pooping baby birds stayed still in their nests and watched.

The shrubbery in the clearing disturbed the silence. "Just let me know when to begin the countdown." Dizzie, Dozie, and Rarelief let out loud sighs and rolled their eyes. "I'm only joking. I'm only joking," the shrubbery called back, chuckling to himself. "Two minutes left."

"You are easily amused," a flat gray shrubbery near him said. The plants turned back to look in the direction of the River Gargle, and as they did so, Granny and Dani, soaking from head to foot, trudged up the bank and made their way back to the base of Rarelief the Splendiferous. They slumped down onto the bench that Rarelief had prepared. Dizzie and Dozie sighed. Rarelief beamed.

"Well now. What brings the two of you back here so soon?" Rarelief asked Granny and Dani.

"We couldn't get across the river," Dani mumbled.

"Excuse me? I couldn't quite catch that. A wee bit louder please," Rarelief said, trying his best not to sound smug.

"We couldn't get across the river," Granny said. "We walked over the bridge, but we didn't get more than halfway when it stood itself up on one side, and we slid all the way back to where we started. It was sort of fun at first—"

"We did it a few times," Dani admitted.

"—but then the bridge started to get angry and started shaking and lurching first, and then it just flung us back onto this side of the river," Granny said.

"It hurt," Dani said.

"So then we did what we saw Hamish do," Granny said.

"We came down the bank a bit and tried to wade across, but the water started flowing in the wrong direction. It swooshed us into the whirlpool."

"And the whirlpool swung us around and around and around until I thought we'd drown or get sick," Dani said.

"Or both," Granny said.

"Or both, exactly," Dani said. "Then the whirlpool rose right up and spat us out on the bank again."

"We only did that once," Granny said.

"I'm sure," Rarelief said.

"It was quite scary," Dani said.

"Very scary," Granny agreed.

"I hear you," Rarelief said.

"We thought we'd try one more thing then," Dani continued. "We thought we'd try to walk behind the waterfall. But that didn't work either."

"I don't believe it!" the oak said, barely suppressing a laugh.

"It spat at us," Granny said.

"It spat at you?"

"The waterfall, yes," Dani said. "It turned itself clean around and sent big jets of water into us, knocking us backward onto the rocks on the ground. So we thought we might just come back here, Mr. Rarelief, sir, and take you up on your offer, if you didn't mind terribly. And we thought that we'd, you know—"

"Listen to what you had to say," Granny finished. "We thought you could help us after all. If you didn't mind."

"I don't mind one bit. Sit there and dry yourselves, and I'll tell you all my knowledge about this day." And Rarelief peeled off big sheets of dry moss from between his roots, which Granny and Dani used as towels.

"This day?" Dani asked.

"Christmas Eve. And all the Christmas Eves. And don't be anxious. You will be off again in search of the Boy King—"

"The Boy King?"

"The boy. What did you call him earlier? Small Brother King of Nowhere?"

"No, I mean, he's not a king—a Boy King or a Red King. He's no kind of king. He's Ruairi. His name is Ruairi, and he's my little brother."

"Fear not, small girl. You'll be back on your way after him in no time at all." And Rarelief began to tell Granny and Dani all they needed to know to help them get safely onwards, across the island.

All the Christmas Eves

"Things started going downhill after King Dudo the Mightily Impressive's fiftieth year. You realize, of course, that fifty years old in Viking times is getting on to being ancient," Rarelief began.

"Fifty in our times is getting on to being ancient," Dani muttered to herself.

Granny turned and looked at her. "You might think so, Dani, but I know a lot of fifty year olds and indeed sixty, seventy, and eighty year olds who would disagree vehemently with you."

"Of course *they'd* think fifty isn't ancient. It's all relative, Granny," Dani explained.

Rarelief chuckled. "A fifty-year-old oak tree is a sheer baby."

"By the way," Dani said, "just one quick question."

"Ask away," Rarelief said.

"So King Dudo and Queen Ursula didn't stay here on Yondersaay?"

"They spent a lot of time here over the years, but after the big splash wedding in the harbor, the Mightily Impressives went back to the king's castle in Denmark. He had a kingdom to run, you know, and of course, no one there knew for sure that he hadn't died a gruesome and bloody death on the ice floe at the hands of the ravenous bear. He had to get back to let his people know he was alive and kicking."

"Ah, I see," Dani said. "Another quick question?"

"Shoot," said Rarelief.

"I don't mean to be rude, but my brother has been kidnapped and all. Is there any chance we can hurry this along?"

"I'll skip ahead where I can. Now ... where was I?" Rarelief said.

"You and he have a lot in common," Dani muttered to Granny.

"Fast-forward a bunch of years," Rarelief continued, "and King Dudo the Mightily Impressive had grown rather fond of the quiet life at home with his Heart's True Love of a wife and their gorgeous wee daughters.

"He was so content he didn't keep himself on top of state affairs the way he used to. Someone made the suggestion to him that he hire a secretary, and so he did just that. Alas the secretary, who had come highly recommended, took advantage of his position and abused the power King Dudo gave him. He signed decrees and made orders in King Dudo's name without consulting King Dudo.

"Things got quite dire. King Dudo and Queen Ursula came back from their summer holidays on Yondersaay one year to find the people of Denmark rioting in the streets.

Dudo got his council together. The secretary said the riots were a result of certain particular investments coming to nothing. Right there and then, he ran through a long list of risky loans and investments made with the Danish sovereign coffers, which had shriveled up or disappeared.

"Dudo shook his head; he had no recollection of making any of these decisions. But the secretary had Dudo's ear now. He convinced Dudo that the mistakes were Dudo's and Dudo's alone. Many believe, but none have a shred of proof, that this secretary used potions and charms to weaken Dudo's mind and make him doubt himself. But, like I say, there's no proof of that.

"Not wanting to believe that this trusted confidante could have deceived him so despicably, Dudo accepted the blame for all the troubles that had befallen his beloved country. He apologized profusely to his subjects and took to his castle, defeated, and ashamed.

"The secretary said he would take care of everything and refused to allow Dudo to see anyone, including his council. Dudo's men, those close to him, those who'd fought with him, were not fooled by this secretary and did their very best to help him. They sent secret messenger pigeons to the castle. But Dudo, convinced utterly and surely of his guilt and tied to the secretary who never left his side, sent the pigeons back, unanswered.

"Dudo, who had lived his entire life with the welfare of his people as his primary concern, finally accepted that this man had undone all his good work. But it was too much to bear. Dudo, known for being a man of action, did not act.

"It wasn't long before Dudo started to get letters from fuming creditors in other lands. He responded with messages promising that the pennings were in the post. The messages kept coming. When pressed, he sent out messages saying that the first boat with the pennings was pillaged, that he was sending another boat with more pennings. But of course there were no boats. There were no pennings. The state coffers were as empty as the head of the man who ran by here a wee while ago, Hamish Sinclair, who runs the butchers.

"When the creditors started arriving at King Dudo's castle in person to ask after their payments, Dudo took to hiding himself in his quarters. When the king of Groenland came, Dudo sent a parchment out to the hallway where he was waiting. Written on the parchment were the words *'I'm not here. I'm off in Antwerp pillaging diamonds to pay you back. Kind regards, Dudo.'*

"The king of Groenland was an old adversary of the Danish king's. Each had great respect and admiration for the other. Sensing something was not quite right, the king of Groenland forced his way past the guards in the castle hallway and stormed into King Dudo's quarters. The secretary, at the door, made only a vague attempt to stop the king from bursting in.

"The king of Groenland slammed open the door to find King Dudo in his bath, up to his armpits in bubbles, with nothing on except for his large, golden, winged helmet and a pair of stripy blue armbands. Dudo was playing with a flock of yellow rubber duckies and a longship bubble machine.

"'Leave us!' the king of Groenland said to the secretary, and the secretary, for once, retreated. The king and the king talked in private. Eventually, the Groenlandish king emerged and demanded to be taken to the kitchens for a bite to eat before he was to make the long journey back to his kingdom.

"The secretary spoke quietly to Dudo while the king of

Groenland was eating in the kitchens. He told King Dudo that he would make all his problems disappear and would negotiate on his behalf with all Denmark's creditors. He would do it, he said quietly to King Dudo, in return for one miniscule favor.

"King Dudo, all dried and dressed, asked what the secretary wanted. The secretary stooped down in that crooked way he had, he put his lips to Dudo's ear, and he whispered with his soft yet high-pitched voice.

"King Dudo listened and took a moment to think. 'I assent, I agree to this request on the understanding that you will undo all the strife you have caused, go to this place at once, and never come back to Denmark.'

"'I promise,' said the secretary, bowing low. He left the king's quarters and made his way to the kitchen where he spoke to the Groenlandish king.

"You see, the secretary hadn't squandered everything at all. He just made it look that way. He had actually stolen it all and hidden it away.

"He told the Groenlandish king there had been a big misunderstanding, and he took him to where all the jewels and pennings were kept. He paid him back, and he gave him enough to give to all the other creditors.

When all Dudo's debts were paid and all the hungry people of Denmark were fed, the secretary went to King Dudo's quarters to bid him farewell. 'It is settled,' the secretary said.

"'Then we are agreed.' Dudo looked him square in the eye and said, 'I hereby invite you to Yondersaay, I bestow the title 'jarl' upon you, and I allow you the right to attempt to claim it as yours.'"

"No!" said Granny.

"No!" said Dani.

"He did NOT just give away Yondersaay to that scheming, double-crossing—" Granny said.

"—poisonous, lying, two-faced—" Dani interrupted.

"—calculating, conniving, underhand—" Granny continued.

"—manipulative, son of a—" Dani went on.

"—secretary, did he?" Granny asked.

"It would appear that way," Rarelief said.

"And what did Ursula have to say about this?" Granny asked. "No way bear-wrestling, dolphin-surfing, eagle-gliding Ursula Swan White took this lying down. No way!"

"When Ursula entered King Dudo's quarters a short while later," Rarelief said, "she noticed that her husband, for the first time in many months, seemed to be back to himself. She was happy, of course, but she was a tad suspicious. And for the first time in many, many months, the ever-present lingering secretary was nowhere to be seen. King Dudo told her about his arrangement with the secretary fellow.

"Queen Ursula was furious. She was fuming, outraged, and livid all at once. Her husband had thrown away their children's birthright, the island of her forefathers, Odin's land of treasures. She screamed and shouted and exploded out her rage. Finally, after a prolonged fit of frothing anger, Ursula turned to her husband and with white-hot calm, she said, 'And to think, for all these years'—she paused, took a deep breath, and pierced Dudo with an angry glare—'I shaved my toes for you.'

"King Dudo came to Ursula, he wrapped her in his arms, and he took her face in his hands. And he whispered something in her ear. Finally, Ursula calmed down. She sat on the enormous royal bed. Dudo sat beside her and took her hand in his. They smiled at each other, their love for each other as strong as on the day by the gargling brook when they first declared their feelings.

"'At least,' she said eventually, 'we can be certain we've seen the last of that secretary of yours. I never liked him. I never liked the way he stooped or appeared as if from nowhere or the greasy way he smiled. I never did warm to Silas Scathe.'"

"Silas Scathe!" Granny clutched her chest.

"Mr. Scathe!" Dani gasped.

Violaceous Hall

Violaceous Hall was a castle of colossal proportions, but you would not know that to look at it from the outside. If you scan the entirety of Fenrir's Seat, otherwise known as Volcano Mount Violaceous, all you can see is a little stone shack the size of a toolshed perched halfway up the side of the mountain with no discernible path to the door. Abandoned and unused looking, it might possibly be used as a shelter for climbers lost in a blizzard but may not even be very effective at that; it's hard to tell if there's a sound roof or if it's properly balanced on that rock. It looks precarious. Perhaps if you went in there, you would fall through disintegrating timbers. You might be better off, as a climber caught unexpectedly in a storm, to shelter in the cave twenty feet below the shack. That's what you might think if you scanned the entirety of Mount Violaceous. Looking up at the mountain from the Beach of Bewilderment or from the Crimson Forest, you would have no idea that something truly magnificent was staring down at you.

Even if you did have an idea or if someone traced the outline for you of the windows set back into the hill—antiglare glass preventing accidental detection—and the various stories and levels, you would still be overwhelmed by the magnitude, the sheer vastness of Violaceous Hall, the expansive chambers and high ceilings, as soon as you set foot inside it.

You do not expect a castle which has been carved into rock in such a way that makes it almost impossible to see with the naked eye to be as flooded with light as a greenhouse in summer. You might also reasonably assume that a vast castle hewn into the side of a mountain with walls and floors of rock would be cold. But even when fires don't blaze in the huge fireplaces, Violaceous Hall is comfortably warm. As the hallways and rooms retreat deeper into the rock face, light and heat penetrate the tightest corners, the smallest back room, and the most spiral of stairwells. Lavishly furnished and decorated, there is an atmosphere of elegance and grandeur.

Every part of the castle is like this. Except for the dungeon. Where the Great Hall is filled with light and is warm even on the frostiest day, the dungeon feels like the coldest winter all year round and like nighttime at all hours of the day. Light sometimes trickles down the stairwell into the tiny passage that leads to that deadly chamber. That light is stopped abruptly by the heavy metal doors that seal off the rooms of torture from the rest of the world.

There is no escape from the Violaceous Hall dungeon except through those metal doors. They are locked and guarded night and day. The walls of the dungeon are impenetrable rock.

Heavy, and slow to open and close, the metal gates are in need of an oiling. No matter where in the castle grounds the jarl is, he can hear the creak of the door. It's a subtle sound if you're far away. But distinctive. If anything went into or out of the dungeon at Violaceous Hall, the jarl knew about it.

Hamish brought Ruairi straight to the dungeon at Violaceous Hall. The jarl was hunting in the meadow on the farthest edge of the castle grounds. At the precise moment Hamish creaked open the dungeon doors, Jarl Silas Scathe's head shot up, and he bade his hunting partners be still. Then he announced confidently without a hint of doubt, "The Red King of Denmark has arrived."

Silas Scathe Lands on Yondersaay

Granny and Dani were now fully dry. They got comfortable on Rarelief's roots as he continued.

"Scathe arrived on the island easily enough, to tell you the truth," Rarelief said. "He had been invited, after all. And he had taken a small following of men with him.

"He found the place handily; he had directions. Mr. Scathe had conducted in-depth research into the island and its history, had read all the literature available, and listened to all the theories. He had even consulted Brother Brian the Devout and Handy with Numbers, and Brother Brian, believing Mr. Scathe to be a friend and close colleague of the king's, was very forthcoming. Brother Brian gave him detailed maps and told him all he knew. In fact, he told him more than he knew; he embellished wildly and greatly played up his closeness with King Dudo.

"It was only when Mr. Scathe set foot on Yondersaay

and wandered about that he realized his odious error. The conniving upstart Mr. Scathe had himself been outsmarted by King Dudo, with the very kind help of the king of Groenland. Not to forget Queen Ursula Swan White, who had conducted another hissy fit before Mr. Scathe left, right under your man's nose. She was a born actress, that one. She threw vases, stamped on garments, tore down tapestries, ripped important-looking documents, and screamed and shouted until Mr. Scathe had left the castle in Denmark. He did not notice the glint in Ursula's eyes nor the growing delight in Dudo's.

"But here on the island, walking along the main promenade, wondering how to announce himself as the new jarl of Yondersaay, he started to realize something was amiss. The villagers mostly ignored him. He finally stopped an old man, who looked very like the king of Groenland, now that Mr. Scathe thought about it, and asked him where the Valhalla treasure was buried. The old man, who had a small bird perched on his shoulder, a raven, asked him to repeat the question, a bit louder this time. When Mr. Scathe did so, the old man laughed and walked away.

"Mr. Scathe ran up the promenade after him and turned him by the shoulder to face him once more. 'Old man, I have asked you where the Valhalla Treasure is, and I demand an answer.'

"'You will never find it,' the old man said with a thrust of his chin, 'and no one here will tell you where it is or how to find it.'"

"I bet it was Odin," Dani said.

"You'd be right to think that, small girl, for indeed the old man was none other than Odin himself," Rarelief said.

"Mr. Scathe was about to declare himself, was about to announce his ownership of the island and everything on it, when the old man straightened and looked Mr. Scathe in the eye. The old man seemed in that instant of straightening to lose about twenty years. His wrinkles flattened out, his eyes took on a deeper hue of blue, he looked bigger and stronger and younger now than he had two seconds previously. Mr. Scathe was beginning to feel uneasy.

"'You made a deal with King Dudo, is that correct?'

"'Yes, that is exactly right; I am now the jarl, and I'm literally the lord and master of Yondersaay!' Mr. Scathe said and pulled himself up to his full height and tried to look as lordly and masterly as possible.

"'You are no such thing!' said the old man. 'You asked to be invited onto Yondersaay and to be allowed to make a claim on it.'

"'Yes, therefore I am literally lord and mas—'

"'Again, Mr. Scathe. You are no such thing,' the old man said.

"'How do you know my name?'

"'I know all there is to know. And I can tell you that you are lord and master only of yourself. You are nothing to Yondersaay. You are here, and that is all. There are only two ways to become lord and master of Yondersaay.'" And here Odin told Scathe what I had told Dudo many years before: kill everyone in Ursula's line, or marry into the family.

"Mr. Scathe was devastated. He swore and cursed and lost himself in such a rage that it would have put Ursula's make-believe tantrum firmly in second place in a tantrum-throwing competition. Mr. Scathe took a stride in the direction of his boat in the harbor when the old man turned to him.

"His appearance returned at a stroke to what it previously was—his eyes lost some of their luster, his back gnarled itself into a hump once more, and wrinkles deepened around his eyes. He spoke softly. "'You may not return to Denmark or to any of the king's lands for the entirety of your life, Mr. Scathe. King Dudo fulfilled his part of the bargain. You are here on Yondersaay as a direct result of his invitation, and you have the right to attempt to claim the island as yours. That the conditions are not favorable to such an outcome is by the bye. You must uphold your part of the agreement.'

"The old man was right and correct. If Mr. Scathe left the island now, he would never make it back again; Mr. Scathe was betting the invitation was good for one visit only. And it was true; he had nowhere else to go. Silas Scathe halted in his tracks. Best not to be too hasty. He veered off his course and turned from the harbor. He walked a little way and sat down to have a think.

"In hindsight, of course, Odin should have kept his mouth shut. He was gloating a bit, you see, rubbing it in. The unfortunate outcome of this, however, was that he gave your man reason to pause and to think, and delayed Mr. Scathe's departure from the island. Odin realized his mistake, but he realized it too late. Still, he would not panic yet; Mr. Scathe would probably get up from his seat on the rock, gather his men, and take to the seas. Any minute now. There was nothing here for him in Yondersaay. Odin tried not to think that there was nothing for him anywhere else either.

"But the sad truth was Mr. Scathe had nothing to lose by staying here, and potentially everything to gain.

"Mr. Scathe sat on the rock thinking until late into the night, long after the sun's hovering descent and the nighttime owls began their hunt. When he finally got out of his think, Mr. Silas Scathe had a new plan. A long-term plan."

The Long-Term Plan

"During the first few hours of Silas Scathe's second day on Yondersaay, the islanders, who had only pretended to ignore him, noticed a subtle shift in his behaviour. Gone were the swaggering self-confidence, the sharpness of his tone, the arrogance. Instead, there was a serenity, which seemed to suggest Silas Scathe had reconciled himself to the fact that he was not Lord of Yondersaay and wouldn't ever be. Another thought piled itself on the others and that was that Mr. Scathe could not go home. He was stuck here, good and proper.

"Over the days and weeks that followed, he and his men went about the island in a quiet way. They were polite and friendly with everyone they came across. They built a little group of dwelling places on the outskirts of the settlement, close enough to the action to know what was going on, far enough away so as not to be seen to be sticking their noses in. Mr. Scathe's was the largest, naturally.

"Mr. Scathe attempted charm. He made himself useful where possible and was generally pleasant and unobtrusive. He made sure his men were nice to everyone too.

"He stayed just like that, on the surface, for a long time. Weeks went by, then months. Without much ado, a couple of years passed and, would you believe it, Mr. Scathe was still on the island. He was known to everyone, and although he had been regarded with a lot of suspicion at first, people had started to forget that this was the secretary who had tried to swindle the island from King Dudo. He was not exactly popular, now, don't get me wrong, but he was put up with. He was insinuating himself into island life slowly, calmly, politely. It had to be said, he did it successfully.

"Up to a point.

"Scathe was an outsider, an incomer, and he always would be. He could exist alongside the locals, but he would never be able to charm and manipulate anyone here the way he had done in Denmark. He would never find out the secrets of the island from the islanders. Mr. Scathe knew this. The islanders knew this. The people on the island didn't feel the need to run Mr. Scathe out of town; their secrets were safe from him. General feelings on the matter about town were that, ignored and defeated, he would eventually give up and move away.

"It was known to the villagers that he spent his nights wandering the island searching for the treasure. He dug hundreds of holes all around the island by moonlight and filled them back in again before morning. He thought no one knew what he was up to. But everyone knew.

"It took Mr. Scathe awhile to notice that the puffins and the trees and the sands and the rocks could talk. The islanders were so confident that Mr. Scathe was no threat to them and to the island that it didn't occur to anyone to warn the animals and the trees and the sands and the rocks and the waters."

The Animals and the Trees, the Sands and the Rocks and the Waters

"Four more years went by. Mr. Scathe spent the nights wandering the island, exploring caves and coves, digging holes and filling them in again. Becoming friendly with all the nonhuman life on the island.

"After a goodly amount of finagling, Mr. Scathe infiltrated a flock of younger puffins. He did this by staging a tarantulafish attack on the flock and arriving just in time to pummel the spider with the end of an old oar. The young puffins were so grateful to be saved, none of them thought to wonder why this man, whom they'd seen trying to get close many times before, suddenly appeared at the edge of their cliff, miles up the steep side of Mount Violaceous, with a sawed-off oar.

"Mr. Scathe was particularly happy when he was in the company of a flighty little hatchling called Fluffness. The poor young puffin, in a moment of friendliness, let it slip that the treasure was not on the Beach of Bewilderment. Fluffness was boasting to Scathe, who pretended not to be convinced, about how clever the Yondersaay puffins were, even the baby ones.

"'It's true,' Fluff said. 'The gulls try to catch us when we're small and eat us up, but we're much too clever for them. We hear them coming or catch sight of them and fly like the wind.'

"'Yes, that is very smart,' Scathe conceded. 'But I'm sure no puffin was ever considered smart enough to have been taken into Odin's confidence. I bet Odin never confided in a puffin,' he said, arching an evil eyebrow and waiting.

"'Oh, no, no, no. Yes, yes, yes. For it was the puffins who alerted Lord Odin to the folly of burying his treasure beneath the sands of the Beach of Bewilderment.'

"'Is that so?'

"'It is so,' Fluffness said through his bright orange beak while waddling about on his bright orange webbed feet. 'And the reason for that, which was figured out by the puffins, the cleverest birds on the island, is, the tarantulafish are thieving scavengers. If there was ever anything shiny to be found on or under the sands of the beach, they would dig it up from underneath the ground and take it out to sea to line their burrows.'

"'I see,' Scathe said. 'Yes, young Fluffness, you have convinced me. The puffins are without doubt literally the smartest birds on the island.'

"Fluffness nodded his beak back and forward and strutted about a bit. He flapped his wee black wings over his stocky white body. He was delighted with himself. Mr. Scathe wasn't slow about establishing that this was the full extent of the information to be gotten out of the puffins; they knew nothing more. He made the steep climb to their cliff-top home less and less and less.

"Mr. Scathe played the sycophant all over the island. He found it difficult, however, to make friends in other places in the same way that he had done with the puffins. It is quite a task to make yourself useful to a stream of water, you know, or to rescue a rock from anything "Eventually, Mr. Scathe came across a clinically depressed boulder and decided he would be a shoulder for him to cry on, a friendly ear.

"He discovered that the rock in question, Fritjof Flat-Top, just liked to be listened to. He had terrible daddy issues, and although Mr. Scathe couldn't bring about a reconciliation between father rock and son rock—the father having been eroded into sand by the waters of the River Gargle decades before—he could in some way become the father little Fritjof never had. Mr. Scathe praised the rock's appearance and told him how grand and how powerful he looked on the bank of the river. He told him he was proud of his ability to stand fast and remain firm even when dogs lifted their legs to him. How he admired his ability to provide shade for those wishing to rest propped up against him.

"Mr. Scathe went on like this with the boulder even though, for many months, the rock spoke only of himself and the insecurities he felt as a result of his overbearing father. After asserting many fine things about the rock, Mr. Scathe's lying brought out the compliment he was sure would get him the information he wanted.

"'You are literally the best and most solid and imposing rock I have ever seen,' Mr. Scathe said to him. 'I am positively certain that any man would trust you and confide in you. Any man, any man at all.'

"'Do you think so?' the rock asked.

"'I'm certain,' Scathe replied. 'I'm sure even Odin himself, if he ever passed by here, would have wanted to bury his treasure under you or near you, so that you could protect it.'

"'He did, as a matter of fact,' the boulder began.

"Mr. Scathe's heart thundered in his chest. Maybe this was it! Barely drawing breath, Mr. Scathe nudged Fritjof Flat-Top to continue. 'He did? He buried the treasure here, in your care?'

"'No, he didn't,' Fritjof said. 'But he did want to. He spent many an hour evaluating this spot or that. But in the end ...'

"'Yes ... in the end?' Mr. Scathe said.

"'In the end, he decided against it,' Fritjof said.

"Mr. Scathe was dejected. 'And where did he go instead?' he asked.

"'That I could not tell you, for he did not tell me. He did not tell anyone here. I can just tell you that the treasure is not buried within my sight lines. Or if it is, then it was all buried without me noticing. And I think that hardly likely."

"'You do? Why?' Scathe asked.

"'It is unlikely, isn't it?' the boulder said, looking like he was about to start sobbing. 'You yourself said I was the bravest, proudest, and most respected rock along this riverbank. How could the bravest, proudest, and most respected rock fail to notice a huge haul of treasure being buried right beneath his nose?'

"'Of course, of course,' Mr. Scathe said. 'Literally impossible!' But deep down, he didn't think it at all impossible. So although Mr. Scathe considered it probable the treasure was not buried under the water or on the banks of the river or behind the waterfall, and although he came by there less and less, he didn't stop going completely. He still carried out the odd evening digging session. Because you just never know.

"Mr. Scathe figured out all on his ownsome the unlikelihood of the treasure being within one of the caves on Mount Violaceous. And, happily, it was in the most painful of manners that this certainty dawned on him," Rarelief said, grinning the widest grin possible on a wooden face.

"Late one night, long after dark, Scathe was digging holes in one of the cave tunnels beneath the mountain. He thought he heard a rumbling sound. He paused in his digging and looked up. He sniffed. He could hear something, *and* he could smell something—an ashy type of smell. Scathe put both the sound and the smell out of his head and returned to his digging, but the smell and the sound kept coming at him. He stopped once more to look up and think about what could be happening when he saw a bright light in the volcano end of the tunnel. Now, he was digging in the dead of night with only a small torch, so the light that was coming toward him now was startling to say the very least of it. It was blindingly bright. It was warm too; no, not warm—*hot*.

"Mr. Scathe was overcome with a sudden realization. He dropped his shovel and scrambled to the exit of the cave. He sprinted as fast as he could, not stopping to pick up his torch or any of his digging materials. The volcano was erupting. It was shooting pent-up, fiery-hot bolts of lava from the belly of the mountain through the cave tunnels to the night beyond.

"Mr. Scathe was very fast. He ran at a glacial pace that would have broken many land speed records had anyone been timing him. But he was not fast enough. A flicker of hot lava caught him right on the backside as he jumped out of the cave and swan dived down the side of the mountain. He landed in a heap of rubble at the bottom of a particularly rocky hill, which covered him in millions of cuts, scratches, and bruises. And he had a burned arse. He limped home covering his bare backside, for the lava had blazed through the back of his clothing. Luckily for him, it was nighttime and no one could see him. Happily for us, he was in a lot of pain.

"Laid up for weeks, Mr. Scathe had plenty of time to have another think. By a process of elimination, he thought it likely that the treasure was not buried in the caves nor in the River Gargle nor on the Beach of Bewilderment. It *could* be buried in the Crimson Forest. But he couldn't be one hundred percent sure. He couldn't be sure, for example, that the treasure wasn't buried *near* the River Gargle or in the hillocks *behind* the Beach of Bewilderment or buried deep underground in one of the caves of Mount Violaceous, out of reach of the burning lava. So he couldn't stop looking in those places altogether.

"But from that moment on, Silas Scathe devoted the majority of his treasure-finding attention to the area in and around the Crimson Forest.

"There was a problem, however. Or to be more precise and specific, there were thousands of problems. So many trees grew all around here that it was nigh on impossible to search efficiently. It was going to take *years* of nighttime digging to find the treasure.

"He eventually hit on a plan. Unfortunately, it was the trees themselves that aided Mr. Scathe in their undoing.

"Mr. Scathe, rather than starting in straight away on a digging schedule in the Crimson Forest, decided a better way than blasting in with a shovel and an ax might present itself. He began taking long, leisurely strolls in the forest—he got used to the haunting. He picnicked here. He tried to befriend some of us in the way he had befriended the puffins and Fritjof Flat-Top—he talked to the trees, told us how powerful and beautiful and strong we were.

"He soon realized it was not the trees but the shrubberies who were the real chatterboxes. They were all quite lively; some of them positively giddy. They talked and talked. They talked so much that it would have been a hard task indeed to keep them quiet *if* Mr. Scathe had wanted to keep them quiet. In fact, Mr. Scathe wanted nothing more than to have a million shrubberies shooting their mouths off all hours of the night, telling him everything he wanted to know.

"Mr. Scathe cursed himself for not starting his search here. He had wasted years on the mountain and on the beach and by the river. The shrubberies told him a lot about the island. Some of what he learned was not new to him; he had heard it from his puffin friends and his boulder friends, or had picked it up from overheard banter in the settlement. But he did not let on; he pretended that all he heard was new information and that it was all very interesting.

"Eventually, he started to hear things he hadn't heard before. Scathe had known, of course, that there was treasure on the island, but in point of fact, he didn't know what the treasure consisted of. He just assumed it was a great and wondrous haul of the most beautiful and valuable jewels and weapons the Viking world had ever seen. And of course he was right but not wholly right.

"The shrubberies were able to talk in detail about some of the most fantastical and sought-after components of the treasury and about the traditions of the island and some of the other properties and powers Odin had bestowed upon it.

"For instance, it wasn't long before he discovered, and this was a big surprise for him, that the Gifts of Odin were not actually buried with the rest of the treasure. They had living purposes and would not be buried until the lord and master of the island no longer had a use for them or until it was certain that the final battle in Valhalla was about to begin.

"Mr. Scathe desperately tried to find out more about these items, their secrets and properties. Of course, he wanted to find out where they were. The shrubberies knew the whereabouts of only one of the Gifts of Odin: the Black Heart, or as it's now known, the Black Heart of the Dragon's Eye, which has the ability to alter time. They knew where that was. It was the eye of the cycloptic dragon.

"'There's a dragon?' Mr. Scathe asked.

"'Yes. Have you not seen it?' the shrubberies asked.

"'No!' Mr. Scathe said.

"'You surely must have.'

"'I am sure I would have noticed a dragon. How can one miss a *dragon*?'

"'It usually sits on a plinth at the top of the harbor,' said a little shrubbery from the back.

"'In the harbor? There's a dragon in the harbor? Literally? In this harbor here, in Yondersaay? Are you certain? A *dragon*?' Mr. Scathe was stunned.

"'Yes. It's the dragon that King Dudo gifted to Jarl Olaf Barelegs the Balding on Top upon his wedding to Queen Ursula,' the first shrubbery said.

"'Oh, *that* dragon!' Mr. Scathe groaned.

"'You know the one we mean?' asked the little shrubbery.

"'Yeah, I know the one you mean,' Mr. Scathe said.

"'Well, its eye is the Black Heart,' the larger shrubbery continued.

"'And, em, how does it work, if one were to use it?' Mr. Scathe asked."

"Wait a minute," Dani interrupted. "There's a dragon in this story? Really? A *dragon*?"

"Yes, you'll have seen it, of course," said Rarelief.

"Nuh-uh, I've never in my life seen a dragon—I thought they didn't exist," Dani said.

"You can't be serious. You've never seen a dragon?" Rarelief asked. Dani shook her head. "How did you get here then?" Rarelief asked.

"What do you mean, 'how did we get here'?" Dani asked.

"Didn't you get here on a dragon?" Rarelief wanted to know.

"No," Dani said. "We came on the early Yonder Air flight in a Yonder Air plane."

"So you didn't come by boat then?" Rarelief said.

"No," Granny and Dani said together.

"Wait a minute," Dani said.

"Yes?" said Rarelief.

"Is a dragon a type of boat?" asked Dani.

"Of course. What else?" said Rarelief.

"Ah, I see," said Dani. "You mean *that* dragon. The one on the plinth in the harbor."

"What else could I possibly have meant?" Rarelief asked. "You didn't think I meant a massive animal that flies about on wings and breathes out fire, did you?" And Rarelief burst out laughing.

"No! Of course not," Dani muttered. "I knew you didn't mean that. Obviously. I just didn't know you meant a Viking longship. Why do they call them dragons?"

But Rarelief was laughing too hard to answer straight away. "If I could ROFL, I'd be ROFLing so hard right now. A *dragon*!" A smattering of leaves was shaken loose by Rarelief's hearty laughter and wafted down on top of Granny and a stone-faced Dani.

"This from a talking tree!" Dani said.

"It's all down to the figurehead carved in the prow," Rarelief said, wiping away a tear of mirth from his eye. "It's shaped like a dragon's head."

"So it is," Dani said. "I remember now. And the one in the harbor only has one eye."

"And is it still there?" Granny asked.

"Is what still where?" asked Rarelief.

"The Black Heart of the Dragon's Eye! Is it still the dragon's eye?"

"Yes, I think so," Rarelief said. "You haven't been to a funeral lately, have you?"

Granny thought for a bit. "No, not for many, many years," she said.

"And all your old friends are still lively as ever, even though they've been alive for over a hundred years?" Rarelief asked.

"Well, yes," Granny said, "but I thought that was because of our modest diets of only seven square meals a day and our habit of taking exercise in the form of a ten-minute stroll along the promenade of an evening."

Rarelief burst into laughter again. "The Black Heart of the Dragon's Eye has an effect on time—how it is perceived and how it is utilized," he said. "No one except for Odin knows all of its uses. It's mostly used to heal wounds quickly or to stave off death, which is why people rarely die here. Mr. Scathe found two more uses for it. That we know of …

"The first has to do with why the islanders are Vikings one day of the year and only one day of the year. And the second has to do with my friends and family—all the trees of the Crimson Forest."

All the Trees

"Silas Scathe had decided the easiest and quickest way to hunt for treasure in the Crimson Forest was to get rid of the trees. All the trees. But he couldn't fell them. The islanders would notice, and there was no way they'd put up with that nonsense. He would have to create a diversion. Then he would have to get rid of all the trees all at once and be nowhere near the forest afterward so he couldn't be blamed.

"He devised his plan and settled on a day.

"The plan was this: Mr. Scathe would utilize the powers of the Black Heart of the Dragon's Eye to make all the villagers believe they were behaving in their normal Viking way, all day, on this day. When the sun came up twenty-four hours later, every single incident and event from that day, every thought even, would be lost to their memories, never to be recalled again.

"The day Silas Scathe chose as the day for this to happen was Christmas Eve. Everything was all set up and prepared and ready. Except for one thing. In order to move thousands and thousands of trees on one day, even with the help of the Black Heart, which would speed up the task no end, the job would, on balance, all things considered, go a lot more smoothly if the trees agreed to the move. It's not an easy undertaking, uprooting a hundred-foot-high, hundred-year-old, hundred-inch-wide oak whose roots are clinging desperately to the earth. Much better to have them ready and willing and happy to help.

"Mr. Scathe came into the Crimson Forest the night before Christmas Eve to talk to all us trees. He used the shrubberies to help him, to vouch for him, and tell us what a decent fellow, in all fairness, he was. He told us he had an offer for us. He told us he had found the long-lost Fjorgyn Thunderbolt and had mastered its transformational powers. He could not show it to us because he could not move it. He said it was embedded deep within the belly of Volcano Mount Violaceous.

"'I, Mr. Silas Scathe, of Denmark,' he said that night, 'will grant each and every one of you majestic specimens the ability to walk.'

"We were all taken aback. Could he really do this? Would he really do this? Why would he do it for us? We had not been very overly friendly with him. In fact, most of us hadn't stopped trying to haunt him.

"'Over these past years, I have come to love the entire island and all life on it,' he said to us. 'But most particularly the forest with its pretty flowers, its friendly shrubberies, and its powerfully magnificent oaks and elms. I am more than a little annoyed, however,' he continued, 'at the way the trees are outrageously mistreated. The islanders do not accord you the respect you deserve. I am outraged by this inequality. Outraged! And with your permission, I will stand for this oppression no longer!' He paused for effect. We trees grumbled agreement.

"'Why should the humans be able to walk and not us?' was whispered back and forth.

"Mr. Scathe went on, 'I will change your lives, your destiny, your very nature. But I can only do it tomorrow, and I can't do it here because although I have mastered the powers of the thingummy, I can't move it—it's embedded in the mountain—so I'll just move you all, one by one instead.'

"We trees talked among ourselves for a bit; we sent our leaves twittering to and fro in quiet whispers so Mr. Scathe could not hear our conversation.

"'What do we have to lose?' we asked ourselves. 'If he can't give us the ability to walk, which, let's face it, is something we'd all sort of like, then we'll just come back here, the day after tomorrow, no harm done.'

"The deliberations took a long time. All the oaks and elms and other trees talked, discussed, and argued all through the night. In the end, just as the sun was rising on the allotted day for moving, that first Christmas Eve, we called Mr. Scathe back and said, 'Yes. We consent to being moved by you and your men, so that we can be given the ability to walk.'

"Mr. Scathe's men, operating under his leadership, closely followed his persnickety instructions. They did an inventory of all us trees first, took our names, and wrote down our dimensions and so forth so as to better order us into groups to make our removal less of a hardship.

"It was nearly midmorning before the inventory-making men made their way over to my side of the forest.

I was very excited about being able to walk, I can tell you. We all were. Every one of us was as accommodating as could be. Every one of us except muggins here." Rarelief pointed a skinny branch at himself.

"When Mr. Scathe's man, Harofith the Officious, came by with his clipboard, I stood to attention, ready to answer all his questions. It was on the first question that I went wrong or got confused. Either way, something happened.

"Sometimes, when I think back on it, I feel myself hearing Odin's voice whispering into my leaves or I can feel the touch of the claws of one of his old ravens on my branches. I don't remember being aware of it at the time, so it wouldn't be a huge stretch to say that there's a chance I'm imagining things, but I feel, deep within my sap, that Odin was there with me, the whole time, whispering to me when I answered that first question.

"Harofith stopped before me and looked up. He poised his pen over his clipboard and said, 'What is your name?'

"Now, this is an easy question. What is your name? Look." Rarelief turned to Dani and said, "What is your name?"

"Daniela Octavia Miller," Dani said.

"See? Easy," Rarelief said. "But on that day I did not say to the officious man with the clipboard, 'Rarelief the Splendiferous.' I did not say 'Rarelief,' or even 'Liefie,' which is what my dear father still calls me, or would if he was here beside me. No. What I said was 'Freakylief the Diseased.'"

Granny and Dani gasped.

"Harofith stepped back from me immediately and turned up his nose. He wrote on his pad while saying aloud, 'Freakylief the *Diseased*.' He didn't ask any more questions. I saw him underlining 'Diseased' again and again.

"'No, wait!' I cried out. "It's not really Freakylief the Diseased, not anymore! It's Rarelief the Splendiferous!'

"'Of *course* it is!' Harofith called back over his shoulder. 'I'm sure you're perfectly healthy and not at all diseased.' But that was it; he was gone. I'd lost my chance. I wouldn't be uprooted and carried up the mountain like the rest of my pals. I wouldn't be having Mr. Scathe do the magic-y thing with the Fjorgyn Thunderbolt on me. I wouldn't ever be gifted the ability to walk.

"I hung my branches, and I wept.

"'Never mind, Rarelief,' my mother and my friends said to me. 'We will talk to Mr. Scathe when we get there; we will tell them there's been a mistake, and they will come back for you. We won't forget you.'"

Dani stroked one of Rarelief's branches as he spoke. Just talking about it seemed to bring some of the sadness back for him.

"But they didn't come back for me," he said quietly, slumping into his branches. "And they didn't learn how to walk either! An eagle flew between my dear mum and me and told me everything. They moved all the trees, all the other trees, during that one Christmas Eve and replanted them elsewhere and abandoned them there," he said, snapping upright. "They were duped! We all were. By old Scathe the Scalded Arse! We will get our own back one day, and we're in no rush about it. We have all the time in the world."

"What about Dizzie and Dozie? Why are they still here?" Granny asked.

"Ah," said Rarelief. "They had been uprooted and were being carried out of the forest and up the side of the mountain the same way all the other trees had been from the dawn of the day until dusk. But Dizzie and Dozie, being the practical jokers that they are, kept messing around. If they weren't firing acorns at the men carrying them, they were pretending to be travelsick and puking sap all over everyone. Or they were playing dead and flopping down heavily and were impossible to carry. In the end, the men transporting them had it up to here, brought them right back, and dumped them beside me. Here all three of us have been ever since.

"And I'm very glad about that. They are a bit juvenile, but they've been great pals over the centuries. Isn't that right, lads?" Rarelief shouted over at them.

Dizzie and Dozie smiled back. Dozie started giggling and said, "Stop it, stop it!" as a family of squirrels ran up his bark. "That tickles!"

"As I'm sure you've realized, Mr. Scathe made a little mistake when he was manipulating the Dragon's Eye. He thought he knew how to control it, but he didn't really; he wasn't quite precise enough in his instructions. So the islanders turn into Vikings just the way they were back then *every* Christmas Eve.

"Mr. Scathe only realized his mistake the next year, on Christmas morning, when none of his men could remember a single thing that had happened the day before. Mr. Scathe was about to go and fix the error when he had a thought. Maybe this was a good thing. Maybe he could use his little mistake, his momentary lack of precision when he laid out his instructions, to his advantage.

"He decided he would use the Christmas Eve changing and the Christmas Day forgetting. He has found another purpose every year since. It was the best mistake he ever made. The next thing on Mr. Scathe's wish list was to teach the volcano a lesson. That particular story involves a sliver of a glacier, but I'm guessing you'd rather hear that particular story another time. I have no doubt that right now the pair of you are eager to head back out in search of the Red King," Rarelief said.

"Ruairi," Dani corrected him.

"Oh, yes," Rarelief said. "Sorry. Small Brother, Ruairi King of Nowhere."

"Nope," Dani said. "Just Ruairi. Plain old Ruairi Miller."

The Dungeon

Ruairi was surprised by the speed and agility of Hamish Sinclair. Hamish had run with him under his arm, swapping over only once or twice, all the way from Yondersaay Village, across the Crimson Forest, through the River Gargle, along the Beach of Bewilderment, and up the side of Mount Violaceous.

"I'll leave you in here until I can get the jarl to come down and have a look at you. He'll know what I'm to do."

"Where am I?" Ruairi asked.

"You're in the dungeon," Hamish said. "Is that not obvious?"

"In the dungeon? Of a castle? On Yondersaay?" Ruairi asked.

"Yes, you are in the dungeon of Violaceous Hall," Hamish said.

"So, I'm a prisoner then," Ruairi said.

"No. Yes. In truth, I don't know," Hamish said. "But I daren't bring you upstairs in case you run off. And I need to go find the jarl, and there's nowhere else to put you. So I reckon I'll be leaving you in here, safe and sound, for five minutes, and then it'll all be figured out, I'm sure. Make yourself at home."

"Okay," said Ruairi, looking around.

"It's not so bad, really," Hamish said as he headed for the doors.

"Not so bad!" Ruairi said. "It's stinking and damp and really, really cold. Can I go to the loo?"

"The what?"

"The loo, the toilet," Ruairi said.

"There's a bucket in the corner," Hamish said and pointed into the dark recesses of the dingy cave.

"You're sure I can't just have a quick trip to the bathroom?" Ruairi gave what he hoped was a winning smile.

"That is the bathroom," Hamish said, pulling the creaky doors of the dungeons of Violaceous Hall shut.

It took a while for Ruairi's eyes to adjust to the darkness, but even before he could see properly, he was at the door trying to pry it open.

It was no use. He went to where the door was attached to the wall to see if he could loosen the hinges, but they were massive and soldered in place. He took his cell phone out of his pocket to call home. The battery was full, but there was no signal. He walked around the cave holding the phone up, trying to get reception, when he heard a voice rasp behind him.

"Is that you?"

Ruairi spun around. "Is that who?" he said, his voice an octave higher than usual.

AOIFE LENNON-RITCHIE

"It's Ruairi, isn't it? Granny Miller's great-great-great-grandson?" said the voice.

"Yes, it's me," Ruairi said, cautiously following the sound deeper into the cave. In the far reaches of the dungeon, chained to the floor, sat a man Ruairi knew very well.

"Mr. Lerwick!" Ruairi said, running to see if he could help him out of his chains. "You don't look so fantastic. How long have you been here?"

"Many a year," Mr. Lerwick said softly.

"How come no one's come to break you out by now? How come no one's even noticed? We went to visit you yesterday in your shop, and everyone we talked to said they hadn't seen you in a day or two. No one said you'd been gone for *years*," Ruairi said, struggling with the chains at Eoin Lerwick's ankles and wrists.

"They'll all have had their memories manipulated by that atrocious Scathe," he said.

"Mr. Scathe?"

"Yes," Eoin Lerwick said. "He's been looking for you, and he'll be here shortly, so quick, let me tell you a few things about him before he comes."

While Eoin spoke, Ruairi took the Swiss Army knife that Dani insisted he carry out of his pocket and tried all the attachments one by one on the locks on Eoin Lerwick's chains.

"I believe you have something of mine in your pocket," Eoin said to Ruairi.

"I don't think so," Ruairi said, emptying his pockets onto the ground in front of the old man. Granny had made sure to stuff his pockets full of things to eat and drink. Ruairi stuck a straw into a juice box and let Eoin drink while he organised everything he had on him. As he sorted, he placed mince pies and mini quiches and roast beef sandwiches behind Eoin's back, within reach of his hands.

"In case they come back," Ruairi said. "There's lots of food here; you should be able to get to it when there's no one looking."

"Thank you, Ruairi," Eoin said, smiling benevolently at the boy.

"I don't see anything else," Ruairi said, lining up coins and pens and bits of paper and fluff.

"There it is," Eoin said. "The purple thing under the Post-it note. You found it in my shop yesterday, is that not true?"

"The gobstopper? Yeah, it was in the grape gobstopper jar behind your counter ... but how did you know?" Ruairi asked.

"I left it there for you to find," Eoin said.

"You left a gobstopper? For me? But how did you know I'd take it? I didn't mean to take it. I'm sorry, I wasn't stealing it. It was in my hand, and then I needed my hand, and, then I suppose I must have robbed it by accident ..."

"It was no accident," Eoin said, grinning. "And it's no gobstopper. It's the Violaceous Amethyst."

Ruairi picked up the shiny but rough purply thing. "You're not joking?" He glanced at Eoin to make sure. "This is the Violaceous Amethyst? I expected it to look more, I don't know, more ... jewel-like. But now that you mention it, I could have sworn yesterday that it was a very odd-looking gobstopper. More purply than you'd think."

"Not purply—violaceous," Eoin said. "Its anonymity is part of its power. It can turn the color it needs to be, and last night, it needed to be purple for you to find it."

"Wow," Ruairi said.

"I needed you to find it, or it to find you, so that

this morning when everyone else on the island woke up thinking they were Vikings, you and your family would be safe from that intoxication.

"My ravens watched over you all night until the sun came up," Eoin said. "Memory tells me she wasn't able to keep you all together no matter how hard she tried. She blocked off all your doors with mounds of snow. She tells me that one member of your family shovelled herself out just as the sun was rising."

"Mum!" Ruairi said. "She's a Viking."

"Actually, she isn't really a Viking; she only thinks she's one."

"But how did you do all that, Mr. Lerwick? How could you get Thought and Memory to do those things while they're out there and you're in here?"

"I have a confession to make," Eoin said.

"You do? Are you guilty of whatever it is they have locked you up in here for?" Ruairi asked.

"I am."

Ruairi was not convinced. "You must have done something terrible. What exactly did you do?"

"It's not what I did. It's who I am."

"You're the greengrocer who gives us sweets and has a "Thing" for Granny Miller," Ruairi said, and Eoin laughed.

"Yes, yes, I suppose I am the greengrocer who gives you sweets and has a "Thing" for Mrs. Miller. But that's not all. I am also the guardian of all Yondersaay, the keeper of the treasures, and the souls of the bravest Vikings awaiting their final battle in Valhalla."

"You're Odin!" Ruairi said.

"Guilty."

Ruairi paused and had a look at him. He was not quite sure what to say. "Pleased to meet you," he said finally. "Do

I bow now? Or kneel? I'm not quite sure," Ruairi said, half bowing, half stooping, bending one knee, and then the other.

Odin laughed. "The pleasure is mine. Thought and Memory are small elements of my being. They can exist apart from my body, but they are an intrinsic part of me. It helps me to resist complete capture; I am in here, but they roam free, carrying out my will insofar as I have the strength to facilitate it. It took nearly my last dregs of energy, Ruairi, to help them assist you this morning.

"Now, listen. I fear our captors will come back for you very soon. Scathe is going to threaten to sacrifice you. He will have the support of all his men and most of the islanders. They believe you are the Red King, the Boy King of Denmark, prophesied to return upon the waves after an absense of hundreds of years to take control of the throne once more. You will have to be very brave from now until the end of the day."

"They're going to sacrifice me?" Ruairi said in a trembling voice.

"They're going to *threaten* to sacrifice you," Odin clarified. "They may even try it a couple of times. But I will do my best not to let that happen. You must use all the cleverness and bravery you have to help you survive. They may do very cruel things to you."

"But I'm not clever," Ruairi said. "Or brave. Dani's the clever, brave one. I'm the one who follows her around trying to stop her from being too clever and too brave."

"You must keep strong. You must find your bravery. You have it within you, I'm certain. Remember, sometimes the bravest option is the one that seems most cowardly."

"I will do my best," Ruairi said, very unsure of himself.

"Ruairi, thank you. I am delighted to have the

Violaceous Amethyst back in my possession. It will go a goodly way to removing the spells that have kept me so weak for so long. However, I will not be able to regain my full strength. The Violaceous Amethyst can protect me from manipulation and intoxication, but it cannot restore me to what I once was, nor anything near it. I have a lot of work to do before that can happen, and I'll need a lot of help from my friends."

"But how? If you're stuck in here, how will anyone help you?" Ruairi asked, upset.

"I know a way out," Odin said, his eyes crinkling into a smile. "There are tunnels all around this mountain—there's one just behind me here. Thought and Memory have been loosening it from the other side for months. A good heave, once my hands are free, and it'll be reduced to dust."

Ruairi looked behind and saw what he meant—one patch of wall was lighter than the rest.

"So don't worry about coming to rescue me, you hear me! I'll make it out of here before sundown, and I will meet you at Gargle View Cottage at nightfall. Wait for me there—first I need to make arrangements with some trees—" Odin halted suddenly and tilted his ear toward the door. "Quick! I hear footsteps on the staircase. Just one more thing … we only have to survive until dawn tomorrow when everything goes back to normal. The villagers will stop believing they are Vikings, and Scathe will have no control over them. The animals and birds, the Beach of Bewilderment, the River Gargle—they'll all go back to the way they usually are. So stay strong, stay brave, and stay alive—until daybreak tomorrow. Go on, my boy; go to the front of the dungeon. It wouldn't do to let them know we have spoken."

Ruairi returned to the front of the dungeon near the

heavy doors and was there mere seconds before voices were heard approaching the door. Footsteps got louder and louder on the flagstones.

"And of course, they mustn't know I have the Amethyst!" Odin said.

"Here, take this," Ruairi said, running back to the old man who was still in chains on the floor. He placed the Swiss Army knife in Odin's hand. "I'm sure one of the attachments will open your chains. Try them all again." Ruairi kicked away all the debris from his pockets that was on the ground in front of Odin. He hid his cell phone deep inside his clothing, ran, and made it back to the front of the cave just as the doors opened.

Hamish entered the dungeon and approached Ruairi. There was another man with him who Ruairi recognized as one of the Turbot cousins from Faraway Farm. Close behind was the other cousin.

"Come with me," Henry said. Or maybe it was Lloyd. They didn't look alike, particularly, but Ruairi could still never remember which was which.

Ruairi glanced back at Odin as he left the dungeon of Violaceous Hall. The old man looked terrible. He had clearly not shaved in a very long time; his beard was extensive and a dirty white. He had probably not bathed in just as long a period. When Henry, Lloyd, and Hamish weren't looking, Odin raised his head and gave a wide grin to Ruairi and a big wink. He dropped his head just as quickly and pretended to be asleep. Ruairi, who was starting to get very anxious now, was greatly cheered by this as he was roughly shoved through the large dungeon doors and into the staircase's tight spiral.

The Boy King meets the Jarl

Broad Hamish ascended the stone stairs, the cousins came behind, in step with each other, thin and gray as whippets. Squashed in the middle of them all was Ruairi. They had to stop every few steps because Hamish's shoulders kept getting lodged in the narrow turns. In the end, the butcher rotated and sidestepped up, taking it one slow step at a time.

Henry tied Ruairi's wrists behind his back. Ruairi struggled against his restraints and his breathing got quicker and shallower with every anxious step.

"I can't believe you forgot what you were to remember about him," one of the cousins was saying to Hamish.

"Seriously, Hjorvarth the Big-Boned and Space between the Ears, sometimes we wonder about you."

Hamish, now Hjorvarth, grunted. "I can't be expected to remember every little thing!"

"Jeez, wait till the jarl hears about this," one Turbot cousin said to the other. Hamish stopped dead on the stairs and turned around. He gave a menacing snarl, exposing fat, yellowing teeth.

Henry and Lloyd laughed nervously and instinctively took two steps back down the stairs, dragging a very pale Ruairi with them.

"We're joking, of course, Hjorvarth," Henry said.

"We wouldn't dream of telling the jarl. This will be our little secret," Lloyd said.

Hamish, his shoulders taut with aggression, continued up the stairs. At the top, he stood aside to reveal a most magnificent hallway. Grand and filled with light, Ruairi had never seen anything like it.

Noticing how Ruairi was awed by his surroundings, Henry took the opportunity to cow him even more. "I am Asgrim Finehair the Artistic, and this is my cousin, Isdrab Graylock the Scientific. You are already acquainted with Hjorvarth the Big-Boned and Space between the Ears." Asgrim motioned to Hamish. "And you, we have reason to believe, have come to Yondersaay to plunder her buried treasures."

"No, no. I don't know where you picked that up, but I'm really not," Ruairi said reasonably, trying to smile. "I've just come on my Christmas holidays with my granny. For a holiday, not to, um, plunder."

"What do you take us for? Fools?" Asgrim asked.

Ruairi said nothing.

"How dare you!" Asgrim said. "Your impudence is abhorrent. Look here at my sword of iron and gold." Asgrim unsheathed a sword and put the point of it right under Ruairi's nose. "What you see along the center of the blade, from the steely tip that could shred your skin from your bones, right down to the hilt of aged form, is a channel. A blood channel. Were I to plunge my sharpened blade deep into your chest cavity, here …" Asgrim moved the point of the blade to rest on Ruairi's chest. Ruairi froze, trying not to shake. "… its entrance would not be hindered by an overflowing of your bloody innards. Instead, they would be cast out and would flow easily down this channel and onto the floor. You would perish in an instant. And your blood, as I just said, would be all over the floor."

Asgrim was winding down when a horn was heard by all. It was coming from outside the front of the castle.

"That is Jarl Scathe, our lord and master, returning from his morning activities. He will outline what is in store for you," Asgrim's cousin, Isdrab, said.

With that, the castle gates, fifty feet high and twenty feet across, crashed open. And in stepped Jarl Silas Scathe. He was clearly going for a grand effect of awe. Actually, the doors were so massive and he was so crooked and weedy that it made him look rather small. No one in the hallway would ever tell Jarl Scathe this, of course. The three men bowed down to the jarl as he approached. Ruairi watched as Jarl Scathe strode as majestically as he could toward him.

"So," Scathe said in a voice he considered booming, "we finally meet, Red King of Denmark." Scathe looked piercingly at Ruairi.

Ruairi glanced behind him to see if the jarl was perhaps addressing someone else. He wasn't. "Me?" Ruairi asked.

Scathe nodded.

"Em, I think there has been a mistake," Ruairi said.

"You do?" Scathe asked.

"I do, yes."

"What mistake would that be?" Scathed asked.

"I am not a king—"

"Yes, you are," Scathe interjected.

"—and I've never been to Denmark."

"Immaterial," Scathe said, swatting the air beside him in a limp gesture of nonchalance. "What is your name, Boy King?" he asked and started to walk around Ruairi as they spoke, looking him up and down.

"Ruairi. Ruairi Miller."

Asgrim the Artistic leaned forward and whispered in Scathe's ear.

"Ah," Scathe said. "Ruairi. Do you know what your name means?"

"Yes. I mean, NO!" Ruairi said.

"I think you do," said Scathe playfully.

"It's my mother's grandfather's name. That's why it's my name, not for any other reason," Ruairi said.

Scathe came up behind Ruairi and put his mouth to Ruairi's ear. Ruairi did not like the smell that wafted his way—part herbal toothpaste, part cheap aftershave. "And what does it mean?" Scathe whispered.

Ruairi hesitated. Scathe waited patiently.

"It means 'red king,'" Ruairi said finally. Hamish grunted loudly, and the cousins whistled. Scathe clapped his hands together, walked back in front of Ruairi, and looked triumphantly at the men. All three smiled at their jarl.

"So, it's really him? Your time has really come?" Asgrim said.

Scathe looked delighted with himself. "I do believe so," he said. "We shall follow all the prescribed protocols to make one hundred and ten percent sure."

"One hundred percent," Isdrab Graylock the Scientific murmured.

"Sorry?" Scathe said.

"Nothing, nothing," Isdrab said, shifting on his feet and avoiding eye contact. Scathe turned and glared at him.

"We shall perform all the recommended tests, and then," he said, spinning back around to Ruairi, "once we have established your lineage beyond a hair's breadth of doubt, I shall take my sword of death—" Scathe unsheathed a long and pointy sword and brought it close to Ruairi's face. "Look here at my sword of iron and gold. What you see along the center of the blade—"

Asgrim coughed. Scathe glanced at him, and Asgrim opened his eyes wide and shook his head a little. He moved toward the jarl, and the jarl moved a bit to confer with him. They turned their backs on Ruairi and the other two men.

"Did you do my blood channel speech?" Scathe whispered to Asgrim. Asgrim hung his head. "Why did you do my blood channel speech? I always do the blood channel speech!"

"I apologize, my liege. I lost the run of myself in the excitement of having him here after all these years," Asgrim explained. "I'm terribly sorry."

"I'm feeling somewhat undermined, Asgrim, I have to tell you," Scathe said. "He's supposed to be terrified of *me*. What do you suggest I do now?"

Asgrim pondered a moment, then said brightly, "You could do your plundering speech."

"You mean, 'I'll take to the waves, and no man shall equal my doggedness in war'?" Scathe said, considering this.

Asgrim nodded vigorously. "It is a wonderful speech, my lord."

"No," Scathe said, after a moment. "It's not personal enough to him to really instill fear. It's more a rallying rhetorical than a terror instiller. I need a terror instiller."

"Mmm," Asgrim said, agreeing. They both thought for a moment. "Ooh, ooh," Asgrim said, "I always liked the 'using-your-bones-for-cooking-with' speech."

"Really? You like that one. You're sure?" Scathe asked.

"Oh, definitely!" Asgrim said, nodding vigorously again.

Scathe spun around to face Ruairi once more. Isdrab and Hamish had both been leaning forward and listening intently to Scathe and Asgrim's conversation. They stood straight and looked around at the floor and the ceiling to disguise the fact that they had been listening in.

Scathe took big, striding steps as he spoke and frequently raised his arms slowly and closed his hands into fists, for effect. "You are in my command and in my control," he said, raising his arms and opening his hands. "You are literally at my mercy." He closed his hands into fists. "Indeed, I am a most merciful ruler. However," Scathe narrowed his eyes and lowered his gaze to meet Ruairi's, "if you are impertinent to me, I shall not hesitate to extract the bones from your body, one by one, while you are still alive and screaming in unending agony. I shall cook the torn-out bones in front of you in a cauldron, with you awake and watching and I shall feed them to my hounds. Is that understood?"

Ruairi felt the blood draining from his face, "Yes," he said.

"Good," Scathe said. "We shall perform all the recommended tests, and once we have established your lineage beyond a hair's breadth of doubt—"

Isdrab whispered to his cousin, "He already said that bit."

"He knows!" Asgrim whispered back. Isdrab let go of Ruairi and came to stand beside Asgrim. "A judicious use of repetition is one of the most important tools of terror-instilling oratory. He lent me the book *How to Terrify Friends and Petrify People*."

Scathe cleared his throat and continued. "Once we have established your lineage beyond a hair's breadth of doubt, you shall be sacrificed to the Viking gods at the Great Yuletide Sacrificial Festival tonight at sundown. And I shall finally become lord and master, literally, once and for all, of all Yondersaay."

Scathe paused for effect. Hamish and the cousins bowed before him. One of the cousins started to clap but stopped immediately when no one else joined in.

Ruairi was getting very worried now. "When you say sacrificed …" he said, gulping hard.

"Yes?" Scathe asked, raising an eyebrow.

"What do you mean exactly?" Ruairi asked.

"You know, sacrificed. We donate the gifts of your body to the gods in a gesture of thanks," Scathe said.

Ruairi looked blankly at Scathe.

"You're not getting it," Scathe said.

Ruairi shook his head.

"We kill you," Scathe said matter-of-factly.

Ruairi acted instantly, impulsively. His entire being sprung into action. He lifted his left foot and brought his heel down sharp into the soft part on the top of Hamish's foot. Hamish bellowed and bent double in pain. The cousins, who had wandered closer to the jarl while he was giving his speeches, no longer had hold of Ruairi. Ruairi turned and ran as fast as he could away from the men.

Scathe sighed and motioned for the cousins to bring him back.

The cousins caught up with him easily enough. They were fast. Besides, all the doors to the Great Hall were bolted shut, and Ruairi's hands were still tied behind his back.

The cousins, tall and thin though they were, were also impressively strong. They each took Ruairi under an arm and carried him back in front of the jarl.

"Can I kill him now?" Hamish asked Scathe quietly. Scathe shook his head.

"Torture him a little?" Hamish said.

"Look, Hjorvarth. There will be plenty of time for combat and torture later."

"You promise?" Hamish said.

"I promise," Scathe responded.

Scathe laughed as Ruairi was brought back to him, "By all means," he said, "You have my permission to try one ineffectual escape without suffering at the hands of my wrath. One only. Do not try anything like that again." He gave Ruairi a menacing smile then turned sharply to his men. "Take him away and perform the ritual testing to establish that his is the blue blood of the Red King of Denmark!" Scathe strode to the end of the hall. The massive wooden doors at the far end of the grand room opened at the jarl's approach, and he disappeared deep into the recesses of the castle.

Pedigree

The testing began before noon, and upon its completion, a lab coat-wearing Isdrab the Scientific took Ruairi outside.

Ruairi was led all the way through the castle to the back boundary, a glass wall which curved inward and gave upon an expansive terrace and an incredible vista beyond. Ruairi was stunned by the beauty of what he saw.

The jarl's backyard was, in fact, the mouth of Volcano Mount Violaceous. The upper-most crags of the mountain stretched skyward around a frozen pool of ice—the plugging glacier. Between the ice and the stretching crags was the most striking garden. No, not a garden. A forest. Ruairi, who was always the first to notice there were no trees when the family arrived at Yondersaay airport, and only two or three sprinkled about the Crimson Forest, could not believe what he was seeing now. For all along the sides of the pool of ice, lining the inner edges of the peaks of Volcano Mount Violaceous, were trees. Not just any trees, but majestic, towering trees, hundreds and hundreds and hundreds of them.

The sun, quite high in the sky now, broke upon the remaining winter leaves and splayed their colors across this most spectacular of courtyards. Ruairi watched flocks of birds dance up to the sky and return en masse to the shelter of the forest. He had not been aware of it before, but an absence of trees had meant an absence of the sounds that go along with trees: the birdsong, the animal noises, the groaning of tree trunks, the cracking and sighing of branches and twigs bending and breaking in the wintry breeze. The sun's afternoon light refracted within the solid layers of ice and became a carpet of icy purples and whites which spread forward to where Ruairi now stood, hands bound, guarded on all sides, on the back patio of Violaceous Hall.

Ruairi turned around to face Scathe. The jarl was no longer in hunting attire but adorned in robes of thick furs and velvets. Ruairi wondered if Scathe had a crown hidden somewhere that he was just dying to put on.

Scathe turned to Isdrab the Scientific. "Your results please, my good man."

"Your lordship," Isdrab began, "it appears highly probable that the boy is in some way connected to a family that may or may not be linked to the throne of Denmark and therefore of Yondersaay."

Scathe nodded along with Isdrab as he spoke but looked a bit confused at the end of the verdict. "So, he is the Red King of Denmark?"

"Well—" Isdrab began.

"Well?" Scathe asked.

"The results do point to that conclusion." Isdrab smiled.

"But they are not verifiable." He stopped smiling.

"Not verifiable?" Scathe asked.

"We conducted the prescribed tests and are pleased with the results," Isdrab said, smiling brightly again. "However," he said, no longer smiling, "we've had to throw the whole lot out."

"Because they're not verifiable?" Scathe said.

"Precisely," Isdrab said.

"You'd better have a good explanation for this failure," Scathe began. "You've been testing for hours now, and it'll be sundown before you know it. I have to organize the pyre construction, the longship burning, and I have to make sure the sacrificial rites are performed in the right way—"

"There was no control group," Isdrab interjected.

"No control group?" Scathe said.

"No, I'm afraid not," Isdrab said. "And without a control group, it's not verifiable. We had to throw it all out."

Scathe turned on his heel and shouted into the castle, "Bring me the oracle!"

Footsteps approached from inside, and within seconds, Asgrim the Artistic and Hamish Hjorvarth the Big-Boned were standing in front of Scathe. A handful of other people came running up behind to offer assistance. They were all eerily alike. Ruairi recognized them as the five twins who worked at the airport.

"Em, sir?" Isdrab the Scientific said.

"Yes?" Scathe snapped.

"The oracle? *Really*?" Isdrab said, approaching Scathe.

"Yes. Why not?" Scathe asked.

"Sorry to be a stickler, my lord," Isdrab said, "but do you really have faith in a person who lives in a hovel, talks in rhyming couplets, is physically incapable of giving a yes/

no answer, and makes decisions based on how the bile-infested innards of a torn-apart rat splat on a rock?"

Scathe wheeled on Isdrab. He cast his gaze languidly down from Isdrab's head to his feet and slowly back up again. He wheeled back around. "Yes," he said.

"Her results are not *verifiable*," Isdrab said, the pitch of his voice getting higher and higher. "She moves bloody guts—"

"Entrails," Asgrim interjected, leaning forward.

"Sorry, entrails," Isdrab continued. "She moves bloody entrails about with her fingers and reads messages from the gods in them. It's not scientific. And I've never once seen her wash her hands afterward."

"You're kidding!" Asgrim said. "She always hands out sandwiches to the gathered hordes. Eww. And I usually eat them!"

"Very tasty sandwiches," Hamish Hjorvarth put in.

"Yes, that is true," Asgrim conceded.

"Besides," Isdrab said, "the medicines she sells at the market have been proven to work no better than placebos, her methods have been discredited so many times—"

"Let me guess," Scathe said. "They're not verifiable?"

"Precisely!" Isdrab said.

Scathe thought for a mere second and said, "Let's see what she says; *then* we'll decide whether or not we believe in her divining authority."

"Good plan, sir," Asgrim said.

"I don't think that's very fair, sir," Isdrab said.

"I like it!" Hamish said.

"But … but …" Isdrab said with his hand in the air like he wanted to ask a question.

"Yes, very good plan, your jarlship," one of the five twins said, grinning.

"Then it's settled," Scathe pronounced. "Isdrab, you are dismissed." Scathe turned back to his other men and roared "BRING ME THE ORACLE!"

"BRING HIM THE ORACLE!" Asgrim shouted.

"BRING HIM THE ORACLE!" Hamish shouted.

"BRING HIM THE ORACLE!" the men around them shouted.

Nobody moved.

"Go on then!" Scathe said, and one of the airport twins shuffled off.

"I always have to do everything," the twin muttered to himself as he wandered through the Great Hall and out the front gates.

Greenbottle Blue

Dry now, and over the trauma of having been spat at by a whirlpool, Dani and Granny thanked Rarelief for all his advice, promised to say hi to his mother should they see her, and set off after Hamish and Ruairi as quickly as they could. Following Rarelief's instructions, Dani twisted the large square-looking boulder two times counterclockwise when they reached the banks of the River Gargle. Then they waded through the river, just between the whirlpool and the tumbling waterfall. They were neither spun out nor spat at. They picked their way up the bank of the river on the other side and made across the dunes to the Beach of Bewilderment.

Halfway across the Beach of Bewilderment, they were forced to stop their trek.

"They look green to me," Dani said to Granny.

"They're clearly blue," Granny said.

"GREEN!" Dani shouted back.

Granny stopped dead, turned, and shouted at Dani, "FINE! They're a greeny-blue,"

"No! They're a bluey-green," Dani said.

"Fine, fine, fine. They're not blue. They're greenbottle blue!" Granny said.

"That just means blue," Dani said. "You're trying to win by pretending you're giving in. Why not bluebottle green?"

"Because there's no such thing as bluebottle green," Granny explained, getting agitated again. "And greenbottle blue is an established and very recognizable color!"

"So you say!" Dani snapped.

"I think we're getting off the point a bit here. Is it really that important?" Granny asked, motioning to what was approaching. "Rarelief warned us about this."

"About what?" Dani asked.

"He said we'd get bewildered on the Beach of Bewilderment, and that we must take care or we'd lose focus," Granny said.

"He did?" Dani asked, looking confused. "I don't remember. I don't remember anything. How long have we been here?"

"Look," Granny said.

While Granny and Dani had been standing in the middle of the beach, bewildered, arguing with each other about whether the creatures which had slowly but solidly emerged from the water lapping up on the beach were in fact green or blue, the creatures, the Yondersaay tarantulafish, as large as Mum's mauve hire car, had slowly and quietly, unfettered and unencumbered, crawled closer.

And closer.

And closer.

"We've just been standing here when we should have been running for the hills!" Granny said.

"And now that they're right beside us, Granny," Dani said, "I absolutely see what you mean; they are definitely a bluey shade of greenbottle blue."

"With rusty legs."

"Hairy rusty legs."

"And bright orange underbellies."

"Their faces are black, though," Dani noted.

"Very black," Granny said, and Granny and Dani moved closer together.

"Can they kill you?" Dani asked.

"Well …" Granny hesitated.

"Well?" Dani turned and faced her great-great-great-grandmother.

"Their bites are pretty nasty, I've heard. Poisonous," Granny said. "And they have fangs. But before they even get close enough to bite you, they can sting you with the barbed hairs full of venom that they flick off their bellies with their back legs like poison arrows."

"Poison! Venom! And is it lethal?" Dani was getting very worried now.

"It won't kill you outright, I don't think," Granny explained, "but its effect can be medically significant. When you're down on the ground writhing in agony, they wrap you up in their silk, bring you back to their underwater burrows, and eat you with those things on their faces."

Dani's voice came out in a high-pitched shriek. "Writhing in agony! Eat you! Medically significant! What the *hell* does medically significant mean?"

"I think it means we should get the heckadoodle out of here," Granny said.

"At last we agree on something!" said Dani.

They made to run, but Granny and Dani were completely surrounded. Some of the tarantulafish were already lifting their back legs to pluck poisonous hairs from their bellies, ready to flick them. Granny and Dani could hear sickening clicks coming from the faces of the tarantulafish. The man-eating, venom-flicking, poison-fanged tarantulafish were getting ready to feast on an old woman in her good maroon coat and her good maroon hat with the puffin feathers and a young, red-haired girl in multiple layers of winter clothes.

The Wooing of Róisínín Rose White

Mum was having troubles of her own. "Put me down, Brokk the Chiselled and Kind of Heart," she said. "I have not assented to marry you. You have further wooing to do."

"But you will, you will assent, Róisínín Rose White," he said. "And by the way, you're beautiful when you're angry."

"I mean it, Brokk. I know you're intent on this wooing business, but you are coming on a little strong. It's very kind of you to tell me I'm beautiful, but the compliment loses a lot of its impact when you imprison me against my will. Now please. Put me down."

"You won't run off again?"

"I won't run off again, I promise," Mum said.

"You'll let me woo you?"

"I'll let me *try* to woo me," Mum said.

Just as Brokk was loosening his grip on Mum, they

heard a voice shouting at them. "Hey, you! Let her go!"

"Another one?" Mum groaned.

Brokk looked around and saw a man, soaked to the bone, approaching. "I'm very sorry, Róisínín, I can't really let you go now he's told me to. I'll look weak."

"I'm the only one here; Aldis has gone to fetch more mead. And I certainly do not think you weak, Brokk the Chiselled and Kind of Heart. You really can let me down," Mum said.

"All the same, if you don't mind," Brokk said, "I'll keep hold of you for just a few minutes more. Who knows who heard him shouting like that? It really will not look good for me if I let you down now."

Mum sighed and rolled her eyes. "Men!"

"Who is this dripping person anyway?" Brokk said motioning to the approaching man.

"I have no idea," Mum said.

The man striding up the embankment from the shore was very tired-looking, very wet, and not wearing Viking clothes.

"What has come over all of you?" he said. "Why are you all dressed like that? Lewis, why are you manhandling my wife? Really. I expected more from you." At this, Dad looked Lewis MacAvinney, the baker, up and down. "Or should I say, I expected less of you."

Brokk and Róisínín looked at each other, puzzled. They did not move.

Dad waited for a minute, then said again, "Go on. Let go of her!"

Brokk took a step toward Dad. A big man, Brokk growled fiercely at Dad, who instinctively took a step back.

"Are you all right, Róisín?" Dad croaked.

"Róisínín," Mum said.

"Róisínín then," Dad said.

"I was until you showed up," Mum said.

"Oh, you were, were you?" Dad said.

"Yes. He's wooing me, but he was about to let me go until you ordered him to. Now he can't without losing face."

Dad looked at Brokk, who shrugged.

"What are you talking about, Róisín? Come on now. Stop messing around. Get out of the arms of Tarzan here, and let's go and get a coffee." Nobody moved. Dad tried again, softer this time. "I've had a long night. I'm exhausted, I'm hungry, and I'm wet—I had to wade to shore from a boat. I'm really not in the mood for this!"

"I'm not going anywhere with you," Mum said, pleasantly but firmly. "Sorry."

"Look, if this is about the fight we had before you left with the children, I've already apologized for that. And I've come all the way here. That should be enough for you. You can stop punishing me now."

"It's not about that," Mum said.

"It's not?" Dad asked.

"No, of course not. I don't know you. I've never seen you before. How could it be about … whatever you just said?"

"Don't be ridiculous! I don't have to take this nonsense!" Dad said and blustered off. Mum noticed him glancing back to see if she had relented and was following him. She was not. She was still in Brokk's arms, letting him stroke her hair. Dad stormed straight back up to the two of them and grabbed at Brokk, trying to lever his arm away from Mum. But Brokk's arm didn't budge an inch. Dad put both his hands around Brokk's forearm and pulled. Nothing. Dad walked up Brokk's leg to his knee, and yanked hard.

He was all the way off the ground, almost horizontal, but it didn't work. Red in the face, Dad climbed down. He spoke to Mum again as if none of it had happened. "If it's not that, then what's stopping you?"

"Even if I were to agree to go for a stroll with you, whoever you are, I can't. Brokk still has a pretty firm hold on me, as you can see, and he's not going to let me go just because you say so."

"Right," Dad said and backed up a few feet. He ran at Brokk and barged into him with his shoulder. Brokk barely raised an eyebrow as Dad glanced off his muscles and fell backward onto the ground. Dad tried that one more time with the same effect. "Okay then," he said midrun, "what can I do?"

"You can go away," Mum said.

"I'm not going away," Dad said, standing up again and crossing his arms.

"Or you can meet him in combat," Mum replied.

"Meet him in com—WHAT?" Dad said.

"You know, hand-to-hand or with battle-axes, whatever you decide between the two of you," Mum explained.

"I vote battle-axes," Brokk said.

"I do love a good battle-ax fight, don't you?" Mum said.

"I'm NOT going into combat with him!" Dad said.

"Oh!" Brokk and Mum said together.

"Not much of a catch, is he, Róisínín?" Brokk said to Mum. "Refusing combat in such a cowardly fashion."

"I know!" Mum said. "And for a minute there, I sort of thought he was quite attractive, you know, in a puny, pasty sort of way."

"Please stop talking about me as though I'm not here. Look at him," Dad said. Brokk and Róisínín both looked Brokk up and down, nodded, and smiled, "and look at me."

They turned and looked at Dad and shook their heads.

"I would cleave him verily in two. There is not much doubting it," Brokk said.

"It would be murder—and as he says there would be heaving and in-two-ing—and I really don't want to be responsible for a respected member of the Yondersaay community going down for the rest of his life. It wouldn't be fair on him," Dad said.

"Going down?" Mum asked.

"To prison," Dad explained.

"Oh, he wouldn't go to prison," Mum said.

"He wouldn't?"

"Of course not! You challenged him. I saw you. He'd be hailed a hero," Mum said.

"Not much of a hero, let's be honest," Brokk put in. "He doesn't seem to be the most threatening of adversaries." Brokk turned to Dad. "No offense."

"None taken."

"We're just saying," Brokk said.

"Yeah, yeah," Dad said.

"In fact," Mum said, "I couldn't really get out of marrying him after the heaving in two."

"You would be so impressed by my manliness," Brokk said, puffing out his chest.

Mum ignored him. "It would be bad form on my part. You know, he goes to all this trouble with the wooing and the combat and the heaving, and I reject him anyway? I'd get a reputation as impossible to please. It would be very bad form."

"But if I walk away," Dad said, "then it looks like I've given in, so you're very unlikely to allow me to woo you."

"It wouldn't look so great," Mum said. "I mean, why would I marry a coward?"

So," Dad said, "if I go away, he'll let you down, but he'll be able to woo you and I won't and you'll probably marry him. And if I don't go away, he'll kill me, and you'll definitely marry him?"

"That's about right."

"You see my dilemma?" Dad said.

"Not really."

"What's not to get?" Dad asked.

"I still don't really get your concern," Mum said. "For a start, who are you? What are you doing here? And, honestly, why are you so interested in me all of a sudden?"

Dad said nothing for a moment. "You're my wife," he said finally.

"You say I'm your wife; I say I've never seen you before. What is your real reason?"

Dad thought about what Mum had just asked him. He looked into Mum's eyes and saw no recognition. He was about to speak when he saw that Brokk was looking intently at him.

"Perhaps I could have a word with you?" Dad said to Mum.

"I accept," Mum said.

Nobody moved.

"In private," Dad said.

Róisínín looked at Brokk; they both shrugged. Brokk held Mum out toward Dad and turned his head away from them. "Go ahead," he called.

"This is the best you can do?" Dad asked Brokk.

"'Fraid so."

"No chance you'll let me take her over—"

Brokk was already shaking his head. "I'll count to myself," he said. "I won't listen in, I promise. Not much, anyway. I shall count up in prime numbers."

"Fine," Dad said. "Wait. You can do that?"

"Certainly. It's not hard." Brokk started counting quietly to himself. "Two, three, five, seven, eleven, thirteen, seventeen—"

Alone at last, after a fashion, Dad looked into Mum's face and said to her, "The first time I saw you, I knew instantly you were my Heart's True Love. I have felt that love in my heart every single day since that first day. The real reason I'm here, is you." Dad stood back and took off his coat. "I will do what you ask," he said.

"What do you mean?" Mum asked.

"I will fight Mr. Muscle here," Dad said.

"You will?" Mum asked. "Are you certain? You wouldn't just rather go away while you still can?"

"I'm certain," Dad said uncertainly.

Brokk was whispering to himself, "Four hundred and one, four hundred and nine"

"Lewis—I mean, Brokk," Dad said. Brokk stopped counting to himself. "I wish to invite, or rather re-invite because I think I inadvertently did it earlier, you into combat for the hand of Róisín."

"Róisínín," Brokk said.

"Róisínín, whatever," Dad said.

"No," Brokk said. "Róisínín Rose White!"

"There's going to be a combat! Ooh, I LOVE a good combat." Everyone turned around to see Aldis the Irregular returning with jugs of mead. "Hand to hand or battle-axes? Please say battle-axes."

Dani's Backpack

"I know what to do," Dani said over her shoulder to Granny, as the circle of greenbottle-blue tarantulafish tightened around them.

"I'm all ears," Granny said.

"I'm sure there'll be something in my backpack to help us." Dani swung her backpack down from her shoulders. "If I shine a torch in their eyes, maybe they'll be blinded, or if I swing the rope round and round, it will keep them back for a while. And if that doesn't work, I have my Swiss Army knife. They'd have to be pretty close for that to do any damage though."

"All sterling ideas, my dear Dani. However …"

Dani looked into her backpack. Her face dropped. She lowered her bag, stood up straight, and swivelled to eye Granny. But Granny sensed it coming and quickly shuffled in a circle to keep her back to Dani. Dani took a big step around to face Granny, but Granny was too quick for her; she inched away again.

Dani grabbed her great-great-great-grandmother by the shoulders and yanked her around, so she could look her in the eye. "Kindly explain!" Dani said to Granny as she raised her open backpack and shoved it under Granny's nose.

Granny looked into the backpack.

"Please tell me my matches and my rope and my Swiss Army knife are underneath all this," Dani said as she lifted out handfuls of mince pies and sandwiches and sausage rolls.

"There wasn't enough space for everything," Granny said, throwing her hands up. "I made room for the essentials."

"And what exactly is essential about mini quiches?" Dani said, her voice starting to get high-pitched again. "You have enough food in here to last us a week! Where did you put everything else?"

"In the cupboard under the stairs."

Furious, Dani grabbed a fistful of sausage rolls, wound her arm around and around like an Olympic shot putter, and said, "What good are they to anyone under the stairs?" as she flung them away from her in a rage.

Dani immediately noticed a vicious-looking tarantulafish react by snarling and snapping the things on its face. Coiling back on its back legs, it bounded straight for Dani.

Dani sprang away in terror. Granny caught Dani in her arms. They both stood there with their eyes tightly shut thinking this was it, this was the end.

"Bloody mini quiches," Dani mumbled, opening her eyes to see that the bounding tarantulafish was circling the food she had flung. It wasn't snarling and snapping at Dani or Granny. It was snarling and snapping at another even bigger, bluer tarantulafish. "They're getting ready to fight each other for the food!"

"Quick," Granny said, reaching deep into Dani's backpack, "throw more!" And Granny and Dani threw handfuls of sausage rolls and mini quiches and ham sandwiches into the circle of tarantulafish. In less than a minute, all the tarantulafish were busy eating or fighting each other over the food.

Quickly and quietly, Dani and Granny tiptoed between clumps of tarantulafish. As soon as they were clear, they sprinted up the beach, over the dunes, and onto the slope at the bottom of Volcano Mount Violaceous.

"I think we are being followed," Granny said as she looked back over her shoulder. She was right; a lone tarantulafish scrambled after them across the beach, hissing and baring its fangs. It was nimble … and fast.

"Quick, in here!" Dani said as she dove into a cave opening behind a large shrubbery.

Granny dove in after her. "Let's hope they don't have good eyesight," Granny said. Dani and Granny sat as quietly as they could in the mouth of the cave. They saw the tarantulafish's legs before they saw its head. It was creeping quickly but silently over the top of the sand dune. Its slow movements were purposeful and elegant. It reached one leg languidly out and rested it down before stretching out another slim leg. The tarantulafish cast about in all directions, lowering its head slowly, and dreamily raising it up again.

"He seems to be following a scent," Dani gasped and watched as the tarantulafish effortlessly picked up speed again. "Maybe he's picked up Hamish's scent. Thanks goodness he's a butcher. He reeks of meat."

"Oh, no. Hamish has Ruairi!" Granny said.

The tarantulafish picked its way over the boulders and rocks at the base of the volcano and began a languorous climb.

"It's going up the mountain!" Granny said. "In that case, I have an idea. When Eoin Lerwick and I were little, we used to spend a lot of time in these caves." Granny turned around and squinted into the cave. "This one leads right to the top of the mountain."

"Are you sure, Granny? We don't have time to make mistakes. Rarelief said that Ruairi would be sacrificed at sundown. That must be only an hour or two away."

"I'm sure, I remember. And the firemen often do their drills in this cave. Come on. Let's go." Granny walked forward into the cave.

"You know, my rope would have come in very handy around about now. We could have tied one end to the shrubbery and unrolled it as we walked so we could always find our way back." Dani thought for a minute. "I suppose we could drop bits of food every few minutes."

"Not on your life," Granny said. "That would be a total waste. Besides, have you never heard of Hansel and Gretel? What if another tarantulafish made its way up here and started following the food trail? We'd be leading him right to us, and in a tunnel this narrow, we'd have no escape."

"Fair point. Okay. Let's grab handfuls of these little flowers from the entrance to the cave and drop one every bit of the way. They're unlikely to get eaten."

"That just might work," Granny said. "Stuff as many as you can into your pockets and let's go."

The Fight to the Death of Brokk the Chiselled and Kind of Heart and Dad the Limp and Dripping

"Are you ready?" Aldis the Irregular shouted to the two men standing on opposite sides of the clearing. Brokk had oiled himself up in preparation for the fight. He had fastened a chest plate over his muscles and was wearing a bejewelled helmet. He paced over and back, grumbling and growling to himself, getting mentally prepared for battle. He swung his battle-ax in the air and caught it every time without even looking at it. Clearly, he had done this before.

Dad had changed into Brokk's spare set of Viking clothes. They were more than a little big for him. Brokk's friend, Thrand, had lent Dad a chest plate and a helmet, but Dad was not wearing the helmet. When he first put it on, it came right down over his eyes. On balance, he decided it would be safer to have no head protection and the ability to see what was going on. His borrowed battle-ax was resting on the ground beside him. He was not pacing up and down grumbling and growling to himself.

Aldis, the referee, and Mum, the wooee, sat on a boulder. The combat would take place around it.

The islanders loved a good fight, so a small crowd had gathered. A man was taking bets, not on who would win, as no one was backing Dad the Limp and Dripping. Nor were they betting on how quickly Brokk would win; no one would bet on Dad lasting more than the time it took Brokk to stride across the field of play and heave him in two, and no one would bet on that being more than fifteen seconds. The bets were mostly related to the amount of blood and guts that would spew from Dad's gaping wounds, the trajectory of the spewing blood and guts, and the volume and quantity of Dad's screeches.

Some people bet on Dad running away and Brokk having to run after him for a few seconds before bringing him back to the clearing and heaving him in two with blood and guts spewing from his gaping wounds.

Aldis was warming up the crowd by shouting out a brief summary of Brokk's combat record. She paraded up and down the clearing, calling out the names of Brokk's defeated foes, counting them off on her fingers. When she ran out of fingers, she drew lines in the snow with a twig. Dad could see Aldis adding line after line after line on the ground and was getting nervous. The crowd was looking at Brokk, who was now doing stretches and performing poses as part of his precombat routine.

"It's really going to happen, Róisín," Dad said. "If this is all a big joke, I get it, it's hilarious, but I think now is the time for you to let everyone know so we can all go home in one piece."

"It's not a joke," Mum said.

"If it's not a joke, that's fine; it's a lesson. You're teaching me a lesson, and yes indeed, I get it. Lesson learned. Time to pull the plug now, Róisín. I've behaved badly. I'm very sorry. I won't do it again."

"It's not a lesson either. But really you don't have to do this. You can walk away at any moment," Mum said.

"Not any moment," Aldis said. "As soon as I call 'one, two, three, engage,' he's pretty much stuck. There's no getting out of it then. Once I say 'engage,' it's to the death."

"Right," Mum said. "So you can stop the combat on your own if you just surrender, accept defeat and humiliation, and walk away."

"I can't do that," he said and paced up and down humming to himself.

"What is that song?" Mum turned and asked Dad.

"What song?"

"The song you are humming."

"Was I humming?" Dad said, thinking a moment. "Oh, wait, I know. It's the song my mother used to sing to me when I was a little boy. I still find it calming in times of great stress and emotional upheaval and also in times when I firmly believe I am about to die a horrible and gory death."

"I know this song," Mum said.

"Of course you do," Dad said.

"How do you know I know this song?"

"I know you know this song because I used to sing it to you. I sang it to you on the morning after our wedding day when I woke up knowing I had married the most exquisite creature who ever existed. I sang it to you in the hospital when we were waiting for Dani and then Ruairi to be born. And you sing it to our children when they are unhappy or unwell."

"It's so familiar," Mum said.

"But the first time I sang this song to you was on the first night we met, when I walked you home," Dad said. "When you looked into my eyes, I saw what I never thought I would ever see."

"What did you see?" Mum asked.

"I saw that you were my Heart's True Love," Dad said.

Aldis shouted, "One … two … three … ENGAGE!"

"Angus?" Mum said and got down from the boulder. Dad's heart nearly exploded, and for the first time in a long time, he realized he had not lost his wife.

At that very second, Brokk the Chiselled and Kind of Heart, battle-ax in the air, helmet firmly down over his forehead, charged forward with a blood-freezing cry of war and ran straight for the spot that Dad had just vacated.

Dad, oblivious of Brokk now, ran to Mum. He picked her up and held her tight to his chest. Dad the Limp and Dripping looked at Róisínín Rose White and saw his heart reflected in her eyes. He kissed her.

Behind them, Brokk collided, not with Dad the Limp and Dripping who was a mere foot away holding his Heart's True Love, but with the rolled up, plate-glass window of a tiny blue three-door car that, alarm blaring, was being carried by a squad of Vikings toward the harbor of Yondersaay Village. Out cold and hanging from the broken window, Brokk was swept along with the car and flung onto the sands of the shore.

"How did you get here?" Mum asked Dad.

"I managed to get a last-minute flight to Helsinki yesterday."

"But I thought there was a storm and that all aircraft were grounded until further notice."

"This flight went via the North Pole, so it avoided the

storm front completely," Dad said. "I didn't know if I'd be stuck in Helsinki on my own for Christmas. I checked into a hotel in the harbor to have a shower and a shave and went down to the bar to check the weather forecast on the television. While I was in the bar, I overheard some Japanese fishermen talking."

"すごい偶然！私たちがかつて日本に住んでいたなんて 幸せなことです!" Mum said.

"Yes, indeed," Dad said. "It *is* very lucky that we used to live in Japan. I overheard the men talking about Yondersaay, so I bought them a drink. It turns out their entire crew belong to an illegal Japanese tarantulafish-hunting vessel which had docked in Helsinki overnight. Tarantulafish are a delicacy in Japan, as you know. The fishermen had been roaming the northern-most seas looking for tarantulafish when they heard that there was an outbreak around Yondersaay and were heading straight here.

"I persuaded them to take me with them. I told the captain I'd spent every summer on Yondersaay since I was a boy and knew where the underwater tarantulafish burrows were."

"Wow! I didn't know you knew that," Mum said.

"I don't," Dad said. "I was bluffing so they would take me. And the bluff worked. Here I am."

The Tome of Tiuz

Scathe decided he would sit while he waited for the oracle. He beckoned to two of his henchmen, whispered something to them, and bade them run into the castle's Great Hall. The pair soon emerged with a big purple box. They schlepped it over to where Scathe was standing and stopped in front of him. Scathe pointed to a spot on the ground two feet away. The men trundled the box to the spot. Scathe held up a hand and pointed to another spot; the men shuffled back a bit with the box. Scathe shook his head and pointed back at the first spot, and they shuffled back, more slowly now though, as the box was getting heavy. Scathe nodded, and the men put the box down and started to remove fragments and stick them back on.

"My porta-throne," Scathe said to Ruairi, who was looking quizzically at the men. Once the throne was assembled, Scathe spread his robes out beyond the armrests and sat down. Ruairi was forced onto a tiny stool at Scathe's feet.

"I take it you are not too happy about your imminent sacrifice and certain death," Scathe said as he accepted a beverage from a henchman.

Ruairi turned and looked up at Scathe. "I've been happier," he said.

"I have an alternative arrangement I'd like to discuss with you," Scathe said, flashing a big smile on Ruairi. "We may be able to avoid your death."

"I'm listening,"

"As you are most likely aware, my key aim is to attain the treasures that are buried on the island. It would be nice to be the lord and master of all Yondersaay, but that is literally, at most a secondary goal. I have been on this godforsaken rock for more years than I care to remember, and I am one hundred and ten percent certain—"

"One hundred percent," Isdrab the Scientific whispered to himself. Ruairi noticed the lab-coated man still hung around, despite having been dismissed.

"—that as soon as I find the treasure, I will want nothing more than to leave this place and never come back. So," Scathe said, "if you, King Ruairi, were to renounce the throne of your own free will, and for good measure tell me where the treasure is, I would be agreeable to letting you go."

"Without killing me," Ruairi said.

"Naturally," Scathe said.

Ruairi looked at Scathe's hands to make sure he wasn't crossing any fingers. "But I'm not a king," Ruairi said, "and I don't know where the treasure is."

"Fine," Scathe said. "Have it your way. We'll continue with the sacrifice."

"Wait a minute, I'm remembering. I *do* know where

the treasure is, and would you believe it, I *am* the Red King of Denmark."

Scathe relaxed back into his chair and smiled. "I knew it!" he said. "So you'll renounce the throne and tell me where the treasure is?"

"Sure."

"It's a deal then?" Scathe said.

"Absolutely," Ruairi said.

"Oh, goodie," Scathe said with an evil twist of his lips. He turned to the Turbot cousins. "Isdrab! Isdrab! Where is that ... Ah, there you are. Where have you been? Never mind. Come here. There is a particular spell inscribed in the Tome of Tiuz that allows us to break the family line of the House of Denmark and end it with this boy here."

"Without killing me?" Ruairi asked.

"Absolutely," Scathe said.

"Just checking," Ruairi said.

"That was our agreement," Scathe said.

"Just making sure."

"BRING ME THE ORACLE!" Scathe shouted again.

"Do we really need her, my liege?" Isdrab asked. "I can manage this on my own."

"Yes, bring her," Scathe said, not even looking at Isdrab. Just then, the airport twin who had been sent to fetch the oracle came running back through the castle and stopped before the jarl on the terrace. Panting, resting one hand on his knee for support, and rubbing his side with the other, the twin, desperately trying to catch his breath, informed the jarl that the oracle was busy pre-sacrificing a goat, a hedgehog, and some rats for the festivities in the harbor and would not be able to come just now. The twin nearly passed out from the effort of speaking. Ruairi could see he was not a fit man. He hobbled off toward a chair.

"Isdrab, prepare the potion! You there," Scathe said, turning to the twin who was just lowering himself into the chair, "carry the implements!"

"Me? Again? Sweet mother of—" the fifth twin mumbled as he hoisted himself to his feet and followed Isdrab.

They came back in a matter of minutes. Isdrab, still dressed in his lab coat, was carrying a giant and very dusty-looking book. The twin was straining under the weight of the equipment Isdrab had strapped to his back and his thighs and his arms.

Isdrab laid all his apparatuses onto a little fold-out table he had taken from one of the bags strapped to the twin. He and the twin set about mixing the potion.

Once it was prepared, Scathe ceremoniously took the bubbling, smoking pot of liquid in his hands. He splashed it on Ruairi's face without any warning. Ruairi sneezed. "I hereby sever all of your blood ties to the line of the House of Denmark," Scathe pronounced. He placed the Tome in front of Ruairi. "You have to recite that bit there," Scathe said, pointing at a little poem in the dusty Tome of Tiuz. "For this to work, you have to demonstrate that you are entering into this severing willingly and of your own free will."

Ruairi looked at the book and recited what was written.

"I, of blood blue and true,

"Do turn it red instead.

"I, of lineage royal and regal,

"Do denounce my heritage and make it legal."

Scathe splashed some more of the potion on Ruairi just as he was finishing. Some of it got in Ruairi's mouth.

"That's *disgusting!*" Ruairi said. "What on earth have you put in that stuff?"

Isdrab opened his mouth to list the ingredients, but

Scathe swatted the question away and addressed Ruairi directly.

"Right. That's the first bit done. You are no longer tied to the royal house. You are no longer the Boy King of Denmark. You are just the, um, boy. And you cease to be the Red King. You are just, well, you are just ginger," he said.

"I don't feel any different," Ruairi said.

"Good!" Scathe said. "Now that part A has been dispensed with, tell me, where is the treasure buried?"

"The treasure is buried, um, it's in, well, it's, let me see now," Ruairi said.

"I'll kill you if you don't tell me," Scathe said, quick as a flash.

"I remember now," Ruairi said. "It's buried under the third boulder from the right as the crow flies on the river bed of the River Gargle, starting out two paces from the whirlpool but on the other side of the bridge."

"On the right or the left?" Scathe asked.

"The left," Ruairi answered without a pause.

"On which side of the river?" Scathe asked before Ruairi had even finished speaking.

"No, it's in the river."

"I understand that," Scathe shot back, "but the third boulder from the right as you're coming from the north side of the river or the south?"

"The, um, south," Ruairi said.

"So facing the mountain?" Scathe said.

"Right!"

"Sorry," Scathe said. "Right, it's on the left on the south side, or wrong it's on the right on the north side? I'm getting confused."

"You were right the first time, the first thing you said," Ruairi said.

"So," Scathe clarified, "it's on the left on the south side as you're facing the mountain."

"Exactly!" Ruairi said, smiling.

"Wonderful!" Scathe said.

"So, I can go now?"

"No, of course not," Scathe said.

"But you said I could go," Ruairi said.

Scathe creased over laughing to himself. He stood, threw his arms out, and laughed loudly and heartily with all his body. "I'm going to kill you anyway," he said. "Because on this day I am the lord and master of all Yondersaay, and I can do whatever the hell I want. And I want nothing more than to see you beg and plead and cry like a little baby before I extinguish your life like a, like a, you know, like something extinguishing an extinguished thing. I will literally sacrifice you for the fun of it, simply because I can. And your line will be positively and truly ended, and nothing, literally nothing, can stop me. Wahahahahahaha!

"And then, the treasure in my possession, the island of Yondersaay indisputably mine at last, I will return to piracy like a fish to the sea. I will literally unleash my superior combat skills upon the worlds. I shall show no mercy, and my mighty power will reach no limits—"

"Ahem," Isdrab said and quickly approached the jarl and whispered in his ear. They whispered together for a minute, Isdrab's face going from not smiling to smiling to not smiling again. Scathe gesticulated wildly while Isdrab spoke.

"The witch hazel, apparently, is the problem," Isdrab said quietly into Scathe's ear. "My conclusion is that an error was made when we doubled the quantities stated in the recipe to make double sure it worked.

"Someone," Isdrab said, glancing accusingly at the twin

who was looking sheepishly around him and whistling, "thought that two times a half a teaspoon was a quarter of a teaspoon, and of course that's not correct at all. Two times half a—"

"I know how much two times half a teaspoon is," Scathe put in impatiently. "It's ..." He paused.

"A teaspoon," Isdrab said.

"I know that. I *know that!*" Scathe said. "What are you doing about it?"

"We're brewing up a new batch with the correct quantities right now," Isdrab the Scientific said, "and, well, if it's not too much bother, we'll have to do the wee ceremony just one more time."

"But it doesn't matter," Scathe said, "the copper-haired king has already told me where the treasure is."

"I think it best to make double sure in these cases, sir. You never know. You have come very close many times before only to be disappointed," Isdrab said. "There might be some side effect to this whole spell thing that we don't know about, or there might be some detail that we're overlooking. We're so close, my liege. I'd feel a lot better if we just did the ceremony quickly once more. It'll only take a minute. Just in case."

Scathe sighed. "Fine. We'll do it one more time." He made a flamboyant turn, his robes flaring behind him. He fixed Ruairi with a big smile. "We have to do the silly magic thingy again just one more time. Bear with us. Won't take a minute."

"But—" Ruairi said.

"But what?" Scathe said, not making eye contact.

"But you just said you were going to kill me anyway," Ruairi said.

"Nonsense," Scathe said, half turning away from Ruairi.

"You *DID*!" Ruairi said. "You said I am the mighty lord master, blah de blah de blah. I will show no mercy, fish to the sea, wahahahahaha, extinguishing an extinguishing thing; then you said I was for the chop!"

"I was joking," Scathe said.

"Didn't sound like you were joking."

"I won't kill you. I promise."

"That's what you said last time," Ruairi said. "I must be honest. I'm not entirely sure I believe you."

"Please?" Scathe said.

"Since you asked so nicely," Ruairi said.

"Really?" Scathe said.

"No! Of course not!" Ruairi said. "Look, what's that?" Ruairi gestured up at the sky. Everyone whirled around to look.

"What am I looking at?" Scathe asked. "What are you seeing that I'm not seeing?"

While their backs were turned, Ruairi grabbed the remains of the first potion from the portable lab and chucked it in Isdrab's face. Isdrab's shriek's of "Oh, that is *heinous,* oh my *goodness,"* captured everyone's attention for a crucial few seconds. Ruairi took off across the ice.

He ran as fast as he could and did not stop. He was wearing sneakers, so he could grip the ice and run without fear of slipping. He knew he had only to get a reasonable distance from the leather-shoe wearing Viking henchmen dotted about the ice to have an unassailable head start. Ruairi glanced backwards as he ran and saw Scathe drop his eyes and notice that Ruairi was not in his place on his stool.

Right or Left

"Which way do we go? Right or left?" Dani looked back into the tunnel and asked Granny, who was coming up behind her. They had crawled a long way in the dark and were slowing with fatigue.

"I can't remember. Let me sit and think for a minute," Granny said, breathing heavily. She took a steak and kidney pie out of her sock and bit into it. She looked first at the tunnel that went right and then at the tunnel that went left. "Left!" Granny said finally, handing half the steak and kidney pie to Dani.

"Left. Are you sure?"

Granny didn't look sure, but she perked up and confidently said, "Yes, left!"

Dani led the way again, taking the left fork in the tunnel, remembering to drop a little pink and then a violet and then a lemon and then a pale blue flower behind her every few paces.

"There's light! Up ahead," Dani said. "You were right, Granny; we've reached the end of the tunnel."

"Well done, Dani, my dear. Well done for leading us so excellently. Nearly there now, nearly there."

Dani rounded a sharp bend in the tunnel. After spending so long in the darkness, she was instantly blinded by a blast of sunlight. She groped her way forward and pushed out, feeling the icy twirl of the winter's breeze.

Granny squeezed out next to her. Filthy and sore from all the digging, they let the breeze caress their relaxing limbs.

Then they heard a voice say, "Ooh, lookie here! I do believe we literally have an ace in the hole. No, wait. *Two* aces in the hole!"

Granny and Dani recognized Scathe's voice at once and immediately made to dart back underground. They weren't quick enough; the Turbot cousins grabbed them and pulled them all the way out of the tunnel.

Scathe clapped his hands together, threw his head back, and emitted a loud, cackling laugh.

"Chilling laugh, sir!" Asgrim said.

"Wonderful," Scathe said, throwing back his head and cackling again. Scathe then turned to the other side of the ice field and shouted, "If you do not come back here this instant, I will literally chop this girl and this woman into a thousand pieces and throw them off the cliff into the sea."

"Can I do some chopping? I haven't done any chopping all day," Hamish put in quietly from the back.

"Later, like I keep telling you! If there's time before the sacrifice …"

The escaping Ruairi stopped abruptly. He was close to the edge of the ice, mere inches from a hidden dip. He looked back and was horrified to see Dani and Granny struggling against the smug-looking Turbot cousins. He turned back to the gathering on the terrace. He was terrified for his sister and his great-great-great-grandmother. He took a step toward the crowd but caught his big sister's gaze and halted. He stopped, he looked at her. She was pointing at the strips of fluorescent material on her winter coat, and he instantly knew what she meant.

"Mum! What would Mum tell me to do?" And Ruairi knew that Dani was urging him to "*keep safe and run away!*"

He understood. He knew that that was what he absolutely should do. Scathe was not to be trusted. Ruairi would be no use to Dani and Granny if he was imprisoned with them, or worse, sacrificed at sundown. But it seemed so cowardly to run off and leave two of the people he loved most in the world to the most despicable person he had ever met. Ruairi wished he was relying on Dani rather than the other way around.

He took a moment, stilled his mind, and thought, "If I run, I can get help. If I stay, I am useless." He repeated this thought over and over, but Ruairi couldn't move. He couldn't leave them. He was cold and he was scared and he couldn't move. Ruairi looked up and caught his big sister's gaze again. Dani smiled at him; it was so good to see her. She rolled her eyes, and Ruairi beamed back at her. He would have laughed, but he was afraid he would cry instead.

With a weak smile at his sister and his granny, Ruairi straightened his back and turned it on them. He walked purposefully toward the edge of the mountain, jumped off the edge, and was gone.

"That was unexpected!" Scathe said.

"What do we do now, sir?" Asgrim asked. "We can't

really perform the sacrifice if there's no one to sacrifice."

"THANKS FOR POINTING THAT OUT, GENIUS!" Scathe shrieked. He let out a roar of fury, then spun around and came within inches of his two prisoners. With a quiet menace, he said, "Take the two of them to the dungeon until I figure out what's to be done." Scathe turned to two of the five twins and said, "You two! After the Red King!"

The two men ran across the ice after Ruairi, slipping a bit and falling a lot in their leather and wool foot coverings.

Scathe circled Dani and Granny. Isdrab tiptoed over and spoke in Scathe's ear. "You're not worried about them being in the same place as, you know, the *other* prisoner?"

"The old man is so out of it he doesn't even know who he is," Scathe said, "and so there is literally no chance they'll have the remotest clue that the stinking, emaciated, blubbering, drooling idiot in chains is Odin, father of all the Vikings."

Dani and Granny glanced at each other and looked away again.

"If you're sure," Isdrab said to Scathe.

"Are you questioning me?"

"Yes." Isdrab said. Scathe turned on him and gave him an injurious look. "I mean, no. No! I wouldn't *dream* of questioning you," Isdrab corrected.

"I will literally eat your spleen for breakfast if you cross me," Scathe said, raising one eyebrow.

"I have no doubt. I beg your forgiveness, my lord," Isdrab said, bowing low.

"With a *spoon*," Scathe said as Isdrab went to take the prisoners to the dungeon. "Wait! I have changed my mind," Scathe announced, pointing a finger in the air. "And not because of what you just said right now," he added, more quietly. "TAKE THE PRISONERS TO THE LONGSHIP!" he screeched.

"The longship now, is it?" Isdrab said.

"To be sacrificed," Scathe said maliciously. "If Mohammed won't go to the mountain, then the mountain, and in this case, of course, I mean, the Red King, will come to Mohammed."

"*What?*" Granny and Dani looked quizzically at Scathe.

"The mountain … and Mohammed! You've never heard that before?" Scathe asked Dani and Granny, who both shook their heads vigorously. "You're not getting it?"

Granny and Dani looked at each other, shrugged, and shook their heads again.

"The sacrifice!" Scathe said, throwing his hands in the air and letting out a big sigh. "If the Red King won't go to the sacrifice, then we'll make him go to the sacrifice." Scathe ran through what he'd just said again in his head, moving his lips as he did so.

Asgrim leaned forward and said, "Sounded better the other way, with Mohammed and what have you."

"Anyway, the point is," Scathe went on, "we'll just sacrifice you instead, and if he turns up to save you, we'll kill you and him. And if he doesn't turn up to save you, then we'll kill you and then hunt him down and then kill him." Scathe gave a withering smile, turned to his men, and shouted, once more, with a great deal of joyous feeling this time, "TAKE THE PRISONERS TO THE LONGSHIP!"

The Great Sacrificial Yuletide Festival

The sun was already beginning its evening turn toward the west, the sky was darkening, and day was coming to a close. News had spread that the Red King of Denmark had come to Yondersaay and that there would be a genuine, real-life sacrifice at the Great Yuletide Sacrificial Festival this year. The islanders were fizzing with excitement. And who could blame them? Yondersaanians loved a good entrail examination ceremony and subsequent sacrifice as much as the next Viking. Once the oracle had confirmed the Red King's identity, the sacrificial rites would be performed.

Every person on the island was helping to prepare. After their morning walk down the High Street to the harbour, they cooked, practiced dances, and organized skits and other amusements all day. Chickens, quails, and turkeys had been slaughtered, plucked, and roasted. Casks of mead had been carted to the shore. Now, a pig was rotating on a spit, whole salmons were being grilled on beachside fires, potatoes were baking on hot stones, and cauldrons of stews and soups were seasoned and stirred.

Groups of Vikings sped about lighting hundreds of torches and sticking them into the sand. The men and women drank mead while they waited for proceedings to begin. People sang and danced, and all were in very high spirits.

Children were chasing each other along the beach. A tiny blue car was burning brightly, and some Vikings were dancing around it. The car alarm, no longer piercing, gave a final whinny and fizzled to silence.

At the center of the hubbub, the pyre piled high, a longship resting atop it, awaiting ceremonial torching. The dragon's head at the prow of the longship rose haughtily into the air and bore a ferocious gaze down on the assembled Vikings. The deck bowed out from the dragon's neck and tightened into a tail at the stern. The mast towered over the scene; at its base was a tidy pile of kindling.

On the beach in front of the funeral pyre, beneath the gaze of the dragon's prow, was a wooden platform. Square in the middle, making it sag, was a grand golden throne. It had a sumptuous, purple velvet *downdle* on the seat. The feet of the throne curved into claws as they dug into the planks, and the legs and arms were encrusted with jewels. Evidently, a porta-throne was not grand enough for this particular occasion.

The crowd hushed on their benches and chairs as a group of heavily armed and very tough-looking Vikings—Hamish Hjorvarth and two of the five twins—stood aside to reveal Silas Scathe. The effect was somewhat diminished by the fact that, in the minutes beforehand, Scathe was plainly seen checking his appearance in various mirrors and frantically applying pomade to some stray hairs. The crowd, however, had been coached by Asgrim and Isdrab. They *oohed* and *ahed* as the jarl ascended the platform.

Behind another group of burly men, much more successfully hidden from the crowd and tied up securely but attempting to get away nonetheless, were a defiant, red-haired, puffy-coated girl and a resistant great-great-great-grandmother.

The Oracle Pronounces

The jarl sauntered to the golden throne in the middle of the platform. Spinning himself around to face the crowd, allowing his flouncy jewel-encrusted robes to billow out dramatically, he slowly, regally, sat down.

Almost immediately, he stood up again. "Welcome to Yondersaay's Annual Great Sacrificial Yuletide Festival! This year, we have an added reason to celebrate our annual feast. We have a real, live sacrifice to look forward to as part of the festivities. With your help, wonderful Yondersaanians, I, Jarl Silas Scathe, at last, after many years of constant, literally twenty-four-seven, full-on, unending effort, have trapped the insidious, the evil, the conniving. Red King of Denmark!"

The crowd whooped and applauded.

"You are all aware, of course, of the legend of the Red King of Denmark—that one day this arrogant young sovereign would come to the island to take Odin's treasure as his own—"

A decaying old man at the front put up his hand. "That's not the version I'm familiar with, your jarlship," the old man said in a surprisingly loud voice. "I was under the impression he was supposed to be a rather decent sort—"

Two of the five twins, in full Viking combat gear now, appeared, lightning-quick, one on either side of the old man. The one on the left discreetly pressed a blade into the old man's side. The one on the right glared menacingly at him.

The jarl stopped and looked at the old man. "Are you sure?" he beseeched in a sickly sweet voice. "Is that really what you remember?"

"Em, no! Now that I think about it, no," the old man said.

"Indeed!" the jarl continued. He gestured to the rest of his men who slowly and subtly dispersed themselves within the crowd, ready to intimidate should the jarl be challenged again. "As we all know, the island has been bereft of Odin's benevolent presence for many a year. It is my belief that when we sacrifice the Red King tonight, the gods will be appeased and Odin will return." Scathe dropped his voice to a whisper and mumbled, "We have the tiny formality of establishing the boy's identity." Scathe brought his voice back to full volume. "Then he will be sacrificed by the final rays of the sun!"

The jarl looked into the crowd. He knew that they loved a good sacrifice, but he wanted to make very sure they were all on his side. "But don't take my word for it. Ladies and gentlemen, this afternoon we welcome Yondersaay's most revered inhabitant, the amanuensis of the gods, the interpreter of divine will, the one, the only ... ORACLE!"

The crowd went bananas. They hushed as the oracle approached the platform. In her ceremonial garbs, she looked quite imposing. She had clearly combed her hair for the occasion. She hadn't washed it, mind, but it wasn't sticking out in matted clumps. And with the breeze traveling in a westerly direction, and the crowd being east of her, they didn't get the full force of the smell. The fact that she mumbled constantly to herself only added to her mystique. The intermittent picking of things off her scalp and flicking them off—not so much.

Once she was on the platform, Jarl Scathe lifted the oracle's right arm into the air and paraded her around the stage so that all gathered could get a good look at her. It was clear to Granny and Dani that the poor woman was trying very hard to be cool. She seemed to be making an attempt at haughty and uninterested, but that all fell apart when the crowds got to their feet to welcome her with applause—she guffawed so loudly in delight at all the attention that for a moment it looked like she was having a seizure. The crowd recoiled in horror. She got hold of her senses, just in time, pointed to the heavens, and muttered things like "... the gods ... communing ... messages ... I am vessel ..." and other incoherent rubbish.

The jarl continued. "Our sacred oracle will perform the ancient rites; she will commune with the Viking gods, and they will tell her two things." The jarl raised his robed arms majestically as he spoke. "One: is the boy who roams among us the Red King, the true Boy King of Denmark?" Scathe's voice crescendoed. "And two: will sacrificing him return our beloved Odin to our midst?"

The crowd erupted into whoops and cheers and drank heartily of their mead.

"You may have noticed," the jarl said more softly,

lowering his arms, "that the copper-haired, silver-eyed boy of the legends is not actually, at this moment in time, just right at the present minute, here on the stage. He is literally right here though. He is among us. And he will come forward in due course."

The people looked about them trying to spot the Red King in the crowd.

"Fear not. His presence is not required at this juncture. We are here to perform the identification rites, and the oracle has the power and the connection with the gods to summon the information forth. With or without the ginger brat."

The oracle stepped to the front of the stage as the crowd applauded. First, she made a big show with a stick-type thing with feathers on the end, mumbling to herself the entire time. She motioned for a large, flat rock to be positioned in front of her and placed lots of implements, including stones and bones of various shapes and sizes, in a line beside it.

She motioned for a big bucket to be brought to the stage. The oracle ceremoniously lowered the top of the bucket so that the gathered masses could see that inside were her pre-sacrificed bloody guts. This got a good reaction. She paused to let the picture sink in.

The oracle reached both arms deep into the bucket. She paused and muttered. Alas, she paused just that wee bit too long—strands of her combed hair came loose and tumbled into the bucket. The crowd let out a collective "Eww." Unperturbed, the oracle lifted her immersed arms high above her head. Her hair flicked back at the same time and splattered blood and guts all over everyone in the front row. She held her arms aloft—bloody to her elbows—and in her hands, she clutched an oozing mixture of innards.

She splattered the entrails across the flat surface of the rock and bent to examine them.

She looked up at the crowd. And back at the entrails. Up at the crowd. Back at the entrails. She turned her clotted, moldy head to the heavens. And back to the entrails. She fishugled them about a bit. And finally, she gazed unseeing ahead of her.

Those in the front rows could see that she was now deep in a trance. The colored bits of her eyes were gone. All the while, her head pivoted, side to side. She started to mumble. The mumbles got louder. And if possible, even more incoherent. The volume rose and rose and rose.

The crowd was silent. The islanders leaned forward as much as they could to see as much as they could see.

At last, the oracle let out a monstrous keening. "Eeeeaahaaaaaa!" The crowd jumped back, startled out of their senses. She screeched again, this time throwing her body behind the sound, and she flounced forward and sprawled onto the platform. Seemingly out of control, her body shook and jittered and flailed about. Suddenly she stopped moving.

"Copper hair, eyes of an aged gray," she said in a deathly monotone.

"The sign of the Red King, Boy King,

"Am I to say?

"Yes, I am, I have an inkling,

"To sacrifice, tonight, on the Yuletide fire,

"The Boy King bound and tied on the pyre.

"Denmark the Red.

"For Odin to return, may he be dead."

With that final pronouncement, the oracle heaved with exhaustion onto the stage.

"What does that even mean?" Dani shouted up to

the stage. "It doesn't mean anything! You could go either way with that! It doesn't mean he's the Boy K—!" Hamish came forward and put a massive hand over Dani's mouth, muffling her words.

"That is clear enough for me!" Scathe announced to the crowd. "The Boy King of Denmark will be sacrificed to the Viking gods on this pyre in this harbor at sundown!"

The crowd roared so clamorously that the benches reverberated from the noise. The oracle was helped to her feet. She stepped forward and took a bow. Several bows in fact. Asgrim had to come and lead her off the stage by her elbow. She reappeared within seconds with a big platter of sandwiches and started handing them out to those in the front row. An elderly gentleman passed out as she thrust a cheese-and-egg flatbread in his face with blood dripping from her fingers.

"Prepare the girl and the granny for their sacrifice," Scathe announced to the men.

"*WHAT*?" Dani said.

Scathe looked down his nose at Dani and Granny. "Like I said on the mountain, I don't know if you were listening, but I will repeat myself just this once. What I said was, I said something along the lines of, 'Come back here, you, and if you don't come back, I'll chop these two into bits and pieces.'"

"Most eloquently put, sir," Asgrim said.

"So get ready for the final rays of the sun whence you will be offed."

Dani and Granny were roughly carried into the longship and strapped to the mast.

"Let the Great Sacrificial Yuletide Festival commence!" Scathe announced to the crowd. "Prepare the dragon for burning! And let our festivities begin!"

The Final Rays of the Sun

Dani and Granny, tied to the mast of the longship, had hardly any time left to effect an escape. The sun was setting but probably wouldn't fully sink beyond the horizon for another twenty minutes, give or take. They struggled with the ropes at their hands, chests, and feet.

"Can't help but think, Granny—" Dani said, through a clenched jaw.

"What, dear?"

"—that a penknife would come in very handy around about now!" She cast a sidelong glance at her sheepish granny.

"Frankly, Dani, and I'm not saying a penknife wouldn't be useful, but all things considered, right at this moment in time, I could murder a mini quiche."

Dani glared past her great-great-great-grandmother toward the mountain and the lowering sun.

"And now," Scathe shouted out to the crowd from his podium, taking a lit torch from a stand and thrusting it into the air, "without further ado, we sacrifice the evil Red King of Denmark's accomplices!"

"Hey!" Dani called out. "You said we'd be sacrificed by the final rays of the sun—the *final* rays of the sun! There are plenty rays of the sun left! Plenty."

"Silence, impudent traitoress! When I said 'the final rays of the sun,' I meant 'whenever the heck I feel like it.' And, whaddya know, I feel like it now," Scathe said.

Dani turned to face Scathe and look him in the eye. She saw him try to project an air of supremely confident arrogance, but, behind the bravado she caught a flicker of apprehension. She followed his gaze into the crowd.

"Ruairi will not come," Granny whispered confidently to Dani. Dani didn't say anything; she was not so sure.

They both turned back just in time to see Scathe's quick spin and thrust as he flung a lit torch right at them on the deck of the longship. The torch landed with a *thump* less than three feet from the mast and rolled toward them. It finally came to a stop mere inches from the kindling. The flame didn't go out. Neither, however, did it threaten to light the kindling. .

Dani and Granny let out a big sigh of relief.

"What happens now? Will someone have to climb in here and move it to the bottom of the mast?" Dani asked.

Granny did not answer. Dani looked at her. When Dani saw Granny's face, the relief she had felt seconds earlier drained away. Granny was not looking at the lit torch smoldering beside them on the deck of the boat. She was not looking at the setting sun, nor even at Silas Scathe. Granny was looking out over the side of the longship toward the celebrating Yondersaanians, her lifelong friends and acquaintances, who were approaching the longship in even lines, singing and dancing a looping dance. Hundreds of them. Each holding a lit torch.

Granny and Dani had not noticed the music changing. It had gotten louder, more rhythmic, and that there was an insistent beat. They noticed it now.

The villagers' song of defiance and war accompanied their dance. They approached and retreated in turn, dancing forward, skipping back, then spinning one another around.

At the end of the first chorus, a line of Vikings surged forward from the back, their torches held high, chanting with a fervor to terrify any enemy, "Up HellyAa! Up HellyAa! I'm a Viking. The sea's the place for me. Up HellyAa!" They stopped abruptly at the edge of the pyre and fired their lit torches forward onto the longship.

"I don't like this dance," Dani said.

"I used to love it as a child," Granny said merrily, thinking back. "Of course, nobody was burned alive when *we* did it."

Most of the torches glanced off the side of the boat and landed on the pyre, which lit very easily. A couple made it to the deck of the longship and burned softly there. One landed on the kindling close to Granny's feet. With her feet bound at the ankles, Granny did her best to kick out and tap at the torch and the kindling around it. It wasn't very effective, so she tried blowing, which caused the flames to rear up. Alarmed, she used her toes like flippers and flicked from her knees, back and forth, back and forth, until she was able to scatter the wood and reduce their flames.

"You know it's interesting that they're using kindling," Granny said to Dani.

"It *is*? You're interested in the *kindling* right now?" Dani shouted over the growing din.

"Well, yes, because in Viking times, kindling hadn't been invented yet—"

"WATCH OUT!" Dani screamed as another torch landed a foot away. Its lighted end nudged a stray twig, which glowed orange and then red and slowly broke apart into flickering flame. Granny and Dani watched helplessly as this thin bit of wood, fully ablaze now, spat fat sparks in all directions. While a few of the sparks landed on inhospitable ground, the rest found dry, flammable homes, and the fire spread rapidly.

Granny and Dani concentrated hard on stamping out the flames. They became slowly aware of the villagers beginning the second verse of their song.

"How does the second verse of this song go, Granny?" Dani asked.

"Let's just say," Granny said, "that there is a lovely kind of pattern, a symmetry, if you will, to the verses of this particular song."

"Uh-huh. Is that right? And just how many verses are there?"

"Oh, there could be hundreds! But I wouldn't worry about the song becoming boring or repetitive. We'll be dead long before then."

"Comforting. Thank you. I can always rely on you to see the sunny side of the situation."

"Aaaaand here they come! Brace yourself!" Granny flinched as a new wave of Vikings stormed forward, ready to hurl their torches at the enemies tied to the mast of the longship. They swung backward from their hips, levered from their back feet onto their front, and as they prepared to launch their flaming torches into the air toward the deck of the smoldering longship, a voice rang out from the back of the crowd.

"Stop the music! Lay down your torches!"

"And would you look—here he comes now!" Scathe lifted a robed arm and pointed to a distant spot where a small, copper-haired boy dressed in a robe similar to Scathe's made his way forward. The dancers faltered; the music stopped. The crowd turned to face the approaching red-haired figure.

"Good people of Yondersaay," Scathe shouted out. "The Red King of Denmark has graced us with his presence!

"No!" Dani and Granny shouted together. "Run, Ruairi! RUN AWAY!"

The boy walked calmly forward as the crowd parted with shocked whispers. "You can let them go now. I'm here," he said in a voice booming and crisp. All eyes were on the little redhead as he slowly and steadily approached the pyre. He never once glanced at Dani and Granny, though he did take in the henchmen dotted through the crowd.

Dani thrashed frantically, desperately trying to free her hands. Granny kicked and flailed, and they both screamed and shouted for Ruairi to run away.

Dani, panicking now, bound and helpless, bereft of ideas but still refusing to give up, felt a gentle hand on her shoulder. Startled, she froze.

"Don't move!" came a soft voice from behind her. She felt the ropes around her hands being cut. Once she and Granny were released, they looked around and saw it was … Ruairi. He was standing there in his normal clothes with his Swiss Army knife in his hand.

"What? But how?" Dani said.

"What's happening?" Granny asked, frantically casting her gaze from normal-clothes Ruairi to robed Ruairi and back again.

"Quick, come," Ruairi said and led them off the ship. "I

went back for you; I never really left. It was easy to give the moron twins the slip. I made tracks going one way in the snow and then doubled back. They followed them without even thinking. I hid among the trees and watched. You'll never guess who I found there, wandering around talking into branches!" Ruairi grinned, put his fingers to his lips, and motioned for the two of them to look.

The robed Ruairi mounted the stage next to Scathe, turned to the crowd, and said, "Greetings, good people of Yondersaay," in a voice very unlike Ruairi's. As he spoke, he slowly brought his arms up into the air. Scathe and his men were mesmerized. Instead of grabbing the boy and restraining him, they stood there watching him address the crowd. Slowly, as his arms were raised, his robes parted, and from under them came two ravens of the shiniest black. The ravens flew out and up into the sky. At the same time, the small, copper-haired boy started to transform. He morphed, his back curved into the form of a wizened, stooped old man, back gnarled and twisted, head bent toward the ground.

The villagers were astounded. Some of them instinctively took steps away from the site of this astonishing metamorphosis. But there was something very familiar about this man now, about the way he carried himself. They were not frightened. The old man straightened and rose to his full height. The ravens fluttered and came to rest, one on either shoulder. The man reached into his robes and slowly, carefully produced the staff that had been hidden there.

Instantly, the villagers knew who he was. They threw themselves onto their knees; they bowed before Odin, father of all Vikings.

"Odin has returned!" Scathe announced, rushing

forward to stand beside the man. Quickly, he motioned to his men in the crowd. Scathe approached the old man, took his hand, and shook it heartily. "There is nothing you can do, old man," Scathe whispered to Odin, and he turned to the crowd and smiled a limp, slithery smile. "I know you are weak, and you know I am strong. I'm going to do away with these people"—Scathe cast a glance back at the three Millers, who were right now wending their way through the crowd—"and if you try to save them, I'll do away with those people." Here he motioned toward his henchmen standing, weapons drawn among the oblivious islanders.

"I can tell that you have not regained your powers," Scathe whispered. "My dear Odin, you must accept defeat. Have your party, bask in the adoration of your subjects, but know that these people"— he nodded toward Granny, Dani, and Ruairi once more—"are finished."

"It won't be necessary to kill them," Odin said.

"Is that a fact?" Scathe said scornfully.

"I will make a deal with you, Mr. Scathe, let me address the crowd, and we'll talk."

Scathe nodded, and Odin walked to the edge of the platform and addressed the islanders. "My fellow Vikings, I am delighted to have come home to you on the night of our annual festivities. I shall return forthwith to celebrate with you. Commence your feasting. The night has barely begun! Enjoy it to the fullest."

The Yondersaanians cheered a welcome and took up their singing, torch-throwing dance, and the festivities continued in earnest.

While they were thus occupied, Odin led Scathe, closely followed by Hamish and four of the five twins, off the platform.

"Isdrab! Asgrim! Apprehend those three! They are

coming with us," Scathe snapped, and Isdrab and Asgrim raced after the scurrying Millers.

"I know what you want, and I am finally prepared to let you have it," Odin said to Scathe as they walked up the shore.

"You are going to let me become lord and master of all Yondersaay?" Scathe asked skeptically.

"No," Odin said, and shook his head. "I don't have the power to do that. There are two ways and two ways alone you can become lord and master of all Yondersaay. You know that. Besides, I don't believe that's what you really want."

"In truth, it is not," Scathe said, smiling and bowing to any islanders that happened to pass close by.

"I suspect you cannot wait to leave Yondersaay," Odin said. "All that is stopping you is my treasure."

"You are very perceptive, old man. I want nothing more than to get off this godforsaken rock. With the treasure, of course," Scathe said.

"I will take you to the treasure and show you how to retrieve it," Odin said. Here Scathe stopped and looked him directly in the face, watching for signs of trickery. "I shall show you where it is. In return, you must release your prisoners, *all* your prisoners, and leave the island, never to return."

"These three must mean quite a lot to you," Scathe said, unconvinced.

"They are Yondersaanians, and it is my duty to protect all who are of this island," Odin said.

"I agree to your trade," Scathe said just as Isdrab and Asgrim returned with a struggling Dani, Ruairi, and Granny. "The treasure and my departure for the prisoners."

"All your prisoners," Odin corrected.

"All right, yes. All my prisoners," Scathe agreed.

Odin nodded. He turned and led Scathe, the Millers, Hamish, the Turbot cousins, and four of the five twins up the hill and through the center of the village.

At the brow of the hill, the little group turned toward the Crimson Forest. Odin stopped and looked back at the harbor. Ruairi saw a resigned sadness in his eye. And an unmistakable twinkle.

Everyone in the small group paused to follow Odin's gaze. From that vantage point, they could see that the majestic dragon-headed longship was fully ablaze in the harbor. In the glow of the flames and by the light of the myriad torches in the sands of the shore, the small group could clearly make out the Viking inhabitants of Yondersaay, the enchanted island in the middle of the northern-most seas, having the night of their lives.

Odin took a long, deep breath and turned his back on the view. The group moved away from the top of the hill and followed Odin along the path to Mount Violaceous. He stopped walking when he reached the taut old oak in the hollow of the Crimson Forest. Everyone looked around, wondering why they had stopped. Odin looked up. "Hello, old friend," Odin said to the tree.

"Welcome back, your godship. I hope you'll be telling me you won't be staying away so long ever again,"

"I hope not, Rarelief," Odin said.

"And hello again, you two," Rarelief said to Dani and Granny.

"Hello there, Rarelief," Granny said with a small smile.

"Hi," Dani said and gave a weak wave.

"I hate to interrupt this touching little reunion," screeched Scathe. "But the treasure is literally *not here!* And you will not convince me that it is. I have searched this forest inch by inch a hundred times over. And I have most certainly looked under this tree."

"The treasure is here, Mr. Scathe," Odin said. "You were just never permitted to attain it before."

"Well then, you won't mind if I have my men dig while we all wait," Scathe said, suppressing visible rage.

"I'm afraid that will not work," Odin said. "Whosoever wishes to claim the treasure as his own, whether it was originally his or not, must remove it from the earth himself. In a very particular way."

"You there, give me your spade!" Scathe said to one of the airport twins.

Odin shook his head. "That will not be adequate," he said to an exasperated Scathe. "The treasure can only be released by the battle-ax of a warrior, an ax that has seen battle and bloodshed, and a spade of wooden making."

"So I must go away and get these and come back?" Scathe sounded murderous.

"Yes," Odin said simply.

"What kind of a moronic, dupe of a dithering fool do you take me for?" Scathe shouted, incandescent. "You are trying to hoodwink me! And I'm not falling for it! You'll move the treasure when I'm gone. Or you'll make me forget where it is."

Odin turned to Scathe and with resignation said, "I swear an oath upon the souls of all the Viking men awaiting their final battle in Valhalla that I have told you the truth about the location of the treasure and how to retrieve it."

"Don't do it, Odin," Ruairi said quietly, desperately trying to think of a way out of this situation.

"Odin, no!" Dani said, defiant.

"I swear an oath upon the souls of all the Viking men awaiting their final battle in Valhalla," Odin continued, with vigor now, resolute, "that I will not move or disturb the treasure or the tree in any manner, nor will I have either of them moved or disturbed in any way by another."

"Please," Dani said.

"I swear an oath upon the souls of all the Viking men awaiting their final battle in Valhalla that I will not alter your memory of these events," Odin said and paused to look at the gathered men. "In fact, Mr. Scathe, I will assist you in your recollections." At this, Odin lifted the hem of Scathe's purple robes and tore a long stretch of material from around the bottom.

"Hey!" Scathe said, jumping back, gathering his robes about him.

"I will wrap this purple ribbon around this tree so there can be no forgetting. I will tie it tightly so it cannot float away. I will let it flutter gently in the breeze while it serves as a reminder to you that the treasures of Yondersaay lie here. Are you satisfied?" Odin asked.

Scathe searched Odin's face. "I am satisfied," he said at last.

"So you will let all your prisoners go?" Odin said.

"I will," Scathe said after a moment's hesitation. He turned to Isdrab and Asgrim. "Men, take the prisoners back to the harbor. Be careful to keep them there in full view until dawn breaks over the waves. Do not harm them—allow them to partake of nourishment—and do not under any circumstances release them before the sun rises. The rest of you, stay here. We have work to do."

Asgrim and Isdrab turned to the Millers and pushed them forward, marching them back up the hill toward the village.

Scathe turned to Hamish and said, "Seize him."

Hamish came forward and grabbed Odin by the shoulders, and the four twins gathered round.

"No!" Ruairi called out as he was being dragged toward the village by Isdrab. He broke free from Isdrab and darted back to the clearing by the tree. He placed himself between Odin and Hamish and stared defiantly into the large Viking's face. "You made a deal!" he said to Scathe.

"I made a deal for *your* lives, Boy King, not for his," Scathe said to Ruairi without even looking at him. He flicked a hand, and Isdrab roughly forced him out of the clearing.

Dani, Ruairi, and Granny struggled against the cousins as they were dragged away from the forest. They kicked; they flailed. Granny tried biting. But their strength was as nothing against the Viking men.

Odin turned to the Millers and said, "Grieve not. It is correct, I am prepared for this. Leave and be safe and think not that I suffer."

"It does not matter," Scathe said, shrugging. "The sun is about to set, the new day is mere hours away, and when the sun rises, all that has happened today will have disappeared from their memories. I am the only one who will remember. The only one. And I will savor the memory of this moment for the rest of my days."

Granny, Dani, and Ruairi reached the brow of the hill that turns onto the High Street. They stopped and looked back at the dimming forest.

"Let us go back," Dani implored Asgrim and Isdrab.

"Please," Ruairi said. "This isn't right. Please let us go back and help him."

Isdrab and Asgrim looked at each other. They looked down into the hollow by the oak tree.

"I'm sorry," Isdrab whispered, his head lowered. "We can't."

"We just can't," Asgrim said.

The final rays of the setting sun gave the Millers a clear view of Silas Scathe forcing Odin, shoulders sagging, onto his knees. They watched as Scathe stooped and spoke in Odin's ear. What he said was lost on the wind.

Thought and Memory, their vibrancy dimming visibly in the cool dusk light, swept once around the clearing and descended at last, clinging helplessly close to Odin. Jarl Silas Scathe took his sword from underneath his ceremonial robes. He took a step back and examined the heavy blade. He swung it high above his head, left it glinting, towering there for an endless moment, and then brought it forcefully down. He plunged the long blade deep into Odin's side.

Ruairi, startled and shocked, could not move. He could not think. He grabbed his sister's hand. Dani screamed. Granny's knees buckled—Isdrab supported her and turned her away.

Ruairi caught Hamish Hjorvarth, who had been itching for violent combat all day turning his head away at the final moment. He did not look back again.

Odin's lifeless body fell forward onto the earth in front of Rarelief the Splendiferous. The elms heaved and cracked, and the oak cried a pitiful roar that sent ripples through the forest bed. Rarelief shed a blanket of radiant purple leaves onto the ground around his old master and the perishing ravens. The two black birds reached out their wings in one last glorious extension as they closed their eyes to the world.

Scathe motioned to his men. They carried Odin's body out of the forest toward the mouth of the River Gargle. No one spoke.

Silas Scathe the Victorious strode across the dank bed of the Crimson Forest in the direction of the towering castle carved into the cold rock of Mount Violaceous. And the sky went black on this particular Christmas Eve on Yondersaay.

Home

Granny, Dani, and Ruairi finally made it home, exhausted, in the early hours of Christmas morning. Released as the sun started to rise, they stepped across the threshold of Gargle View Cottage just as the golden rays announced the new day to the village.

Once they'd removed their winter layers, Granny said, "let me have a look at it," and took into her hand the pendant that could was hanging around Dani's neck.

"You would never know," Dani said, "never in a million years, that this is the Violaceous Amethyst of legend."

"Where did you get that?" Ruairi asked.

"Odin slipped it to me on the way out of the village. You remember he stopped at the top of the hill and looked down at the harbor?"

"Yes," Ruairi said. "We all looked down too."

"When no one was looking, he winked at me and

looked at his hand. I followed his gaze and saw him drop something onto the ground and then cover it with snow. When he passed by me, he whispered to me. He told me what it was and to make sure I wore it all day, so that we wouldn't be intoxicated by any spells of Scathe's. I bent down to tie my shoelace, made sure the moron cousins weren't looking, and put it in my shoe."

"So we'll be able to remember everything that happened to us, everything Scathe did," Granny said sadly.

"I'm not sure I want to remember what he did," Ruairi said, a lump rising in his throat and a tightness constricting his chest.

"Don't say that, Ruairi," Granny said sharply. "We must remember! So he doesn't get away with it."

"Shh!" Ruairi said, spinning toward the living room. "I hear a noise!" Ruairi walked toward the door.

"No, wait!" Dani said. "Don't just go in there."

"Stay here," Ruairi said to Dani and Granny, and the newly brave boy marched forward and opened the door. Dani and Granny were fused to the spot for a moment, they looked quizzically at each other, and rushed to follow a very confident Ruairi. They were all taken aback by the two figures cuddled together under what looked like a large sheepskin waistcoat.

"Mum! Dad!" Dani and Ruairi shouted and ran to their parents.

Delighted to see them, Mum started to laugh as she hugged and kissed her children.

"There you are! Dad said, getting in on the hugs.

"Were you having fun at the harbor with everyone else? I do hope so," Mum said. "We found your note and decided the clever thing was to wait here for you for a bit and then go out and look for you. What time is it? We must have fallen asleep."

Dani and Ruairi hugged their parents, happy to find them both safe at home. They told each other about their Christmas Eve. After the harrowing stories reduced the family to sadness, Ruairi pretended to only now notice that Mum and Dad were still wearing their Viking clothes. "*Please*, cover *up*! My eyes! My eyes!" he said, stomping about with one hand over his eyes and the other out in front like a blind man. Dani almost laughed as Ruairi walked straight into a door. Mum laughed and half cried, and then laughed again. Then she blushed. Mum put an arm around a grieving Granny as she led her family to the warmth of the Gargle View Cottage fireplace.

An Ordinary, Everyday Christmas Morning

Early morning sunlight penetrated blinds and curtains and brought one islander after another out of their strange dreams of burning longships and yuletide sacrifices. Smells of frying bacon, sausages, and black and white pudding woke the rest.

It was a clear Christmas morning, bright and cold. A fresh smattering of snow concealed the last shreds of evidence that the day before had been anything other than an ordinary, everyday Christmas Eve.

The draper, as he did every Christmas morning, left his house early to collect his mother from the far side of the

AOIFE LENNON-RITCHIE

island in his little blue car. Still half-asleep and with a splitting headache, he was thirsty, he smelled rank, and he was hoarse from all the drunken singing he would never remember. He also appeared to have spilled an entire kebab and fries down his front.

The draper, a teetotaler who had never knowingly swallowed a drop of alcohol, was utterly unfamiliar with the effects of overconsumption and did not know, therefore, that what he was suffering from was the mother of all hangovers.

Discombobulated, he took out his car keys before he reached his garden gate as he normally did. He stopped a foot from the curb and leaned forward to put the key, as he normally did, in the lock of the driver's door. Usually, at this point, his key would meet resistance in the form of a car lock and the draper would stop leaning forward. However, on this particular Christmas morning, there was no resistance. Because there was no car. The draper leaned farther forward, all the time thinking only about his headache and the furry taste in his mouth. He leaned, and he leaned. He did not remember, of course, that the day before, he had lifted his little blue car over his head with the help of some Viking friends and hauled it to the harbour, its alarm shrieking, and set it alight on the shore. He leaned until his center of gravity tipped irrevocably and he found himself falling flat, right hand out, full on his face in the middle of Yondersaay High Street.

Hamish Sinclair, the butcher, woke up and went straight to his kitchen. Hamish was hungry. His kitchen, still shuttered, was dim. He stood in the light of the refrigerator and scratched his head. He couldn't understand what it was he was seeing. He closed the fridge and stood back. He opened it again. He hadn't been mistaken. His fridge was full of vegetables. Full of them. And fruit. They were bursting out of it. Hamish, still not fully awake, and more than a little confused, let the door swing open as he stared in, trying to figure it out.

As he stood there, a slender arm came from behind him, reached in, and took out two oranges, an apple, a carrot, and something green that Hamish did not recognize.

Hamish turned to look at the person who owned the arm.

"Smoothie?" Alice Cogle said and smiled.

Hamish shrieked like a schoolboy and recoiled in fright. Then he just stood there, staring. Alice moved to the kitchen counter and started preparing breakfast. She was wearing Hamish's shirt.

"Not yet," he said eventually, looking her up and down. He came over and scooped her up in his arms and kicked the fridge door closed. Hamish Sinclair, who believes real men eat only meat and the occasional Cadbury's creme egg, picked up a squirming and giggling Alice Cogle, who believes meat, all meat, is murder and kissed her.

"Hello! Hello! HELLO!" the fifth twin said when he woke up on Christmas morning. "Is anybody there?" As his eyes adjusted to the lack of light, he looked around and could not for the life of him figure out how he had gotten here. The fifth twin was in a very dark, cave-like tunnel. Once his eyes were accustomed to the dim light, he spotted a tiny purple flower a few feet down the slope from him. He crawled toward it. A bit farther was a minute yellow flower, and beyond that was a teensy cornflower blue flower. The twin followed the colorful flowers, on all fours, all the way into the light.

Finally, he made it clear of the tunnel into the bright Christmas morning. "How am I going to explain this at home?" he said as he took himself in and saw that he was dressed in strappy sandals, a leather miniskirt, and a fringed string vest.

The Millers

Dani and Ruairi could not stop talking to each other and to their parents. Dani told them about Rarelief and the whirlpool spitting them out and about the tarantulafish. Ruairi talked about the oracle handling bloody guts and then passing sandwiches around. Mum said she could remember her time as a Viking but was still struggling to come to terms with everything that had happened to her and to her family on Christmas Eve. They were talking, but they were subdued. Mum decided the best way to take their minds of Odin's traumatic end was to get stuck into Christmas Day preparations. They all got involved, finalizing the decorating, arranging presents under the tree, getting the food ready

All except Granny Miller. Try as she might, she was not feeling the Christmas spirit. She listened as her great-great-great-grandchildren recounted their adventures for their parents, but she did not feel up to talking herself. Granny tried her best not to think of the boy she had grown up with. She tried her hardest not to dwell on memories of her dear friend Eoin Lerwick who it turns out was Odin, father of all the Vikings. Eoin had entered Granny's thoughts the same way he had entered her heart—irreversibly and without her even noticing, and he would remain in her heart forevermore.

She would hold a little ball of anger in her for the treacherous Silas Scathe for eternity. If he should ever cross her path again …

When no one was looking, Granny moved away from the others and sat alone in the window that looked out onto the village. From the window seat, she idly watched her friends and neighbors go about their Christmas morning business. It was clear they hadn't an inkling concerning what had happened the day before.

"You miss Mr. Lerwick, don't you?" Dani appeared beside Granny.

"I do." Granny nodded. "There is no doubting that he went willingly. But his loss leaves an ache in my chest I fear will linger for a long time." Dani hugged her.

Ruairi came up and stood with them. He wanted to say something comforting to Granny to make it all better. He wanted to tell her it didn't matter or it wasn't real or she would feel fine again soon. But he couldn't. He didn't know how. He put an arm around her shoulder and sat with her on the window seat. Dani mirrored him and sat on the other side. Ruairi saw the fresh snow covering the tracks of the day before. He saw some Yondersaanians Christmassing in the usual way. Then he saw a fleck in the sky. He looked closely, and it moved. It broke apart in front of him. He watched as the flecks moved closer.

"Look, Granny," he said, pointing into the sky. "Look!"

Dani and Granny turned their gaze upwards and saw what Ruairi saw. Ruairi and Dani jumped to their feet. "It's Thought and Memory!" Granny said, stumbling and falling off the window seat onto her feet. She was right. The flecks were not flecks; they were two sparkly black ravens—Thought and Memory. There they were clear and in plain sight, fluttering in synchronized patterns all over the northern-most sky.

Dani grabbed Granny's arm and squeezed it tight. Ruairi hugged her. Ruairi and Dani jumped onto the window seat so they could get a better view.

"They are part of Odin, they can't survive without him," Ruairi said. "'You must release your prisoners, all your prisoners,' that's what Odin made Scathe promise. All his prisoners, including Odin. It was a trick. By making Scathe promise that, he made it impossible for Scathe to kill him."

Granny eased herself back onto her seat and raised her face to the sky. Her shoulders relaxed as she broke into a smile. "You must release your prisoners, all your prisoners, and leave the island, never to return," Granny said. And then she put a hand over her stomach, and allowed the tiny knot of tightly-wound pain that had been building there unwind, disintegrate, and disappear.

Mr. Scathe

Silas Scathe woke up early on this crisp, clear Christmas morning. He was alone in his castle. All his men and all the islanders had returned home to their families and their habitual lives. He could not be their jarl for another year—the spell of Christmas Eve was broken.

Usually, on Christmas morning, this would make Scathe's stomach turn over a little, the realization that it was all done with for three hundred and sixty-four more days. Usually, on Christmas morning, he would have breakfast and go back to the village, blend in, and begin his nightly search for the buried treasure of Yondersaay all over again.

Usually, on Christmas morning. But not today. Because on this particular Christmas morning, Scathe had bounded out of bed as cheery and optimistic as it was possible for him to be. Today was different. He, Silas Scathe, had single-handedly—indeed single-mindedly—defeated that despicable old fool Odin and had forced him to surrender his treasure. To him. Silas Scathe. The one and only. The victorious!

Scathe took his espresso on the terrace. It was a beautiful morning, crisp and clear, if cold. Something was different—he couldn't put his finger on what exactly had changed, but *he* was different now; *he* had changed. This must be how the Victorious feel every day! The sun was bright, if not warm, and the ice gave off a subtle purple hue. Scathe sipped his coffee, had a croissant, and went inside to get dressed in his ordinary, everyday, non-Viking clothes.

When he was ready to leave, he turned off the lights and locked the doors. He remembered to empty and unplug the refrigerator. As he was carrying out his chores, Scathe was getting more and more excited thinking about the treasure that was finally his after all these years.

He gathered up the old warrior's battle-ax from the armour in the Great Hall and his wooden spade, remembering that Odin had said they were crucial. How could he have been so foolish all these hundreds of years? How could he not have realized that the ancient skalders' poems, which sang of using the battle-axes of warriors and spades of wooden construction in the uncovering of the earth's greatest treasures, applied to Odin's great haul?

Scathe closed the heavy front doors and took one last look at Violaceous Hall as he descended the mountain. He was singing to himself as he walked. He was swinging his battle-ax, chopping the heads off flowers and shrubberies as he went, no longer pretending to be gentle and kind. He could not hear their cries of pain or protest anyway; it was no longer Christmas Eve—they no longer had a voice. Nor would they for another whole year.

And he'd be long gone by then.

Scathe decided to stroll along the Beach of Bewilderment one last time and to approach his treasure trove from the River Gargle. He ascended the dunes and crossed the bridge between the whirlpool and the waterfall. He sauntered to where he remembered the Tree to be. The Tree he now knew as Rarelief the Splendiferous. The Tree with the purple leaves and the purple ribbon tied around it. The Tree with the treasure buried among its roots.

Scathe approached the entrance to the Crimson Forest. The birdsong echoed his feelings of joy and triumph. Usually there was only such voluminous and various birdsong in his back garden. How apt that they would sing for him down here like this today!

He cast his mind back, before the sauntering and the strolling and the one last look and the locking up. He was sure there was something he was forgetting … He drank his espresso and ate his croissant and cleared out and unplugged the refrigerator. Then he had glanced out over his icy courtyard, he had seen the purple glint off the ground and the peaks of the mountain, but something was different. He was sure of it; something he wasn't able to put his finger on was missing.

Scathe stopped and finally looked ahead of him into the Crimson Forest. Then he realized what it was, that little something not quite right.

His battle-ax dropped heavily to the ground, and his spade fell beside it. He took a small step forward, and then another one; his jaw went slack, and his mouth fell open.

There, in front of Silas Scathe, at the entrance to the Crimson Forest, was not one oak but thousands of oaks. Not two elms but thousands. The forest was replete. It was living and thriving. All his trees were there, back where they had first been all those hundreds of years ago. Every tree that he had had his men uproot and transport to his private courtyard in the topmost part of Mount Violaceous was back, here, in the Crimson Forest.

All around were trees, encroaching onto the banks of the River Gargle, sidling halfway up the mountain, creeping forward toward the village and backwards over the dunes to the sea. Densely packed: hundreds and hundreds and hundreds of them.

Scathe dropped to his knees and flung back his head. The scream came from such a deep and black place; it was so piercing and so pained that it affected all the island creatures no matter who or where they were. Every last bird in the forest took flight in terror; creatures ran for cover. Babies shivered, and grown men wept.

The sound that emerged from the rankest, most fetid place within Scathe came at the precise instant, the very millisecond he realized something else was desperately, desperately wrong.

Tied tightly so it could not float away, fluttering in the early morning breeze was a purple ribbon. Not just on the Tree, but on *every* tree—every oak, every elm—on every one of the thousands and thousands of trees that encroached all around and up and beyond. Toward the village, scaling the mountain's slopes, even receding over the dunes to the sea. A purple ribbon on every tree. Literally.

THE END

Acknowledgements

I owe a debt of gratitude to a great many people. The book started out as my Masters in Creative writing thesis at the University of Cape Town. I'm grateful to my teachers for their expert advice, encouragement, and support, especially to Ron Irwin, Jean McNeil, and the late Stephen Watson. A shout out to my fabulous classmates: Hazel Woodward, Sue Sega, Sally Cranswick, Penny Busetto, Mo Ismail, Marcus Low, Paul Leger, Sam Wilson, Charlie Human, Monica Jacobs, Lisa Lazarus, Ellen Banda-Aaku, and Nape Montana.

Massive thanks to my writing buddy Kira Schlesinger for her daily chats in the research commons and for keeping me sane, well, more sane that I otherwise would have been. Thanks also to Robin Moger, another research commons desk mate for his friendship and support and for being an astute and constructive early reader of the book.

Luke Fiske was an inspirational teacher and supervisor, always kind, thorough, thoughtful and encouraging. I wouldn't have written this book if not for Luke, he believed in it from the beginning – if you didn't like it, it's all his fault.

Thanks to Michelle Magwood and Olivia Birdsall, the first anonymous readers of the book, for their words of praise and encouragement. Extra love to Michelle for her continued friendship.

I'm so thankful to early readers of the book, Mary Auxier for her exquisite editorial advice, and to Libby Ferda, Ciaran MacGlinchey, Rachel Ferriman, Michele

Rowe, Joanna Trollope, and Jack Ritchie. Thanks to Emer Horgan and her friend Tatsuo Kitagawa for translating the line of Japanese.

To the best agent in the world, Ali MacDonald, you are the cat's pajamas and the bee's knees.

Thank you to Georgia McBride for saying yes to this book, and for everything that's happened since then - it's been a wonderful ride. Huge thanks to my lovely editor Tara Creel for her diligence and support, and to Jaime, Nicole, and the rest of the indefatigable team at Tantrum Books.

AOIFE LENNON-RITCHIE

Aoife Lennon-Ritchie is an Irish writer and actor. She lives in Cape Town, South Africa with her husband and two children. She is only one-sixteenth Yondersaanian, but she has red hair and white skin so is often mistaken for a full Yondersaanian.

If you would like more information on Yondersaay, have a look at the author's website www.aoifelennonritchie. com and the book's website www.extremelyepic.com. For even more information, or to go to the island over the school holidays, try emailing the Shetland tourist board, the Yondersaay tourist board, and the Scottish tourist board and ask to be invited to Yondersaay.

OTHER MONTH9BOOKS TITLES YOU MIGHT LIKE

Poppy Mayberry, The Monday
Polaris
Artifacts

Find more books like this at Month9Books.com

Connect with Month9Books online:

Facebook: www.Facebook.com/Month9Books
Twitter: https://twitter.com/Month9Books
You Tube: www.youtube.com/user/Month9Books
Blog: http://month9books.tumblr.com/
Instagram: https://instagram.com/month9books

Monday isn't just another day of the week.

Poppy Mayberry,
The Monday

Nova Kids Book 1

Jennie K. Brown

Don't open the door.
Don't invite him in.
He is not from here.

Polaris

BETH BOWLAND